The Girl with Glass Feet

e returned on c

'tem

ALSO BY ALI SHAW
FROM CLIPPER LARGE PRINT

The Man who Rained

The Girl with Glass Feet

Ali Shaw

W F HOWES LTD

This large print edition published in 2012 by
W F Howes Ltd
Unit 4, Rearsby Business Park, Gaddesby Lane,
Rearsby, Leicester LE7 4YH

1 3 5 7 9 10 8 6 4 2

First published in the United Kingdom in 2009
by Atlantic Books

A CIP catalogue record for this book is available
from the British Library

ISBN 978 1 47120 295 7

Typeset by Palimpsest Book Production Limited,
Falkirk, Stirlingshire
Printed and bound in Great Britain
by MPG Books Ltd, Bodmin, Cornwall

MIX
Paper from
responsible sources
FSC
www.fsc.org   FSC® C018575

CHAPTER 1

That winter there were reports in the newspaper of an iceberg the shape of a galleon floating in creaking majesty past St Hauda's Land's cliffs, of a snuffling hog leading lost hillwalkers out of the crags beneath Lomdendol Tor, of a dumbfounded ornithologist counting five albino crows in a flock of two hundred. But Midas Crook did not read the newspaper, he only looked at the photographs.

That winter Midas had seen photos everywhere. They haunted the woods and lurked at the ends of deserted streets. They were of such multitude that while lining up a shot at one, a second would cross his aim and, tracking that, he'd catch a third in his sights.

One day in mid-December he chased the photos to a part of the woods near Ettinsford. It was a darkening afternoon whose final shafts of light passed between trees, swung across the earth like searchlights. He left the path to follow such a beam. Twigs crunched beneath his shoes. A bleating bird skipped away over leaves. Branches swayed and clacked against each other overhead,

1

snipping through the roving beam. He kept up his close pursuit, treading through its trail of shadows.

His father had once told him a legend: lone travellers on overgrown paths would glimpse a humanoid glow that ghosted between trees or swam in a still lake. And something, some impulse from the guts, would make the traveller lurch off the path in pursuit, into the mazy trees or deep water. When they pinned it down it would take shape. Sometimes it would form a flower of phosphorescent petals. Sometimes it drew a bird of sparks whose tail feathers fizzed embers. Sometimes it became like a person and they'd think they saw, under a nimbus like a veil, the features of a loved one long lost. Always the light grew steadily brighter until – in a flash – they'd be blinded. Midas's father hadn't needed to elaborate on what happened to them after that. Lost and alone in the cold of the woods.

It was nonsense, of course, like everything his father had said. But light *was* magic, making the dull earth vivid. A shaft of it hung against a tree trunk, bleaching the cracked bark yellow. Enticed, Midas crept towards it and captured it on camera before it sank back into the loam. A quick glance at his display screen promised a fine picture, but he was greedy for more. Another shaft lit briars and holly ahead. It made the berries sharply red, the leaves poisonously green. He shot it, and harried another that drifted ahead through the undergrowth. It gathered pace while Midas tripped on roots and snagged his ankles on strands of thorns. He chased it all the way to the fringe of the wood, and followed it into the open, where the scrubland sloped down and away from him towards a river. Crows wheeled in a sky of oily rags. Hidden water gurgled nearby, welling into a dark pool at the bottom of the slope. Above the pool, the ray of light dangled like a golden ribbon. He charged down the slope to catch it, feet skidding on mushy soil and sharp air driving into his lungs as he stumbled the last distance down to the banks. A sheet of lacy ice covered the water and prevented reflections, so all he could see in the pool was darkness. The ray had vanished. The clouds had coalesced too fast. He was panting, hanging his head and resting with hands on knees. His breath hung in the air.

'Are you okay?'

He spun around and felt his foot skid on a clot of soil. He fell forward and stumbled up again with filthy hands and cold muddy patches on his knees. A girl sat neatly on a flat rock. Somehow he'd not seen her. She looked like she'd stepped through the screen of a 1950s movie. Her skin and blonde hair were such pale shades they looked monochrome. Her long coat was tied at the waist by a fabric belt. She was probably a few years younger than him, in her early twenties, wearing a white hat with matching gloves.

'Sorry,' she said, 'if I surprised you.'

Her irises were titanium grey, her most striking feature. Her lips were an afterthought and her cheekbones flat. But her *eyes* . . . He realized he was staring into them and quickly looked away.

He turned to the pond in hope of the light. On the other side of the water was a field marked out by a stringy barbed-wire fence. A shaggy grey ram stood there, horns like ammonites, staring into space. Past that the woods began again, with no sign of a farmhouse attached to the ram's field. Nor was there any sign of the light.

'Are you *sure* you're okay? Have you lost something?'

'Light.'

He turned back to her, wondering if she might have seen it. It was on the rock beside her, beamed through a hole in the clouds.

'*Shh!*' He spent half a second aiming, then took the shot.

'What are you doing?'

He scrutinized the image on the camera's screen. A fine photo, all told. The girl's half of the stone steeped in a tree's forked shadow, the other half turned to a hunk of glowing amber. But wait . . . On closer examination he had made a mess of the composition, cropping the ends of her boots. He bent closer to the screen. No wonder he had made the mistake, for the girl's feet sat neatly together in a pair of boots many sizes too big for her. They were covered in laces and buckles like straitjackets. A walking stick lay across her lap.

'I'm still here, you know.'

He looked up, startled.

'And I asked you what you were doing.'

'What?'

4

'Are you a photographer?'

'Yes.'

'You're a professional?'

'No.'

'Amateur?'

He frowned.

'You're an unemployed photographer?'

He waved his hands in vague directions. This complicated question often worried him. What other people could not realize was that photography wasn't a job, a hobby or an obsession; it was simply as fundamental to his interpretation of the world as the effect of light diving in his retinas.

'I cope,' he mumbled, 'with photography.'

She raised an eyebrow. 'It's rude to photograph people without their consent. Not everyone enjoys the experience.'

The ram grunted in its field.

She carried on. 'Anyway, may I see it? The photograph you took of me.'

Midas timidly held out the camera, tilting it slightly towards her.

'Actually,' he explained, 'um, it's not a photo of you. If it were I'd have framed it differently. I wouldn't have cropped the tip of your, erm, boots. And I'd have asked permission.'

'Then what's it a photograph of?'

He shrugged. 'You could say it was the light.'

'Can I take a closer look?'

Before he'd had a chance to figure out how to word a sentence to say no, not really, not quite, he wasn't that comfortable with other people handling his camera, she reached up and took it. The carry strap, still slung around his neck, forced him to step unbearably close to her. He winced and waited, leaning backwards to keep as much of himself as far as he could from her. His eyes drifted back to her boots. They weren't just big. They were enormous on a girl so thin. They reached almost up to her knees.

'God, I look awful. So shadowy.' She sighed and let the camera go. Midas straightened up and took a relieved step backwards, still staring at her boots.

'They were my dad's. He was a policeman. They're made for plodding.'

'Oh. Ah . . .'

'Here,' she opened her handbag and took out her wallet, finding inside a dog-eared piece of photograph showing her in denim shorts, yellow T-shirt and sunglasses. She stood on a beach Midas recognized.

'That's Shalhem Bay,' he said, 'near Gurmton.'

'Last summer. The last time I came to St Hauda's Land.'

She offered him the photo to take a closer look. In it, her skin was tanned and her hair a roasted blonde. She wore a pair of flip-flops on small, untoward feet.

A snort behind him made Midas jump. The ram had made a steamy halo for its horned head.

'You're quite a jumpy guy. Are you sure you're all right? What's your name?'

'Midas.'

'That's unusual.'

He shrugged.

'Not so unusual if it's your own name, I suppose. Mine's Ida.'

'Hello, Ida.'

She smiled, showing slightly yellowed teeth. He didn't know why that should surprise him. Perhaps because the rest of her was so grey.

'Ida,' he said.

'Yes.' She gestured to the speckled surface of the rock. 'Do you want to sit down?'

He sat a few feet away from her.

'Is it just me,' she asked, 'or is this an ugly winter?'

The clouds were now as thick and drab as concrete. The ram rubbed a hind leg against the fence, tearing its grey wool on the barbed wire.

'I don't know,' Midas said.

'There've been so few of those crisp days when the sky's that brilliant blue. Outdoor days I like. And the dead leaves aren't coppery, they're grey.'

He examined the mush of leaves at their feet. She was right. 'Pleasing,' he said.

She laughed. She had a watery cackle he wasn't sure he enjoyed.

'But you,' he said, 'are wearing grey.' And she looked good. He'd like to photograph her among monochrome pines. She'd wear a black dress and white make-up. He'd use colour film and capture the muted flush in her cheeks.

'I used to dress in bright colours,' she said, 'saffrons and scarlets. Jesus, I used to have a tan.'

He screwed up his face.

'Well, *you* were always bound to enjoy black-and-white winters. You're a photographer.' She reached over and shoved him playfully in a way that stunned him and would have made him shriek if he weren't so surprised. 'Like the wolf man.'

'Um . . .'

'Seeing in black and white like a dog. As for me, I like colourful winters. I really want them to return. They were never this dreary before.'

She kept her feet still as she sat, not shuffling them about and poking at the ground as he had a habit of doing.

'So what do you do? If you're not a professional photographer?'

He remembered from nowhere what his father had said about never talking to strangers. He cleared his throat. 'I work for my friend. At a florist's. It's called Catherine's.'

'Sounds fun.'

'I get paper cuts. From the bouquet paper.'

'A florist must be a nightmare for a black-and-white photographer.'

The ram hoofed at slushy dirt.

Midas gulped. These had been more words than he had spoken in some weeks. His tongue was getting dry. 'What about you?'

'Me? I suppose you could say I'm unemployable.'

'Um . . . Are you ill?'

She shrugged. A fleck of rain hit the rock. She smoothed her hat further on to her head. Another raindrop fell on the leather of one boot, making a reflective spot above the toes.

She sighed. 'I don't know.'

More rain fell icy on their cheeks and foreheads.

Ida looked up at the sky. 'I'd best head back.' She picked up her walking stick and carefully pushed herself to her feet.

Midas looked back up the slope he'd charged down. 'Where's . . . back?'

She gestured with her stick. Away down a winding river-bank path. 'A little cottage that belongs to a friend.'

'Ah. I suppose I'd best be going, too.'

'Nice to meet you.'

'And you. Get . . . Get well soon.'

She waved gingerly, then turned around and moved away along the path. She walked at snail's pace, cautiously placing her stick before each step, like she was rediscovering walking after a bedridden spell. Midas felt a tug inside him as she left. He wanted to take a picture, photograph *her* this time, not light. He hesitated, then shot her from behind, her shuffling figure back-dropped by the water and the ram's grey field.

CHAPTER 2

She'd developed a particular way of walking to accommodate her condition. Step, pause, step, instead of step, step, step. You needed that moment's pause to make sure you'd set your foot straight. Like the opening gambits of a dance. Her boots were thick and padded, but one accidental fall or careless stumble could do irreparable damage that would finish her off for good, she supposed. That would be that.

And what was it like, walking on bone and muscle, on heels and soles? She couldn't remember. Now walking felt like levitation, always an inch off the ground.

The river stayed quiet, here pattering down a short cascade, there brushing over a weed-covered rock that looked like a head of green hair. Ida kept hobbling, occasional raindrops dissolving into her coat and making the wool of her hat wet. That was another problem with this bloody stupid way of getting about: you couldn't move fast enough to keep warm. She pulled her scarf over her chin and ice-cold nose.

Thickets of holly dipped branches in the river.

A moth landed on a cluster of bright berries. She stopped walking as it fanned its wings. They were furred brown and speckled with lush greens.

'Hi,' she said to the moth.

It flew away.

She walked on.

She wanted the moth back. Sometimes when she closed her eyes she saw more colour than she could in a whole day on St Hauda's Land with them open.

She had always liked to be in places where tightly packed hips, shoulders and backsides danced against yours, a dazzle of colours whirling on dresses and shirts. She'd held off sleep using the sheer pleasure of company, be it huddled in a freezing tent wearing a thick jumper or trading stories over card games in friends' flats until morning came. There was none of that to be had on these islands.

She had with her the tatty St Hauda's Land guidebook she had bought on her trip to the archipelago in the summer. When she had opened it that winter, for the first time since the trip, grains of white sand fell from its spine.

She'd had more enthusiasm for the place in summertime. She had read, with pity for the islanders, about the lurching industrial fishing boats that trawled from the mainland to intrude in the archipelago's waters, scooping whole pods of speared whales from the water and turning them to blubber and red slop on their slaughterhouse decks. She had read of local whalers who sailed farther and farther out to sea in little boats their

11

fathers and grandfathers had fished in. Some had not returned, either when storms blew up or generations-old vessels failed them. She had read of how, when they returned with dismal catches, the market was already saturated by the meat from the mainland. Whaling families began to move away, taking their youngsters with them. Ida's guidebook tried to draw a line under this, but sounded delirious instead. Tourists would never be attracted, as the authors hoped, by the drab architecture of Glamsgallow's seafront. Nor by the plain rock walls of Ettinsford's church. Nor by the fishery guildhall at Gurmton, whose painted ceiling of seamen and sea creatures, all depicted with underwhelming skill in the muted colours of the ocean, was optimistically compared to the ceiling of the Sistine Chapel.

It was wrong to count on the landscape, although it could be impressive at times. Other island destinations had more dramatic coastlines than St Hauda's Land, which showcased more than anything the insidious sea. Ida had wondered when the guidebook's map was sketched, for entire beaches shown on it were these days buried under the weight of water. An impressive natural rock tower called Grem Forst (known locally as the Giant's Lamphouse) was described in flowery prose as a star attraction. The lumberjack sea had been at work, cutting away at the rock with its adze of waves. Unwitnessed one evening, the Lamphouse toppled. It broke into a string of boulders peeking meek faces out of the tide.

Inland, the archipelago had only foul-smelling bogs and haggard woodland to attract holiday-makers. Ida doubted the islands could survive the peddling of this kind of tourism. If anything, the guidebook should trumpet the one thing it was careful to avoid.

Loneliness. You couldn't buy company on St Hauda's Land.

He'd been an odd one, that boy with the camera. Such a distinctive physique: pale skin so taut on his skeleton, holding himself with a shy hunch, not ugly as such but certainly not handsome, with a demeanour eager to cause no trouble, to attract no attention.

Made sense. She reckoned photographers wanted you to behave as normal, as if they and their cameras weren't there.

She liked him.

She hesitated, taking her next careful step along the river path. There were more pressing things than one skewed island man. Like finding Henry Fuwa, her *first* skewed island man.

Henry Fuwa. The kind of man who was either pitied or scoffed at. The kind of person who might be seen on a bus paired with the only empty seat, while passengers chose to stand in the aisle. A man she had come back all this way – braved the heaving sigh of the ferry deck and the retreat of colour – to pin down. Out of everyone she'd met since what was happening started happening to her, only Henry had offered any clue about the

13

strange transformation beneath her boots and many-layered socks. She had not even known it was a clue when he offered it, because back on that summer trip she had still been able to wriggle her toes and pick the sand out from between them.

Wind stirred the branches of the firs overhead. The memory of the clue he had given her was like a dripping tap in the dead of night. The moment you blocked out the dripping, you realized you'd done so, and that made you listen again.

He had said it in the Barnacle, that ugly little pub in Gurmton, six months ago when the earth was baked yellow and the sea aquamarine.

'Would you believe,' he had said (and back then she had not), 'there are glass bodies here, hidden in the bog water?'

Night mustered in the woods. Shadows lengthened across the path and Ida could barely see where track ended and root began. The half-moon looked like it was dissolving in the clouds. A bird called out. Leaves rustled among worm-shapes of trunks. Something shook the branches.

She hobbled onward in the dark, eager to be inside, to root out colours in the safety of the cottage. Tomorrow she would look again for Henry Fuwa. But how did you find a recluse in a wilderness of recluses?

CHAPTER 3

After meeting Ida, Midas dawdled back to his car, scrolling through his camera's image bank as he walked. The photos of the light shafts had worked wondrously, but he'd lost all interest in those. Both Ida pictures were awful. In the first, on the rock, she looked too shadowy. In the second, where she walked carefully away down the path, she looked plain and her boots clumsy. By the time he got back to his home in Ettinsford he'd deleted all the photos of her.

Ettinsford was one of the few settlements on St Hauda's Land whose population was dwindling, rather than plunging to desertion. Families on St Hauda's Land had always been whalers, ever since (it was said) a fatigued Saint Hauda drove his staff into the water at Longhem and was rewarded with the plump corpse of a narwhal calf, whose fire-charred meat kept his mission from starvation. The whaling ban of a decade back ended all that, and with the loss of the whaling families the coastal towns were falling empty. Built on slopes sinking away from the woods on both sides, Ettinsford's roads led steeply down to a wide body of water, whose banks were designated as parkland due to regular floods rather than the need for green space. On the other side of the river the wooded slopes rose steeply. All attempts to build on these had failed. Root-infested soil gave way under houses, bricks and mortar collapsed and rolled down to splash into the water.

The town had a grocer, a fishmonger and a clutter of specialist shops with haphazard opening hours, since trade in Ettinsford happened mostly on market days and market days alone. There were two churches, one a whitewashed shack beloved of Midas's mother before she moved to Martyr's Pitfall on Lomdendol Island, the other an old stone chapel, the church of Saint Hauda.

Midas pushed open the gate of his front yard and walked up the path to the door of his narrow, slate-built house. Winter had perished most of the weeds but he kicked a nettle off the path while patting down his pockets for his keys. He went straight through to the kitchen, turned on the kettle and slumped into one of the wooden chairs there. Coffee rings patterned the white table. On its underside hung handfuls of sticky tack like chewing gum under a school desk, convenient when he needed to stick up a picture. He wished he had a perfect picture of Ida.

The kitchen walls were a hedgerow of black-and-white photographs. Landscapes, strangers, loved ones. A picture of a man trying to ride a bike without tyres, a mongrel cat nursing a baby pit bull to its teat, a burning boat, a streaker at a bullfight. In the only photo of himself, Midas's hair stuck up like a crow's wing in the wind while he helped his mother up a frosty hillside. There was another photo of his mother, hanging beside the sole picture of his father. Once he had used his computer to join them together and make it look like they were happy. He couldn't make it real.

The kettle wheezed and clicked off. He got up, found the cafetière and rinsed his cracked white mug. Then he crouched by the fridge to get the coffee out of the freezer compartment.

Denver had stuck one of her narwhal sketches to his fridge door. He closed his eyes and took a deep breath. He'd asked her to stop sticking things there. She still did it. Hard to get cross with her when she was only just turned seven and had taken the time to sketch him such a beautiful narwhal. But sometimes Midas suspected that life was a film with subliminal messages. Things would move along with an acceptable degree of predictability, then be punctuated by some horrible childhood memory. He was in the kitchen. He had found the cafetière. He was going to open the freezer for the coffee. Then all at once he was finding his father's suicide note on the door of another fridge, some ten or twelve years ago.

He carefully unpeeled Denver's sketch. She'd have come around to see him and let herself in. He hoped she'd had an okay time at school. He hoped those other girls hadn't been cruel to her that day.

He found the coffee and spooned some into the cafetière, then added water.

Something about Ida had caught him off guard. Not just her boots, her hair, her face. It was that strange thing . . . The way the *real* Ida was somehow more alluring than the filmic one.

Old-fashioned film could fix that problem.

If he had a second chance to shoot Ida, with real film, he'd get a good picture. He knew he could. The digital camera was dimming his instincts. If only he could shoot Ida somewhere brighter: set up lamps, umbrella reflectors, everything.

He plunged the filter through the cafetière. Coffee swirled inside.

But she would be company, and he was steering clear of company. It was his recurring New Year's resolution, and it would seem a shame to break it now December was upon him. Besides, he didn't have enough intact heartstrings to hand them to people to pull. Ever since he'd split up with Natasha (that was a long time ago now) he'd been chaste, alone. The occasional afternoon with Denver and her daddy, Gustav. All those evenings with only a camera for company.

It lay on the table with its crappy shots inside. He'd removed the lens cap to clean the glass beneath. The lens gleamed.

He *enjoyed* being alone.

CHAPTER 4

Six months ago, Ida had seen Henry Fuwa lope across a cobbled road. She didn't know him then, didn't know anyone on St Hauda's Land. Just a tourist enjoying some summer sun. All she had known for certain was that there'd be a collision. Henry Fuwa was so focused on his jewellery box he didn't lift his head to look out for traffic. A cyclist, puffing downhill towards the seafront, yelled as his brakes squealed and his wheels juddered over cobblestones. He was tossed through the air by the impact, the bike upending and clattering into the road with its front wheel spinning. Henry fell backwards with his breath knocked out of him. His jewellery box flew up, turning and opening. He groped after it, then it dropped to the ground where the lid snapped clean from the hinges and the contents scudded into the gutter.

Ida sprang forward to check that both men were okay. Henry pushed his large pair of spectacles back on to his face and crawled towards his smashed box, but before he could reach its scattered contents the cyclist, who had groaned to his feet, hauled him up by the collar and snarled, 'What the fuck do you think you're doing?'

Ida, trying to be helpful, crouched to scoop up the box's contents. A little nest of straw, a square of silk and some kind of dried bug, which she picked up with finger and thumb.

It had butterfly wings, like flakes of patterned wax. Under the wings it had a hairy body with tiny horns. Its fur looked very dry in the hot summer rays. It had an ox's head, no bigger than her thumbnail, with a pink muzzle drawn into a grimace. A white splodge between its nostrils. The impossible detail of a scar on its bottom lip.

There was warmth and a heartbeat in its body like that of a newly hatched chick.

She shook her head and came to her senses. She could no longer feel the heartbeat. She must have imagined it. Likewise she had imagined the warmth of its breath on her fingers, and the rolling back of its eyes in their sockets. It must be a toy, some kind of ornament.

She looked up with a start when she heard a shout of grief. Henry Fuwa was shoving off the angry cyclist and barging towards her. He snatched the little ornament from her hands and cupped it in his, bowing his head of shaggy hair. His legs buckled under him and he fell to his knees on the cobbles. Tears dripped down the inside lenses of his glasses like droplets down a windowpane. The cyclist stormed away with his bike. Henry Fuwa gathered up the broken jewellery box and laid the ornament inside. He tugged at his beard, moaned, thumped both fists on the road. His shoulders jerked up and down so hard the vertebrae in his bowed neck showed, quivering. A pedestrian skirted wide around him and hurried on her way, but Ida, not knowing what else to do, crouched down and put a hand on his shoulder.

The road became hushed, the only sounds the distant sea, the tiptoe of gulls' feet on the eaves of square houses and the snivelling of Henry Fuwa. He was a tall man, even knelt on the cobbles. In his late forties, she'd guess, with a smell about him, not unpleasant, like moist soil.

Ida looked down the road at a pub sign hanging over a doorway. The Barnacle, with a painting of a shipwreck for its sign. She squeezed his shoulder.

'Come on,' she soothed, 'come on. Why don't you stand up? Why don't we go inside? I'll buy you a drink.'

'It's dead,' he said.

She slipped her arm under his and helped him up, then led him like a child into the pub.

When she had booked her summer holiday on these islands, this little archipelago thirty miles north-west of the mainland, she had reserved two seats on the ferry, one for herself and one for her boyfriend. Then he had dumped her. With a week to go, everything booked in her name, and a forecast of gorgeous summer sun, she took the trip anyway. She enjoyed stretching her legs on the hotel bed, flexing her toes in both bottom corners of the mattress. Not that she'd have been getting terribly intimate if her ex had been there. The boy was the offspring of a preacher mother and a policeman father. Their first conversation sparked from that: how to get by when your parents represented not only domestic law, but between them the laws of the state and the soul. Her own dad had been a lay preacher as well as a copper, so she sympathized. Her mother, thank heavens, had been something of a smuggler, which had helped to ensure that Ida escaped the inhibitions her ex struggled with. *Mouth* the word sex to him and his neck would retract like a turtle's into its shell. His teeth would grit, his eyes would bow.

She guiltily found she didn't miss him as much as she missed company in general. In most places she'd travelled to she'd quickly found like-minded people with whom to chat long hours away, and socializing had become a vocation. On St Hauda's Land she found only cautious, secretive people, well-mannered but closed to strangers. In the evenings the little towns and villages became deserted and deathly quiet, but this far north in the world the summer sun didn't sink until late, and even then light loitered. A summer day here was a long time to spend on your own.

She led Henry Fuwa to a corner table of the Barnacle, where tracks of dried bitter stained beer mats. She sat him on a stool and asked him what he'd like to drink. He shrugged.

'Come on,' she said, 'it's on me.'

'Ugh . . .' he wiped his eyes with his wrists. 'A gin, if you please. Just a neat single gin with ice.'

'What's your name?'

'Henry Fuwa.'

'Pleased to meet you, Henry Fuwa. I'm Ida Maclaird.'

He dried his glasses on a tatty sweater. 'Thank you for your kindness, Ida.'

The Barnacle's landlady leant one flabby arm on the bar while the other gesticulated in time with blurred vowels as she held forth to two regulars. The regulars sat on stools at the bar, dressed in short trousers and identical pairs of red socks stitched with white anchors. Pictures of St Hauda's Land's football team through the ages hung in chronological order along the walls. A sepia band of moustachioed, felt-cap-wearing gents morphed slowly down the years into a mix of spiky-haired and gap-toothed lads dressed in the club's ice-blue strip.

The jukebox played guitar solos from the seventies, and Ida thought how badly aged some of the tracks sounded, trapped like flies in the jam jar of the pub. Broken air-conditioning snored behind the bar and did nothing about the muggy summer. She glanced back at the table where Henry Fuwa sat motionless with his head in his hands.

She wondered what her ex would make of this, proposing drinks with oddballs off the street. She sometimes wished she possessed the flawed kind of taste that drew girls to arseholes who wanted that one thing alone. You knew that kind of guy, that breed of ox-necked brute who would not be averse to wearing the same football shirt every day of the week. Who had a glamour model screensaver that made him fiddle in his pants each time it was displayed.

Not that this was a romantic endeavour. This guy was nearly as old as her dad. She took a long draught of her lager while she waited for Henry's gin to be served.

She wasn't that kind of girl. Instead (at times it seemed uncontrollably) she went after blokes who were wound into knots over who they were and how they tied into the world. The first time she'd lured her ex to a restaurant it had been all she could do to snap him out of the reverie he entered, only for him to emerge spouting nonsense about how she was a princess, a goddess, even a fucking mermaid one time he called her.

And now he had ditched her. He was too introverted for her, he'd said, swallowing between every word. Sweet idiot. *A girl like you shouldn't be hanging out with a guy like me. I'm worried I'm holding you back.*

She carried the drinks to the table. Henry Fuwa looked a little more composed. He rubbed his sleeve across his nose.

'So,' she began, 'are you from around here?'

'Some miles away. But I live on St Hauda's Land, yes.'

'Did you make that ornament? Is that why you're sad? A lot of work went into it, I bet.'

'No. It was an old jewellery box that belonged to my mother.'

'I mean . . . the figurine inside. Did you make that?'

His lips began to wobble again.

'It was a kind of music-box, right? Such a shame. I thought it was pretty. How did you get the wings to stay attached to the little bull's body?'

He studied her for a moment, then gave a dejected shrug. 'I raised it.'

'I'm sorry?'

'But the most unfortunate thing happened. They like to fly down to the water – to the beach near where I keep them. If they ever escape I know that's where they'll head. It's the salt, or something in the make-up of the ocean. They weigh very little, you see. Little enough to stand on the surface like that fruitfly floating in your beer.'

The sight of the bug, all six legs cycling in the dissolving head of her drink, distracted her for a moment from her incredulity.

'But yesterday . . . the tide was in. And there were jellyfish in the shallows. The bull in that box landed on the surface and, as I explained, they love to . . .' He ran his hands through his hair and stared ashen-faced into his gin.

She fished out the fruitfly and wiped it on to her beer mat.

He started up again. 'The sting . . . it received . . . *People* don't always recover from jellyfish attacks, so what hope is there for a moth-winged bull? My last resort was a clinic down by the seafront, set up to treat jellyfish victims. I would have had to explain *everything* but . . .'

He took an unpractised slurp of his gin and put it back down with a lick of his lips.

She had yet to decide whether he was lying (to try to impress her?) or just nuts. The latest tune from the jukebox was a tedious soppy love song. She sipped her lager. 'I take it this . . . moth-winged bull . . . was the only one in existence?'

'No. There are sixty-one in known existence. All back at my pen. Sorry . . . There are only sixty now.'

'That's . . . incredible.'

She knew he could tell she didn't believe him. He shrugged gloomily. 'They eat and shit and get themselves killed like everything else.'

'And you're the only person in the world who knows about them?'

'They're my secret.' He took a longer sip of his gin and blinked hard as he swallowed it, his expression describing the descent of the alcohol in his throat. She wondered when he'd last had a drink, then wondered if he were plain drunk. He leant across the table as earnest as hobos she'd seen in her dad's police cells.

'Would you believe there's an animal in the woods who turns everything she looks at pure white?'

She sighed. 'No. I don't. Believe it.'

He leant back, scratching his beard. Then he tried leaning forward again. 'Would you believe there are glass bodies here, hidden in the bog water?'

'No. You've got black hair and a healthy complexion for one thing.'

'I don't see what that's got . . . Ah, wait. I didn't say she'd seen *me*.'

She watched his eyes boggle as he drained the gin. He held a hand to his forehead and wagged his finger. 'You bought me a double . . .'

'What kind of animal is she?'

'She's white all over, as you'd expect, except for on the back of her head where she can't see herself.'

Ida had been through three fingers of her pint in the space it had taken him to finish his glass.

'What colour?'

'*White.*'

'What colour's the back of her head?'

'Blue.'

She smiled sweetly. 'What do you do for a living, Henry?'

'I'm too occupied with the . . .' he snapped his mouth shut and looked suddenly sober. 'Of course. You think I'm some kind of nut.'

'It's not that . . .'

He stood up, fiddled through his wallet and stacked the cost of the gin on the table in coins.

'It was on me,' she said.

He walked out of the pub. After a moment of feeling frustrated at herself, she left the coins and jogged after him, but he was nowhere to be seen in the hot street. White gulls pecked at the remains of fish and chips, gobbling batter and polystyrene tray alike. For a moment she thought the whitest of them had white eyes, but it was only a trick of the light.

CHAPTER 5

From an aeroplane the three main islands of the St Hauda's Land archipelago looked like the swatted corpse of a blob-eyed insect. The thorax was Gurm Island, all marshland and wooded hills. The neck was a natural aqueduct with weathered arches through which the sea flushed, leading to the eye. That was the towering but drowsy hill of Lomdendol Tor on Lomdendol Island, which (local supposition had it) first squirted St Hauda's Land into being. The legs were six spurs of rock extending from the southwest coast of Gurm Island, trapping the sea in sandy coves between them. The wings were a wind-torn flotilla of uninhabited granite islets in the north. The tail's sting was the sickle-shaped Ferry Island in the east, the quaint little town of Glamsgallow a drop of poison welling on its tip.

Glamsgallow boasted St Hauda's Land's only airport, but most aeroplanes crossed the islands before turning to land, flying over the other settlements. In the north of Gurm, walled off to the public, was Enghem, the private property of Hector Stallows, the local millionaire. Built at the foot of Lomdendol Tor, Martyr's Pitfall was a town for the elderly. On Sunday afternoons the shadow of the tor covered the buildings and streets. Couples trickled from retirement homes to walk and sit in landscaped graveyards. By contrast, Gurmton attracted the young and nocturnal. Thousands of lights twinkled on its seafront, from the frantic flashes of fruit machines and jukeboxes to the spotlights slicing the sky at night, beaming the rival logos of two sleazy nightclubs on to the clouds.

Behind Gurmton the woods began suddenly. Lost partygoers looking for the seafront sobered up in seconds when they stumbled upon the eaves of the forest at night. Likewise, people driving the shadowy roads inland through the trees became aware of the din of their engines. Stereos would be turned off and conversations postponed. The woods felt like a sleeping monster worth tiptoeing past.

And at the heart of the woods cowered Ettinsford, where leaves and dead branches blew across the streets, where roads disappeared on leaving the town, as if their builders had been seduced from their intended paths. Ettinsford's river was technically a strait, the narrowest point in the division between Gurm and Ferry islands. An old stone bridge breached the water at the point, as local legend had it, that Saint Hauda himself had been carried from one landmass to the other by a flock of one hundred and one sparrows.

In Ettinsford, in Catherine's, the island's florist, the bell chimed as Midas opened the door.

Gustav wiped a fleck of mayonnaise from his lips and looked up. He was red faced and red haired, but his hairline was dissipating faster than it should for a man who had just turned thirty. A cocktail stick pinned together the fat club sandwich on his desk. Three slices of wholemeal bread, rashers of bacon and half a pot of mayonnaise. Midas could smell it through the pollen.

'Morning,' he said, rubbing his eyes.

'Bloody hell.' Gustav gulped down his mouthful. 'You okay?'

Midas's hair stood on end and his eyes had bags beneath them. His whole body felt like collapsing. 'Slept badly.'

Gustav folded some foil over his sandwich and wiped his hands on an old piece of bouquet paper. 'What's up? You going down with a cold? Denver's got it. Going to be off school by the end of the week, I reckon.'

Gustav scrunched the paper he'd wiped his hands on and tossed it at the bin. It overshot and disappeared into a dense area of sea hollies with regal blue heads.

'Damn.'

He climbed out from behind the desk and pricked himself on the hollies as he foraged for the litter. He found it and dropped it in the bin, slapping his hands together as he walked back around the desk.

'Are you going to tell me what's wrong? Did you get drunk? You have a *good* night for once?'

Midas played with a lily head. 'I told you. I couldn't sleep.'

Gustav opened a drawer and pulled out the clipboard they used for deliveries. 'But there's something else, isn't there?'

Midas hesitated, but they'd been best friends for a long time.

'A girl.'

Gustav dropped the clipboard. 'Say again?'

'I met this girl yesterday and she –'

'Midas! That's great! Secretly I've been worried that – '

Midas shook his hands. 'Nothing, you know . . . it wasn't a romantic encounter. That's not why I mentioned it. It's just . . .'

Gustav grinned deliriously.

'. . . just that there was something unusual about her.'

'There bloody had to be, to keep Midas Crook up all night.'

'She wore some boots. As large as this vase.' He tapped it. Blue and tall.

'She's . . . big-boned, then?'

'That's the thing. She's about my height. And thin, almost unhealthily thin.'

Gustav was confused. 'She's not one of those weird fashionable chicks from the mainland . . .'

'No. I don't think so. She *is* from the mainland, but she wasn't weird, apart from the boots. Gustav, do you know anything about conditions? Foot conditions?'

He didn't, though he gave him a list of names: Achilles heel, athlete's foot, fungus nails. None of them seemed right for Ida.

The pair of them carried on with the business of running the florist. Midas drove some bouquets around town and thought about Ida the whole time. Just after midday he came back shaking raindrops off his jacket. Gustav sat at the desk, on the phone, one hand to his ruddy forehead. He glanced up gloomily when the doorbell rang.

'Yeah, okay,' he said into the receiver, 'I'll see you then.'

The phone clunked as he put it down and puffed out his cheeks. He sighed and ran his hands back through his thinning hair.

'What are you doing on Saturday, Midas?'

'You want me to work?'

'No. That was my mother-in-law. She's found some old boxes of Catherine's stuff. Wonders if I want any of it.'

'Catherine's *mother* doesn't want it?'

He shrugged. 'She doesn't like to see it. Said she might throw it away. I told her I'd take anything.'

'You're going over to the mainland on Saturday?'

'Yeah.'

'And you want me to look after Denver?'

He nodded. 'Just for the morning, if the traffic's light. I don't want to bring her with me. I'll be in fucking floods of tears.'

It had been three years that felt like nothing. Sitting in Gustav's car with cold cups of coffee in plastic thermos mugs. The green and neon jackets of paramedics.

Clearly Gustav was remembering too. After a while he pushed himself out of the chair and shambled over to the tap at the back of the shop. He turned it on. Water drummed into a watering can.

And it had been what? Only eight years since that hot day when Midas was best man and his collar bit into his sweaty neck and he played with the ring in its box – so easy to lose in his pocket – and he watched the noxious wedding photographer going about everything wrong and then . . . he was swept away by how beautiful Catherine looked and all the whiteness of her wedding dress.

He had been friends with Gustav since he was little, when they lived at opposite ends of the same street. Gustav had been an overweight, unambitious child more interested in football stickers than homework, but he had been several years older than Midas and that had made him an invaluable friend to the unpopular weirdo who answered to the name of Crooky in the playground. Countless times the sheer height and bulk of the bigger, older boy had saved Midas's wallet and his lunch money, or his skin from the punches of other children. Even when Gustav had left school (at the earliest opportunity) and was working for his keep, he had arrived after-hours to mind Midas on his way home, and to talk knowledgeably to the smaller boy about football leagues, a subject Midas had never been able to grasp. In return, Midas had been Gustav's sounding board, listening intently to his romantic woes and his morose talk of being washed up and in crisis aged only twenty.

Then Gustav fell in love. Midas had worried it would mean the end of their friendship, but instead it led to the second friend of his young life. Catherine was sparkling, ambitious, and the new owner of the town's florist. Gustav had been working in a newsagent's for half a decade since leaving school; this hadn't equipped him with an extensive knowledge of botany, but through a sheer lack of other applicants he was successful in securing a job at the florist's. Over the course of two years among curling arum lilies and brilliant yellow arctic poppies, Catherine slowly but surely fell as much in love with Gustav as he had with her in their first instant together. Denver arrived almost at once, a happy accident. They married soon after Catherine discovered she was pregnant, and for a short while their home had been the warmest, most welcoming place Midas could think of on St Hauda's Land.

Gustav twirled a strand of raffia. 'I could phone around and try to get you the afternoon off. Today. To make up for the short notice. And apologies in advance if I'm late getting back. You know how Catherine's mum likes a natter.'

'You don't have to give me the afternoon off. I love looking after Denver. You know I'll help.'

34

They stood side by side in silence. Midas remembered how they had stood side by side over Catherine's body, with the policewoman insisting they said it out loud when the sheer looks on their faces should have been enough. *Yes,* Gustav had croaked, *it's her.*

Gustav cleared his throat and turned off the tap. 'I tell you something. Listen. Don't mess up with this new girlfriend of yours.'

'But . . . She's not a girlfriend . . . I only met her yesterday. It's because of her boots that she sticks in my mind. It's nothing to do with attraction. If anything, I thought her peculiar. Flimsy. Easily snapped.'

Gustav raised his eyebrows. Midas blushed. He hadn't meant to sound derogatory.

The bell above the door rang and a customer came in.

Midas's guts clenched. A drop from the tap splashed into the watering can.

Ida, hair stuck to her head by rain, entered the florist. She carried a white umbrella blown inside out by the wind, and wore a knee-length coat over a black woollen dress. She wiped her nose and cheeks dry with one hand, the other resting on the handle of her stick.

'Good afternoon,' said Gustav. 'Can I help . . .' he faltered because he'd seen her boots '. . . you. With, um, anything?'

She blushed. 'I just sort of came in. To see Midas.' She gestured back to the doorway. 'I recognized the name on the sign. Catherine's. Um. Hello, Midas. You remember you told me you worked here.'

Gustav drummed his hands on the table and sat up straight. 'That's *great*. Great. Wow. And you two, you two are doing what? Going for a coffee, or something?'

During the silence that followed a moment's sunlight broke on the street outside, made even brighter by the still falling rain and the wet sheen on buildings.

'I just came in . . .' Ida mumbled. 'Just, you know.' She drew herself up. 'Well. You're both busy. Midas is working.' She waved at Midas.

'H-hello,' he said.

'Actually,' said Gustav, 'I just gave him the afternoon off.'

The sunlight vanished.

'Midas,' said Ida, 'would you . . . would you like to go for a coffee?'

She ended up drinking lemonade, while Midas sipped an Americano in a café with steamed-up windows and a murmuring black-and-white television on the counter. They'd been drenched on the short route from the florist to the café (Ida hobbled so slowly). When they sat down his trouser legs clung damp to his thighs. It was a typical Ettinsford café, with a patterned carpet and plastic tablecloths. Watercolours by a local artist portrayed the town not as the pit of sagging masonry that Midas had photographic proof of, but as a citadel

36

of stone flushed peach in improbable light. Were this artist's eyes designed differently to his? He cleared a salt shaker and blocked pepper pot from the table, then settled back to let Ida do most of the talking. He thought about panel lights and umbrella reflectors. Then she shifted about in her seat to get comfy and Midas felt her boot brush his shoe beneath the table. Touch made him shudder, like hearing a bump at night. He swung his legs back tight beneath his chair and screwed up his eyes.

When he opened them she was sipping lemonade and regarding him curiously. He tried to stop himself from examining her. Bags under her eyes: dark as bruises. Skin thin and veined like set glue. But even looking unwell he itched to have a photo of her, to pore over it in magnification.

'So how long have you lived here?'

'All my life,' mumbled Midas, looking down at the table. He wondered whether she'd think he should have been more adventurous. 'What about you? Where are you from?'

'I've travelled around a lot. I'm staying at my mum's friend's cottage just outside of Ettinsford. He's gone to the mainland for a few days.'

'Are you having a holiday?'

She shook her head. 'I came here to find someone I met once on the islands. Only, I've got nothing to go on.' She stirred her lemonade with a black straw. Bubbles drifted to its surface. Hazy ice cubes clinked against each other.

'My mum's friend Carl – the man whose cottage

I'm staying at – he said the island was so incestuous you could ask nearly anyone about anyone else's business. Do you think that's true?'

'No. You can find out what they *think* of each other's business . . .'

'That's not the same, is it? Carl didn't know where I should look, that's for sure.'

This Carl was right. There was something incestuous about the place. Midas knew of three Carls on the island, and hoped none of them were friends of Ida's. 'What does Carl do?'

'He's a professor of classics.'

Midas screwed up his face. His father had been a professor of classics.

'But he's not stuffy, like you think. He's very hands-on. He works with archaeologists on his research – he travels around. I helped him on one project when I was a teenager – when my parents wanted to offload me for a week or two. I did a lot of diving. That was my speciality. Recently he's done something at the causeway at Lomdendol. A lot of diving there I imagine.'

He filed the character description. It sounded worryingly familiar, but conversations were like marathons and you had to press on regardless. Especially when they were flowing with such rarity as this one. 'You . . . like diving?'

'I won medals when I was a kid. In fact . . . It's kind of embarrassing now I think of it . . . I brought another photo to show you.'

She opened her bag and removed a creased

colour photograph of her in her diving gear, giving a double thumbs-up and grinning behind a neon-pink snorkelling mask. In the background the ocean was an impossible ultramarine. He'd never seen sea like that. Even in summer the islands' waters remained secretive, opaque and grey.

'The Med,' she explained. 'Off the coast of Spain.'

'Oh.' To imagine her as he did now (tanned by roasting Spanish sun, leaving footprints in the golden sand, laughing her watery laugh, in nothing but a neon-pink bikini) spoiled her. He tried to focus on the present, her modest dress sense, her elegant monochrome complexion. 'I . . . I . . . take it you can't dive at the moment? With your foot condition.'

She shook her head. On the counter, the black-and-white TV lost its reception and made a cracking sound like a whip. She obviously didn't like to talk about her feet, but it was all he could think of to keep the conversation running. He accidentally slurped his coffee and felt embarrassed at the bubbling noise. The television reception settled. A news anchor was reading a finance report about ascending shares in companies owned by Hector Stallows, known infamously on St Hauda's Land as 'the perfume man', since scent was how he'd amassed his fortune.

'So,' she said, pushing her straw around the glass, 'this man I'm looking for . . . His father was Japanese. There can't be many Japanese names on the island. His name is Henry Fuwa.'

Midas looked at her eager, fascinating face, and wanted to turn into a wave so he could spill away.

'Well? Have you heard of him? He's got a mop of black hair and a thick black beard. Gangly. Bug-eye glasses.'

Midas hung his head. The television news report went to the weather. On the islands' limited-service television they still stuck card cutouts of clouds to a poster map. He closed his eyes and remembered Henry Fuwa on local TV, something he'd watched on a damp afternoon a few years back. Henry Fuwa crouched on a riverbank, wearing a checked shirt and battered broad-brimmed hat. Dressed and dirtied like a prospector panning for gold, mannered like a bank vole. He'd looked wild-eyed into the camera, his name flashing across the bottom of the screen, and Midas then remembered Nihongo characters written on a bouquet tag. An order for white orchids in the florist. To be delivered. He remembered his shocked and shaking hands as he held, in his left, the inscription and, in his right, the delivery address Mr Henry Fuwa had requested.

The bouquet was to be delivered to Midas's mother.

'Well, *have you*?'

He shook his head quick.

'That's to be expected, I suppose. Nobody has. I met him in Gurmton, but he said he lived some miles away. I had no luck in Gurmton, so I thought Ettinsford was my next-best bet.'

'I don't think he lives here.'

She sighed. 'Any suggestions?'

'Maybe in the countryside.'

'This whole place is the countryside!'

Midas drew composure back from the four winds, and looked up. 'To . . . to someone from the mainland it might look like countryside, but I've never, um, thought of Ettinsford like that. It's town. In the countryside there are a hundred nooks with cottages secluded in them.'

'But short of driving to *every single one* . . .'

'You wouldn't even find them all on the map . . .'

'Great.' She tapped her fingers on the table. 'I've nothing else to go on. I've got his name, and his smell.'

He didn't ask her to elaborate, but she did.

'Of peat.'

Midas's nostrils twitched and conjured a whiff of it. She'd said it flippantly, but it had prompted . . . The air that came from opened packages in his childhood. *This is the time*, he told himself, *to finish your coffee and never see this girl again.*

'Well,' she puffed, 'this investigation's going nowhere. Tell me about you. You and your family must be close.'

'No,' he wiped his forehead, grateful this conversation was going elsewhere. 'Why? Why do you ask?'

'If you've lived in Ettinsford all your life. You must have strong roots here.'

'Well . . .' The truth was he lay awake some nights asking himself why he'd never moved away. He

41

normally concluded he was a coward: too much like his father. But once in a while he believed that moving away would be cowardly. He could have left after Catherine's death, after his father's death. But ties remained. There remained Gustav and Denver. There remained his mother . . .

He blinked and the bouquet from Henry Fuwa was waiting as if it were a photo on the insides of his eyelids.

'I suppose,' he said carefully, 'there are roots.'

'Family?'

'My mother lives near Martyr's Pitfall. It's not a long way away. But I don't see her.'

Ida raised her eyebrows.

He drank his coffee.

'The raised eyebrows mean carry on.'

'Oh. Sorry. Well, it's straightforward. She doesn't care much for me: I don't care much for her. It's best not to be involved.'

'That's awful. How can you say it so frankly?'

'Because I'm being frank. There was more between us once . . . But she's in her own world now. If you were to see her . . . it would be like watching an animal through a screen at a zoo. Sometimes she regards you blankly. Other times she paces across the room, or loafs in her damned chair.'

He dreaded to think what happened in his mother's head when she sat like that. You could see from her vacant eyes and silently moving lips that she was reimagining her life.

Ida watched him levelly. 'What about your father?'

He snorted.

'Go on. What about him? Do you see him? Does he see her?'

He shook his head.

'Then where is he now?'

Even after the discomfort of the bouquet memories, he found himself grinning, relishing what he was about to say. He didn't think he believed in an afterlife but he liked to imagine a little something for his father. 'Somewhere where he'll never get used to the heat.'

CHAPTER 6

In a hammock of moss the size of a cupped palm, dangling between green-barked branches, a moth-winged bull slept. It had folded back its papery wings and drifted to sleep kneeling on the dank threads of its makeshift bed. Around it the bog stretched to the horizon in every direction, a mottle of glistening peat, ochre grass and trees whose bent trunks formed low archways. In their shadows toads sat alone or piled on each others' backs, throats pulsing into pink balls. Winter sunlight warmed nothing. Heat came from the juicy soil and the occasional pop of a bubble of foul gas.

A toad croaked and disappeared into an opaque puddle. The bull woke at the splosh, lifted its head and tested its wings. They whirred, a flipbook of blot tests, before it took off with its legs dangling beneath it. It skimmed from tree to tree, jinked through the traffic of droning bluebottles and gliding mosquitoes.

In this way it flew for some time, until gull shrieks pierced the humming of the mere. Stones slick with algae like upturned boats punctuated the landscape, turning the bog into a realm of rock pools and drooling rivulets. The bull paused on one of their granite tops, fanning its wings in the light and lapping water from a pock on the stone. Then it flew onward. The smell of brine joined the recipe of gas. Not far ahead the land dropped suddenly away and the sea crashed against it. Along the cliff top, a man wearing waterproof trousers and wellington boots walked home.

He would introduce himself on occasion as Mr Fuwa, the name he had been called back in Japan, but plain Henry was easier if he were to make a new acquaintance, something that happened so rarely as to make the whole business of names redundant. Similarly redundant were razor blades and shaving foam, hairbrushes, clothes irons and deodorant. None of which meant he was scatty or absent-minded. His glasses were kept immaculate because his line of work required meticulous observation of minute detail. On the rare occasions when he made an acquaintance, that person's face would be seared in his mind's eye for months.

The moth-winged bull flew past him.

At first he could scarcely believe it. He clapped both hands to his head and watched it flitter. 'What are you doing here?' he cried, instinctively reaching out his palm. It touched down on his skin, light as balsa-wood. It stared at him impassive, stretched its wings and closed them across the tiny blue brand on its back.

They were forever escaping their pen these days,

even though he checked and double-checked the locks every morning and evening. They got out if the fierce bog wind swept a tile from the roof or niggled loose a chip of mortar, creating the tiny openings that were all they needed to escape. Nowadays they were flying further afield into danger, be it stray jellies in the sea or curious toads, adders or bats in the bog.

Not far away stood his cottage, on a flat of rock in the mere. He had a kind of garden, a little square of marsh enclosed by a fence, where ground-hugging flowers grew cups of white petals. At the end of the garden was an old slate-roofed shed: his cattle pen.

Looking into the distance, he could see the hump on the horizon where Lomdendol Tor rose tall on westernmost Lomdendol Island. Geologists said it had been a volcano in prehistory, slobbering the islands into being, fire transforming into land.

That metamorphosis was in the rock of St Hauda's Land. In quarries, blown-apart boulders showed their insides turning to quartz, or revealed fossilized prisoners. The sea gnawed at the coastline, remoulding it with every year. And in nooks and crannies uncatalogued transmogrifications took place . . .

Henry jogged along the stone garden path that served as a run of stepping-stones when the rain came heavy. He unlocked the pen door and turned the latch, but didn't open it at once. The moth-winged bull had followed him home, and he offered it his palm again, making throaty noises to set it at

46

ease. It touched down indifferently and he cupped his other hand over it, feeling the drum of its wings as it butted against his palms. He slipped into the pen, kicking the door shut behind him.

In here was a chickenfeed smell from the slop that fed the cattle, and a second door that functioned as a makeshift airlock. He backed into it and entered the pen proper, where a battery-powered lamp glowed in a corner, lighting the many birdcages stacked against the walls or hanging like mobiles from the ceiling. The bulls used them as perches and beds, although they were empty now because the herd was in full flight.

They whirled through the air like a cloud of leaves in a gale. Sixty brown and grey and cream-coloured bodies borne in circles around the pen by glittering, opalescent wings. Henry threw the bull he'd recaptured into the air to join them. Wings humming, it flew back to the door and knocked itself over and over against the woodwork. It always made him smile when they needed his help. He cuffed it lightly towards the herd and it shot up and lost itself among them. Henry sat on a three-legged stool that creaked beneath his weight. A herd of moth-winged cattle on the ground could stand still for hours with all the docility of common cattle in a field, but in the air they delighted in the power of flight, and there was something kaleidoscopic about their movement. You started to see patterns, and before long you'd be hypnotized, your thoughts fluttering in the air around you. You thought how you'd been sitting like this admiring the cattle since you were young (perhaps you had been doing it for too long now).

He took off his glasses and folded them on his lap as he leant back against the pen wall, exhaled, closed his eyes and listened to the drone and rustle of the cattle wings.

He had only ever trusted one person enough to deliberately reveal the secret of the moth-winged cattle, but he could picture the face of the girl who had found out by chance. Ida Maclaird.

She had caught him off guard that time when he smashed the jewellery box and she had dragged him to the Barnacle. On occasion he worried about her and who she might tell. He wished he hadn't stormed out of the Barnacle. It seemed inevitable to him that she would be out in the wider world telling anecdotes to her friends about the wacko she'd met on holiday. If she had believed in the moth-winged cattle *she* would be the wacko, and as such might not tell them. He often prayed for her silence, for a revelation to come to her, wherever she was, that the fragile cattle were real, and should remain undiscovered.

CHAPTER 7

Young Ida Maclaird.

Carl Maulsen had only had the briefest moment with her. Then he had left St Hauda's Land as if a tempest blew him. He had forced the clips closed on his crammed suitcase. He had wished her a loud *halloo* and given her a bearish hug, noticed her walking stick and boots (no time to comment: the taxi honked its horn in the road), deposited the cottage key in her small soft hand, dived into the cab to speed away.

All the time a horrible panic had gripped him, caused by the sight of her alone. As a man proud to shape his own destiny, he found it shameful when events blew him off course. It didn't take tragedy or war to derail a man. It took only a memory.

Sweat had budded on his forehead. His heart palpitated and his cheek tingled with electrostatic from the feel of Ida's hair brushing his face when he had hugged her. He laughed in open wonder at the uncharacteristic behaviour of his body, which in forty-eight years had only behaved this way around one other woman. With his trouser legs stuck to the leather taxi seat, he finally realized he had forgotten to pack his composure. He had held her figure in his arms, as slight as Freya Maclaird's had been.

As the taxi rushed under the boughs of the woodland he stared out at the grid of branches and tried to get a grip on himself. The taxi drove out of the woods and down a hillside towards the old stone bridge that crossed the strait between Gurm and Ferry islands. Waves marched urgently under the bridge, headed for the wider sea.

The taxi's route wound through the vast meres of Ferry Island, where the pools were full of half-ice and bulrushes grew as tall and thick as saplings. The smell of marsh gas filtered through the car's closed windows. He watched his fists knocking on his knees.

Ida had grown up to look just like Freya. He wondered whether, when people said that women became their mothers, they meant in mere mimicry alone, or whether a girl could really *become* her mother. Could a woman vacate her girlhood and leave it for her daughter, like a hand-me-down dress? Could a man get a second chance at a girl that way? He thumped his leg to stop it jittering. His ideas had not been this whimsical since Freya Maclaird was alive. He knew it was a ridiculous proposition and tried to erase it from his mind. Still it cropped up throughout the journey, as the road arced around the bogs of the south coast and approached the town of Glamsgallow, stacked up against its docks.

On the ferry he thought of Freya. In the coach on the mainland he thought of Freya. In the hotel lobby, waiting for his keys, he thought of Freya.

In the morning he went to the mainland university at which he was giving his lecture. Afterwards, the professors who had invited him wined and dined him, then went back to their studies and left him to find his way back to the coach stop, where now he waited, alone by a main road, screwing up his nose at the artificial wind from the traffic. He saw his coach approaching, his booked return to the port and from there the boat to St Hauda's Land. It pulled up. Its doors juddered open. The driver, in a tie and shirt with yellowing collar, peered down at Carl and waited for a moment before rolling his eyes and asking, 'You getting on today?'

Carl thought about Ida staying in his little cottage. The feeling that had ambushed him yesterday, how in his arms she had brought back his time with her mother, had dulled with the mundanity of a chain hotel, bus stops, lecture halls and microphones testing, on and off, fire-escape signs glimmering green . . . But it had not vanished. It was burrowed somewhere inside him. He needed to brace himself before seeing her again.

The coach doors closed, and only when the vehicle was moving did the driver flip his middle finger.

Carl crossed the road. A truck honked at him and swerved to avoid collision. On the other side of the road, he sat down on the pavement beside the coach stop, waiting for the bus that went south. Deeper into the mainland.

He had first entertained the idea while he ate lunch, while the literature professor who was his chaperone had droned on and on about the Romantics. He had growled assent to her opinions and chewed the meat from the deep-fried chicken he had ordered. He never intended to find himself blathering to bored students or idolized by eccentric professors. He had stood in that lecture theatre and looked into the vacant eyes of a hundred porous undergrads. His lecture had faltered. He couldn't think about the classics. He could only think of Freya.

But when he tried to picture her, he thought of her headstone and the boxed bones six feet under. He had to think of Ida's alive and breathing face to displace them.

The southbound coach arrived and Carl barged to the back, to a seat with little leg room beside a commuter in a khaki trench coat, whose glowing laptop bugged him. He made his discomfort known by spreading his legs and sticking out his elbow.

He had called Ida by Freya's maiden name when last he wrote to her. Ida Ingmarsson. All my love from Carl. He realized his mistake the moment the letter dropped through the slot in the postbox, then made several unsuccessful attempts to prevent it being sent. Of course it had passed without comment, but it had been there in looks when he next saw her, nearly a year after the event. How premonitory that seemed now.

What love he had possessed he had thought dead a long time back, leaving only remorse and a heart like dried meat. But seeing Ida fully grown had saturated it and made it beat again. This image of his undead love amused him briefly, before the social formula of their relationship returned. She had called him uncle as a girl. Of course he should never have let himself get to know her. He shouldn't have kept in touch with her mother. As if you could terminate love abruptly because the one you loved signed papers with someone else in a church.

Outside, suburbs and towns repeated. Then came heavily worked farmland, arable acres and fields of spotted cows. Evening came, traffic thickened. They drove through a city of tower blocks with windows lit yellow and so many telephone cables, wires and aerials that the buildings looked caught in a net. The man beside him snored. A dangle of drool strung his mouth to the knot of his tie.

Carl got off the coach in a town communist in architecture. In the distance, hills and a power station cast a protective cloud over the streets. Double-headed lampposts stood tall on street corners. Fences were tagged with unimaginative graffiti in tasteless colours. He found the best-looking hotel he could, which had at least made an effort (if a rather meagre one) by laying a tawdry red carpet in the foyer and hanging chandeliers made of plastic in the lobby. A jobbing student with a wonky black bow tie gave him a room key, and he took the stairs up to the fourth floor to exercise legs that had become nearly numb on the coach. He threw his bag into his room, locked the door again and headed straight back out on to the streets, ignoring his rumbling stomach.

He strode down the roads that led him to the graveyard. He wished there were a florist open at this time in the evening so he could leave Freya her favourite golden irises. In the graveyard he passed a mourner caressing a memorial bench and found his way between the headstones to the white block of stone carved with that strange name that was only half hers. Freya *Maclaird*.

That bastard Charles Maclaird never even told Carl a tumour was bulging at the top of Freya's spine. Never even informed him of her death. That was his spite towards him, more hurtful even than his legal ties to the woman. More hurtful even than the idea of the two of them sharing a bed with torturous regularity.

Crouching by the gravestone with fists clenched in front of his mouth, he wondered how the girl he had seen, the girl he had given his house keys to, had nothing of Charles about her. She was so like her mother had been in her heyday that she could have been a sister. Holding her in his arms had been like . . . like what he had always imagined holding Freya would be.

If he had only known Freya were dying he would

have come to her bedside and held her, no matter what Charles Maclaird and the rest of the world might think.

When he had last come to this graveyard (could it be three years back?) he had been so distraught that he awoke the day after to find his fingernails cracked and his fingers bruised by bite marks. He had seriously considered digging her out of the earth. He had been deprived of his rightful place at her deathbed and funeral, and he could scarcely believe his hopes were dashed. He had long held a swaggering belief that Charles would wrong-foot one day and Freya would come running. He had held the belief, albeit steadily eroded by the ageing of his body, that there would be nights with her. Her frame and his, her gasp through parted lips.

How clean, so much cleaner, the headstone had been three years back. Only fear had stopped him from scrabbling at the fresh dirt back then. Not fear of the consequences should he be caught, but fear of how he might defile her. Instead he had returned to his cottage on St Hauda's Land.

There were no flowers on her grave now. Charles should have tended it, but here was the rub: Charles had loathed and despised Freya. Called her a whore, so it was alleged. Carl would have wrung the wretch's neck if he had witnessed him call her that. At least Ida saw sense. Ida, from what she had told him in letters, saw her father for the selfish bumpkin he was. She might not despise him as

Carl did, but it made him grimly pleased to know they were on better terms with each other than she was with the dolt who had engendered her.

She was every inch her mother, that girl. He bent down to kiss the headstone.

CHAPTER 8

An army of leaves roved through Ettinsford's low-lying park, charging over the bedraggled turf and the tarmac paths. A child in a pushchair tried to catch them as they poured past her. She strained against her harness and squealed as her fingers snapped at thin air. The leaves kept moving, passed the banks of the strait on to which the park backed, rounded the bottom of the painted clock tower. Finally they piled against a hedge behind an old lady on a bench. She screwed up her face as they scrambled over her and caught in her shawl.

Midas checked the clock tower. Already the sunset was ending, dividing the sky into a yellow wall and jewel-blue ceiling. Robins darted among bare branches. Ducks bobbing on the water tucked their beaks under their wings. A faded crisp packet crackled in the wind.

He wondered whether Ida would show up, because she was late. They'd arranged to get some fish and chips, and he'd come here straight from work, down the winding cobbled road from the florist in the High Street to the exposed grass of the park. He crossed his arms and stamped from foot to foot. Even over two jumpers and three T-shirts, his ropy coat couldn't keep him warm. He was uncomfortable about the fish and chips. When they had left the café the day before, Ida had suggested they meet up again, for a meal. He'd not tried any of Ettinsford's restaurants or bars, so when she asked him for a recommendation the only place he could remember visiting was the chip shop, maybe six or seven years back. She'd said it wasn't what she'd had in mind, but insisted that if it was what he recommended she'd give it a shot.

He was surprised she had wanted to meet up with him again, after he'd told her he couldn't help her find Henry Fuwa. In the café when she'd said his name his gut reaction had been to shake his head and deflect the memory of bouquets. Yet later, in the evening when he boiled the kettle for his hot-water bottle, he noticed he felt deceitful. As if he had betrayed her.

Memories were just photos printed on synapses. As such he justified sharing some of them with the world while keeping others locked in hidden albums. Yet as he'd poured the steaming water down the bottle's rubber nozzle, some queasy emotion made him shudder, splashing scalding water over his hand. Was there some law at work, some authority that required him to submit his memories of Fuwa to her as evidence? He hadn't slept well, had sat up in bed with his bony knees bundled close to his chest, feeling too spooked to turn the light off.

Now, in the park, he wondered how he could tell Ida that actually, yes, the name Henry Fuwa did ring a bell, without making her angry that he hadn't done so before.

A tramp waddled into view on the other side of the clock tower, holding a carrier bag of blue cider bottles. Somebody walked slowly behind him. When the tramp slouched on to a bench, Midas saw that it was Ida. Only, her gait was different. She had abandoned her walking stick in favour of a stout wooden crutch.

He knew the moment she smiled across the park at him that he would let himself down. Braving the queasy feeling was better than braving her anger. His gullet rippled as he willed the guilt back inside. She approached along the edge of the water, wearing the same white hat and knee-length coat he'd seen her in before, and it struck him again that her face and eyes were almost monochrome in pallor. The cold gave everything acute definition, and she was no exception. He wanted to rip off his lens cap and photograph her there and then.

'A pleasant afternoon,' she said, looking up at the sky.

'Yes,' he said, deciding not to comment on the switch from stick to crutch.

'You look freezing. Sorry I'm late.'

'You're not.'

She looked at the clock face. 'I am. Really, I'm sorry. I still find it hard to allow time for these.' She pointed at her boots. 'I was dreading you'd think I wasn't coming. Aren't you cold? Midas, there's a hole in your coat!'

'I've got two jumpers on.'

'But aren't you cold?'

'A bit.'

'Okay. Then let's grab those fish and chips.'

He nodded to show enthusiasm and walked slowly beside her out of the park and across a road to the chip shop.

A wooden fish hung over the door. Cracks and smears of bird shit sullied its blue paintwork. The smell of grease and batter wafted on to the pavement. It smelt even stronger inside, in the hot close air where the blue walls were tiled like a swimming pool's and were painted with murals of shark and octopi. Red-faced staff in white caps shovelled chips into polystyrene trays and dunked fish into sizzling fat fryers.

Midas pointed to a green-hued photo of the speciality fishcake. When she'd asked him what was so great about the chip shop he'd cited them as an example. On cue, a grinning customer left the counter with an open fishcake and chips, vinegar making the breadcrumbs soggy. A lean man in a leather jacket and black polo-neck stepped up to the counter and rested an umbrella against it. He winked at the girl serving, who blushed.

'Double fishcake and chips,' he said in a nasal voice.

'Salt and vinegar?'

'Plenty of salt.'

The girl serving scattered salt over his chips. Midas turned to Ida to ask her not to be disappointed if the fishcakes had gone downhill in six years, suddenly embarrassed about his choice of food. Yet she looked genuinely delighted, and entrusted him with ordering her fishcake while she sat in a white plastic chair at a small table by the window.

'How long do you think they'll stay hot for?' she asked when he came over with two soft packages of greaseproof paper.

'They're just out of the fat fryer.'

She grinned. 'Shall we take them back to my place?'

'Um . . .'

She stood up carefully and tapped his belly. The touch of her finger on his stomach had filled his throat with a gargle and he couldn't speak, even though he thought he should politely decline her offer. *God*, he barely knew her.

She was relentless. 'Are you okay to drive us?'

He looked at her eager face and took the father test: ask yourself what your father would have done and make sure you do the precise opposite.

They stepped out into the chilly street, where the tramp from the park was huddled in an alley mouth with his carrier bag of cider bottles. Midas heard the percussion of his chattering teeth. He led the way towards his car, which he realized now he'd parked in a puddle. She lowered herself carefully into the passenger's side. Night was falling quickly. Soon they were driving through darkening countryside and there were no other cars on the road.

'Those chips smell good.'

'Mm.'

She laughed. 'You get really tongue-tied, don't you?'

He blushed. 'S'pose.'

Dark branches rushed past the window. It started to rain. The car shuddered through a pothole and Ida winced and involuntarily grabbed her knees. Midas tried to watch the road. Coniferous trees shook in the wind and rain.

'Perhaps you think too hard about what words you're going to use and how to make your mouth say them.'

He frowned. Perhaps she spoke her mind too easily. 'Maybe.'

After a silence she pointed out a narrow driveway. He turned up it, headlights sweeping across a tiny bungalow with a slate roof.

Trees lashed each other in the darkness. Cold rain, nearly sleet, tapped their scalps and shoulders as they left the car.

Ida took a deep breath. 'Okay. This is the cottage.'

A blue front door had a horseshoe nailed to it. Dead plants in cracked flowerpots sat on the windowsills. A drop of icy rain hit Midas in the eye. Ida stepped up to the door, holding the key tightly but making no move to place it in the lock. She stared at the woodwork.

'The décor's rather predictable I'm afraid. Carl's

not really interested in it. Think middle-aged academic.'

He thought of his father. She unlocked the door and hit a light switch.

A wide passageway led to some wooden stairs and two doors, one to a kitchen and one to a sitting room with a sofa bed where she had clearly been sleeping. He wondered why she didn't sleep upstairs in the bedroom, and whether the sofa bed made this her bedroom. In which case he was *in her bedroom*. God, he wasn't ready for anything like that.

A bookshelf was stacked with a few photo frames and books with names he half remembered from his father's study: Virgil, Pliny, Ovid. They were like the words of a black magic spell, and he turned his back on them. In a corner sat a neat pile of lifting weights and an aged pair of blue boxing gloves, while on the wall opposite the window hung a small print of a self-portrait of Van Gogh, ear bandaged tightly. A patterned throw, navy blue with silver dots, overlaid the sofa bed.

Ida sat on the bed and started to unlace her boots. Midas tried not to seem too interested. She slid them off and laid them carefully on the carpet beside the bed. Underneath, she wore many layers of thick socks.

'It must have been hard,' he said, looking at her padded feet. 'Underwater.'

She frowned. 'What do you mean?'

'That diving you said you used to do with Carl Maulsen.'

'No, no. This . . . condition hadn't developed when I was working for Carl.'

'Oh.'

'Yes.'

'Is it recent?'

She nodded.

They looked at their laps.

'Midas?'

'Yes?'

'I don't want to talk about it.'

'Sorry.'

She shrugged. She clapped her hands together. 'Right then. Let's eat these fishcakes.'

Midas went to the kitchen and found plates. He unwrapped the greasy bundles on to the crockery and carried them back to the sitting room. He sank into an armchair that was lumpy with springs.

Ida had opened a window to let out the smell of chip grease. Something in the trees hooted as they ate.

'There are owls outside,' said Midas.

'Yes. I heard them. When I couldn't sleep the other night.'

'We should go out and look for one.'

She seemed surprised. 'You'd like to do that?'

'Yes.'

She chewed thoughtfully, finished her mouthful and wiped her lips. 'When I was a kid I used to go down to the beach and look for dolphins in the moonlight. Don't think I've ever gone owl watching. But now . . . it's hard for me to walk in the dark.'

'We won't go far.'

'Sorry.' She blushed. 'Sorry, Midas. I'm too frightened I'll trip.'

He was surprised. He'd seen her superior confidence in every matter, and the sudden role reversal made her look, for a moment, younger, almost a kid.

It was getting colder inside. Ida closed the window, cranked up the heating and got Midas to bring them a bottle of white wine from the fridge, moisture all up its green neck.

'You've got a lot of bottles in that fridge.'

She grinned. 'They're Carl's. But, you know, he told me to help myself.'

She put the wine firmly on a counter beside the sofa bed, along with two glasses, then took a corkscrew, which she brandished like a knife.

'He's been really good to me, down the years. A sort of uncle figure.'

'Are you actually related?'

'No. My mother just knew him from way back.' She jabbed the corkscrew into the cork and twisted it absent-mindedly. 'That's him. In that framed cutting.'

There was a yellowing newspaper column in a small frame on the end of the bookshelf. Midas got up and took it off the shelf. The headline read LOCAL DUO EARN HONORARY MAINLAND FELLOWSHIP and there was a grainy picture at the bottom of the article. Of the two men it showed in crisp suits, the first was undoubtedly Maulsen, squarely built with a dashing grin and silver hair.

'Shit,' said Midas, grip tightening on the photo frame.

Ida looked up, worried. The cork crumbled into the bottle and bobbed in the wine.

He staggered to the armchair and collapsed backwards into it.

'Midas, what's wrong?'

He shook his head quickly. She narrowed her eyes when he looked at her. He thought of how he'd concealed what he knew about Henry Fuwa, and couldn't bear to disguise this too. He handed her the picture frame.

'Read the names.'

She skimmed the article, then squinted at the image. 'Is this *you*?'

'My father.'

'You have the same *name*?'

'Yes.'

She put the photo down. 'You didn't know about this, did you?'

He shook his head. 'I mean, I knew about the fellowship, but not Carl Maulsen.'

'Well . . . it's great news! You said you didn't know much about your father. Carl might be able to help you.'

'I don't want to find out more about my father. And to see a new photo of him after all these years . . .'

She stayed quiet. He wondered whether a mainlander like her could understand the tangles of life here. The gossip chains more powerful than television. The snooping neighbours who could detect secrets like crows detecting carrion. Almost worse than that (because you could ignore people): the way the *place* regurgitated unwanted details. He wanted death to have transformed his father into ashes and dust, as the priest had promised it would at his funeral. Maybe the soil was too thin on St Hauda's Land. '*God*,' he blurted out, 'these islands! They're so incestuous!'

'Why don't you move away?' she asked gently, as if he'd been thinking out loud.

'Because . . .' he puffed out his cheeks, 'it wouldn't make what's happened go away. I have to . . . overcome it.'

She nodded slowly. 'What's happened, exactly?'

He pointed to the newspaper cutting. 'If you went to the *Echo*'s archives you'd find maybe two or three incidents of note from the last ten years. Life is so sleepy . . . When something tragic happens its effects are compounded. You can't walk down the street without people recognizing you as the poor bastard from the paper. And worse – since there's only one thing to talk about – some of those looks you get are ugly. Distorted.'

Ida picked her words carefully. 'Something bad happened. To you?'

'My friend drowned. Before that, my father killed himself. And there have been other things . . .'

'Shit. I'm sorry, Midas.'

He smiled weakly at her. 'I'm okay. It's only the first thing that's still a problem.'

'I meant I'm sorry for gabbling on and on about how everyone here knows everybody else's business.' She looked at the emerald bottle in her hand. 'I'm also sorry I corked the wine.'

He smiled at her. 'It doesn't matter. We can strain it out.'

He found a tea strainer in the kitchen (his *father's colleague's* kitchen). Wine glugged from the bottle and sieved through the strainer.

'Cheers,' said Ida, looking at him fondly as she handed him his glass.

CHAPTER 9

On a quiet summer's evening, Midas's father tumbled from his chair and lay twisted on his study floor. Midas's mother found him and phoned for an ambulance, which arrived shortly and rushed him to hospital, where he spent three days. Examinations revealed an anomalous growth beneath his heart. There was no chance of a cure.

'He may feel fine for weeks, even months,' said the doctor flatly, thumb jittering on the button of a pen. 'Then in all probability he'll have a seizure similar to the one he's just suffered, or worse. There'll come a point where his body won't be able to restore complete control. He'll lose sensation and motor function in the body parts affected. We hope this will occur primarily in appendages but, you understand, if it spreads to a major artery or his digestive system there's not much we can do.'

The doctor twirled the pen between his fingers, then brought it up to his lips and tapped it against his chin.

'If he fights it,' said Midas's mother after a while, hands clasped tightly. 'If he fights it for long enough. If he holds out.'

The doctor gnawed his pen.

Then (on the day when his father stuck the note to the fridge) Midas ran away from school. It was a large school to which children from across St Hauda's Land were bussed every day, yet he could neither fit in nor find anonymity. While other pupils slept with each other and smoked cannabis at the fringe of the playing field he sat in the library studying heavy books of photographs. The teachers had banned his camera as prevention of theft, but at break-time that day he was dreaming about the new zoom lens his aunt had bought him. Still in its shiny box back at home. Still smelling of polystyrene. He had been desperate to tell somebody about it, but there was nobody who would listen. Heavy rain broke over the school, banging off the rooftops and driving the other children inside. And that brought Freddy Clare to the library.

'Hello, Crooky,' he said, sidling onto the chair opposite Midas. His hair stuck to his neck, soaked by rain.

'Hello, Freddy.'

'Look at this, Crooky.' Something silver flashed in his pocket as he opened his blazer. It looked like the handle of a spoon.

'What's that, Freddy?'

Freddy looked around furtively, then pulled it from his pocket. A flick knife, blade folded into the handle. 'Like in *The Godfather*, Crooky. Do you like it?'

'It's very nice.'

'Damn right. Now, you got any money on you?'

'No.'

Freddy gritted his teeth. 'Don't be a silly boy, Crooky. Being a silly boy could land you in trouble. Let's not forget, I know where you live.'

Midas watched Freddy toy with the knife. He had plasters on three fingers and one thumb. There were no librarians in sight and though other kids had noticed, their noses were buried resolutely in books.

'I don't have any money, Freddy.'

'Of course not.' Smiling, he pulled the blade from its handle.

'I . . . I'm not lying.'

'Of course not. Like in *The Godfather*, Crooky.'

To Midas's relief, a librarian appeared from behind the Ancient History section. She saw Freddy's knife and looked horrified, opening and closing her mouth, fiddling with her cardigan buttons.

Freddy sighed and folded the blade back into the handle. 'It's all right, Miss, I was just showing Crooky my new toy.'

He slipped off his chair and looked ruefully at the knife. Rain battered the library windows.

'But I suppose you'll want to confiscate it. Won't you, Miss?'

He held it out to her. She snatched it up.

'Well!' she puffed, 'thank goodness you boys have been responsible about this!'

Freddy beamed. 'No problem, Miss. You caught me fair and square.'

71

The librarian held the knife between finger and thumb, as if it might contaminate her. 'You realize I shall be obliged to report this breach of school regulations?'

Freddy shrugged amicably. 'Just doing your job, Miss.' He stuffed his hands into his pockets and checked the big library clock.

'What do you know? Break-time's nearly over. Time flies, doesn't it, Crooky? See you after school.'

Midas and the librarian watched him saunter off. The school bell rang.

Midas hid in the library toilets until lessons began. Then he made his escape, slipping out of school with his jacket collar turned up, the rain and wind so heavy he had to force his way home. When he got in he was soaked through. He called out to see if his father was home but got no reply. Then, while he made coffee, he saw a note tacked to the fridge door:

In garage. Sorry about mess.
M.

Midas left the coffee and pulled his drenched jacket back on. He went out through the back door, jogged through the yard and down the alleyway to the street's block of garages. Rain fell at a sharp angle, fired up by the wind.

Light shone an outline around the edge of the

garage door. Drops drummed on the metal and echoed off windows. Midas splashed over and hauled the door open, ducking inside as soon as there was space.

His father stood on a stepladder, a pale moustached man in a sweater and smart trousers, tearing at a strip of tape with his teeth. He was sticking bin liners to one wall. His nervous hunch was pronounced, even on the ladder.

'What are you doing?' Midas asked.

His father almost fell off the ladder in surprise, then held a hand to his heart. '*My God,* Midas, you frightened the wits out of me.' He hurried down the stepladder and kicked shut a case in which lay some sort of tool, something L-shaped and black-handled. Midas didn't see it for long enough to tell what it was, although he noticed a bag of tiny metal cylinders beside it in the case.

His father put his hands on his hips. 'What are you doing here? You're supposed to be in school.'

'I ran away.'

'Oh . . . *Midas*!' He plodded over, looking his son up and down. 'You're going to get pneumonia if you don't dry yourself off. You picked a filthy day to run away. Let's go and get you a towel.'

'What are you doing with those bin liners?'

His father looked over his shoulder at the black bags on the walls and floor. 'Those? Well . . . Shall we get you that towel?'

He turned off the garage light. Midas opened the door and they dashed back to the house together, their feet kicking up puddles. They leapt through the back door.

'Towel, towel . . .' murmured his father.

'I can find you one,' Midas said.

'I'm trying to find *you* one. Here.' He passed him one of the dishcloths. 'Now. You can't just run away from school.'

Midas rubbed the dishcloth over his hair.

'They'll be worrying about you.'

'They won't miss me.'

'Oh, they *will*, Midas. Institutions like that, they never miss a beat. They'll have the police out by now, I'm sure.'

The phone rang. Midas's father rubbed his moustache with forefinger and thumb.

'That'll probably be them now,' he said. 'Phoning to let me know you're gone. Come on.' He walked into the hallway and lifted the phone off the wall. 'Crook household. Mr Crook speaking. How may I help you? Yes. Yes, I'm afraid so. With me, yes. Oh, I will. Hm, well, good day.' He put the phone down firmly and sighed. 'Put your shoes on. I'll drive you back.'

'I've already got my shoes on.'

'Ah. Ah-hah. Then let's go. The car's in the road. I was, er, using the garage.'

'What were you doing with those bin liners?'

His father checked his pockets for his car keys but stopped before he opened the door, fingers on the handle. 'Don't worry, Midas. You can take them down this afternoon.'

'But what were you—'

'Midas. Please?' He opened the door. Rain flew in and slapped his face. 'Good Lord, you'd think the world was flooding.'

They stared up at the black clouds.

'I don't want to go back to school. If I do, Freddy Clare will either beat me up or stab me to death. Depending on whether he gets his knife back.'

'Yes,' murmured his father, watching plumes of water jump in puddles.

'I'm serious,' Midas said, 'and so is Freddy. He's crazy.'

'Come on then, into the car. Bring a bucket if you like, to bail us out as we go.' He chuckled to himself. Midas followed him through the rain, still holding the dishcloth, and climbed into the passenger seat. His father stopped, his keys halfway to the ignition.

'Your mother would have had you go to Sunday school if I hadn't objected. Can you believe that?' He leant back in his seat. 'I did you a favour, holding you back. Not for my son, the dogmatic belief in a monotheistic deity. No, my son is fully aware of the symbolism of a pantheon – the impossible coexistence of a multitude of ruling drives. Isn't that so, Midas?'

Would it be a fast puncture, if Freddy had the knife back, or something drawn out? Excruciatingly slow, a sliver at a time . . .

'You know, Midas, I'm glad we stumbled across each other this afternoon.' He tapped his fingers against the steering wheel while the keys still hung, unturned, in the ignition. 'This talk of Sunday school, and this torrid downpour, has taken me with thoughts of the Flood.'

Rainwater sloshed down the windscreen.

His father began to talk about arks settling on mountain peaks, about snow-white doves and drowned crows floating on oceans. Midas lost himself in worry. Then he realized his father had stopped talking. His knuckles were white on the steering wheel. His glasses had slipped halfway down his nose. That was how he got when he was excited. His father was never enthused or merry, but once in a very long while he was thrilled.

A blackbird, pummelled by rain, landed on the car bonnet and staggered over it before hopping down on to the tarmac and stumbling in another direction.

Midas's father clapped his hands. 'Boats, Midas! A fine way to do things. Finer than this nonsense with the bin liners.'

'What *about* the bin liners?'

'A fool's business. Boats, Midas! My God, but you're a stimulant.'

He turned the ignition suddenly. 'Let's get you back to school.'

Midas hung his head. He arrived back at school in time for double maths, with only a soaked dishcloth to show for his escape.

CHAPTER 10

When Midas woke, his head hurt and his joints felt stiff. He'd fallen asleep in the armchair in Ida's room, where it was pitch dark. They'd talked about easier things, books (they figured he'd read one for every twenty of hers), the news (he was out of touch) and cinema (he told her he couldn't cope with movies: he wanted to study every frame as he would a photo, but the effort made him dizzy). Eventually tiredness caught up with them. They fell asleep where they sat.

They'd left the curtains open and the world outside was visible now in vague blue layers, like looking out of a submarine. Soft breathing came from the bed. Midas's mouth felt dry and still tasted of white wine. He tried to settle back to sleep but that failed. He reached for the lamp. A spider raced up the wall, away from the soft orange glow that suddenly filled the room. Ida lay on the bed, her silver-dotted blanket folded over and beneath her. Her feet poked off the end of the bed. He watched them for a while, in a kind of doze. She snuffled and turned her head every so often, but her feet didn't move once. Even when she clenched her fists and drew them protectively to her chest, her toes remained still as stone.

Night-time seemed to upheave his curiosity, like the moon swelling up the tides. His camera nestled in his satchel beside the chair. He took it out, removed the lens cap, then realized what he was thinking and clipped it back on. He put down the camera on the bedside counter and refused to look at it.

It looked so innocent, but with Ida sleeping in the room it also looked weirdly alien, as if it were an accessory. He took hold of the strap, felt the coarse weave of its threads on his fingertips. He had thought of it for so long as an extension of his body, as others might think of a wheelchair or a pair of spectacles, that to consider acting independently made his shoulders tense and his toes go cold. He'd be blind without its guidance. Looking at Ida's motionless feet, he doubted he had the courage to investigate them without its cool.

His knees clicked when he got up and crept to the foot of the bed.

The top pair of Ida's socks were creamy white. He glanced back at the camera, the dull plastic of the lens cap masking its eye. His fingers twitched. He steadied his breathing, then gently placed a thumb on Ida's big toe. She didn't notice. The unexpected coolness of her foot meant it didn't feel like touching another person. She breathed regularly, lips parted, a fleck of saliva in the corner of her mouth. He pressed lightly. Her socks were soft. But her toe was hard like diamond.

He pulled his thumb away at once and stepped back from the bed. The white wine must still be addling him. What he'd touched hadn't felt like a toe.

He returned to the armchair and cradled his camera. Soon he was happy to believe he'd deceived himself.

He was ninety-nine-per-cent happy to believe that.

Drawing the strap of his camera over his head, he moved back to the end of the bed, took a deep breath and took her big toe between finger and thumb. He squeezed until he couldn't deny how icy hard it felt. And she surely couldn't feel it. She mumbled in her sleep. He shoved his cold hands into his pockets. On the ceiling, the spider cantered back and forth, in and out of the arc of the light.

He reached for the top of Ida's socks and gripped them gently together. Then he rolled them towards her ankle. She mumbled something and he froze, but left his fingers in place. She was still deep in her dream. He eased the socks down, over her ankle and a few inches of her foot.

He stared.

Kept staring.

Peeled off the socks entirely.

Her toes were pure glass. Smooth, clear, shining glass. Glinting crescents of light edged each toenail and each crease between the joints of each digit.

Seen through her toes, the silver spots on the bed sheet diffused into metallic vapours. The ball of her foot was glass too, but murkier, losing its transparency in a gradient until, near her ankle, it reached skin: matt and flesh-toned like any other. And yet . . . Those few inches of transition astonished him even more than her solid glass toes. Bones materialized faintly inside the ball of her foot, then became lily-white and precise nearer her unaltered ankle, shrouded along the way by translucent red ligaments in denser layers. In the curve of her instep wisps of blood hung trapped like twirls of paint in marbles. And there were places in the glass where the petrification was incomplete. Here was a pinprick mole, there a fine blonde hair.

Still she slept deeply.

His fingers inched their way towards the buttons on his camera.

When he had taken enough photos he stood for a while holding her removed socks. He tried to put them back on her, but as he pulled them up around her ankle she gasped in her sleep and he stopped very still. He hadn't woken her, but he couldn't get the sock back on. He left the sock scrunched over her toes and returned to the armchair where he gave careful consideration to running away. She would wake up at some point, notice her socks, and draw the obvious conclusion. He groaned quietly. He was still a little drunk, and very tired. The image of her foot hung in his mind, feeling like the memory of a dream he knew was about to dissolve.

Ida ran with her pulse and hip-hop in her ears. On her left towered giants of concrete and glass: office blocks and tenements whose laundry and hanging baskets brightened their drab sides with a hundred colours. On her right the city's river laboured under boats and buoys. Ahead a bridge crossed the honey-coloured water, bearing hundreds of pedestrians honked at by traffic. The sun turned each and every windscreen to a plate of opaque orange.

She jogged under the bridge and her footfalls echoed unevenly off girders decorated by graffiti artists and the tide. The echoes were uneven because she couldn't maintain a steady pace. Each time her right foot struck the pavement something sharp dug into her toe. She'd been trying to ignore it and had already stopped several times to shake stones out of her trainer with no result. She kept running for almost a mile before she tried again, this time sitting on a bench that looked across the river to the city's cathedral. A web of scaffolding wrapped the church's twin spires. Builders in hard hats moved across it like spiders. A party boat was moored on the far bank, its guests staggering about hugging each other and hooting across the water.

She removed her shoe and shook it, then did the same to her sock and felt for stones. Still nothing.

Putting it back on she felt something like a splinter and took her foot in her hands to try to find it.

The sun blinked off a speck on her big toe's underside, picked out an orange twinkle in her flushed skin. She tried to brush it off. It remained. Looking closer, she saw what looked like an embedded crystal. A thin layer of skin had grown over it.

Later, in a steaming bath back at her flat, with the noise of agitated traffic incessant even through closed windows, she tried to pick out the crystal with a needle and tweezers. She got a grip and yanked. Fiery pain coursed through her foot and she hissed and clamped a hand around her toe, squeezing hard as she waited for it to die out.

The crystal remained in its cushion of reddened flesh. She took a deep breath and tried to pluck it with the tweezers again, but the pain was even fiercer now the flesh was inflamed. A siren started outside and she had a sudden sense of the vastness of the city and the country beyond it, the landscape of the continent, cloud formations above, oceans undermining the land, and herself barely a speck within it all. She shivered. The bathwater had turned cold.

From nowhere she remembered the man from St Hauda's Land. Henry Fuwa and his jewellery box drilled with air holes.

She woke in the night and pulled the duvet tight around her. Her knees and legs felt bloodless and clammy. She looked at Midas, who slept in the chair with a shrill snore. He had turned the bedside lamp on. She wouldn't be surprised if this was due to a fear of the night, and she found that endearing. He held his camera on his lap like a teddy bear. Ida wondered whether she could trust him.

Trust him enough to tell him everything about her feet, she'd need to find out more about him.

She sat up and moved stealthily across the bed. The socks on one foot fell to the carpet. She stopped and stared from them to Midas.

He opened his eyes. A clock ticked somewhere in the darkness. This was the time of night when things seemed unreal, when a thought that could be dismissed in daylight might take hold of the guts and not be uprooted until morning. But he was awake, no doubt about it. He *had* seen what he had seen. He'd dreamt of lightning striking beaches and fusing sand grains into glass. And . . . he had not meant to fall asleep again. He had meant to run away before Ida woke up.

He yawned and was about to stretch when he realized his camera wasn't on his lap. The bedside lamp was still on. His whole body tensed.

Ida was sitting up in bed with her back to him, the camera's strap dangling from her hand.

He panicked. He feigned sleep. He couldn't tell which photo he wanted her to see least. That one where he'd filled the shot with the area of transition, so that the crystallised ribbons of blood reminded him of nebulas in photographs of deep space? Or the close-up of her toes, when he'd hovered his free hand behind them so they filled up with the pale pink of his fingers? He faked a snore. After a while, he heard Ida moving closer. He felt the camera's weight return to his lap. The bed sheets rustled and the mattress creaked. The light went out.

Ida woke him, nudging his arm. Wintry light filled the bedroom. He shut his eyes again.

'Come on, Midas. I've got something to show you.'

She smelt fragrant and her hair was wet. She wore a dove-grey jumper and a black skirt over which she'd tied a white apron. She had her boots back on.

'Come on.'

He forced himself up and followed her into the kitchen where she stopped by the window, leaving space for him to stand beside her. Fine snow had settled outside, blanketing the fields that sloped up to the tangled woods. Halfway up the slope, deer were walking. A small herd, the closest maybe twenty yards away. A young stag patrolled solemnly among them, occasionally shaking snow from his immature antlers.

'Beautiful, aren't they?'

'Yes.'

Oh *God*, he thought as the memory of Ida hunched over his camera rushed back to him. She knew he'd seen her feet. Why hadn't she mentioned it? Oh *God.*

She went to the cooker. Blue flames on the hob heated a frying pan, bacon and tomatoes sizzling in its oil. She peeled back the plastic cover of a packet of sausages.

'I'm cooking you a full English,' she said. 'To say thanks for staying over last night. Are you hung over?'

He tried to smile.

She flipped the bacon and pushed it around the pan. 'Coffee or tea?'

'Coffee please.'

Outside, one of the deer nudged its face against the stag's.

Ida poured coffee into a big white mug while steam rose in the air.

'Orange juice?'

'Listen, Ida . . .'

She glanced up at him, then back at the bacon. 'Well?'

'Coffee, please.'

'You've already got coffee.'

He looked into the black circle in the mug. 'Yeah. I mean, it's fine, thanks. No juice. Just coffee's fine . . . um.'

She cracked a pink egg and the insides ran into the frying pan. The white hissed and turned cloudy.

'One egg or two? I got them from a farmer who lives around the corner.'

'Er . . . Ida?'

She sprinkled a little salt on the egg, then glanced irritably at him. 'You're determined to bring it up? I suppose I thought we could pretend it never happened.'

She ran her wooden spatula around the rim of the egg. Outside, the deer moved across the field in slow motion.

'Look,' she said eventually, 'I thought I'd be angry but I'm not.' She tapped the spatula against her other palm. 'At least not very. I don't understand why, but I actually feel a little relieved.

'This morning I've tried to think of all the reasons why you might be so intrusive. Did you know already? Or perhaps you just have a foot fetish?' She laughed. 'But you wanted to take a photo, didn't you? There was no malice.'

She stirred the bacon. He shuffled.

'Midas, I *like* you.' She pointed the spatula at him. 'But don't you tell a soul about my feet. I swear to God I'll kill you if you do.'

'Okay,' he said, swallowing.

'Breakfast's done. Sit down.'

He pulled out a chair and sat at the table. A checked tablecloth lay diagonally, leaving the wooden corners bare.

'So,' she said, 'do you want this egg?'

'Do they *hurt*?'

She stared intently at the food as she slapped it on to two plates and dumped them on the table, rattling the knives and forks. Midas shrivelled into the chair.

'Listen, I've told you I trust you. I forgive you for prying, although I still think you've been incredibly rude even if you didn't mean to be. But I'm not sure I want to go into the gory details. I like to forget about them.'

'They frighten you, don't they?'

'When you've dug yourself a hole, Midas, and someone offers you a way out, it's customary to take it, not keep digging.'

'Sorry.'

She sat down, then stood up again, tore at the apron strings to undo the knot, took off the apron, scrunched it up and threw it across the room. She sat down again. She picked up her knife and fork and sawed into her egg, spilling the yolk everywhere. She took a deep breath and laid her cutlery against her plate. She put her palms to her eyes and rubbed them. 'I'm sorry. You're right. They frighten me.'

'I won't tell a soul and I won't ask questions.'

'Thanks.'

'My coffee's lovely.' He took another sip and began on his bacon.

'Midas?'

He chewed. 'Yes?'

'The glass is spreading. I'm frightened. One month ago only the very tips of my toes were affected.'

He swallowed. The kitchen seemed so quiet now he'd stopped chewing. 'Have you . . . I mean, do you mind if I ask . . .'

'If I've seen a doctor?' She shook her head. 'You

think a doctor could help? *Here, take these antibiotics. It'll clear up in a fortnight.*'

'Maybe you could find some kind of . . . alternative treatment?'

'Like what? Holistic medicine? Acupuncture? I'm in deeper trouble than . . .' She stopped speaking because her eyes were brimming.

He looked down at his breakfast. He cut into a fried tomato and watched the seeds float out on its juices.

Ida wiped her eyes and tried her tea but pulled a face because it was getting cold. 'I'm scared, Midas. Although it won't stop me.'

He nodded slowly. 'And what can I do?'

'I told you. Tell no one.'

'I want to help.'

He watched her stand up and hobble delicately towards the kettle. He thought she'd tell him to stop interfering again. Outside, the deer were slinking back into the trees.

'The simplest thing you could do to help . . . Like I said before . . . I *am* frightened. I can't feel my toes, for God's sake. I don't know where I end and my socks and boots begin. You could, if it's not too much trouble, just hang around.'

He stood up. He supposed in a movie this would be the moment where he put his arm around her waist and said something manly. At the very least he'd place a firm hand on her shoulder. But his arms were dead.

'Okay,' he said, 'that shouldn't be a problem.'

'Thanks,' she said. 'I need to go to the bathroom.'

He sat there and poked his bacon while she was gone. This was a big deal. A very big deal. He looked down at his camera and wondered if it had got him into this as some kind of jealous punishment for spending too much time thinking of her. Yet he was relieved that he might still get his chance to photograph her with her consent.

He closed his eyes and felt some happiness for that, set as it was against the unsettling idea that she was turning into glass.

CHAPTER 11

Carl Maulsen gripped the ferry railing and watched the waves rear and spit like cobras. Close fog reduced the world to the painted white metal of boat rocking on sea. Wind brushed him with ribbons of fog that lingered wrapped around his limbs or noosed around his neck.

He took a deep breath of briny cold air. To say that he had been haunted by Freya Maclaird these last few days would not be metaphorical. He didn't believe in ghosts but he had seen her, like a projection on the wall, one night when drowsy in his room. He thought he had glimpsed her in a crowded street and barged towards her before coming to his senses and glaring back at the strangers he'd elbowed aside. Nevertheless he was sure he had recognized her outfit and the sunburn across her nose from when he was twenty-one and the two of them were on their way back to their university campus from the beach.

Then the other night he had been ill. He had woken up bathed in pins and needles. He squirmed in his bed, knotting himself in his sheets. The blankets were by turns his only shelter from teeth-chattering cold and made of a fabric as hot and sticky as lava. He had thrown himself under his hotel-room shower and sat coughing and sweating under a trickle of tepid water. But after that he had felt better. Stretched, yet refocused. He had not imagined seeing Freya since. He had got a grip.

Now on the ferry, he looked at the white hairs dashing along his forearms and the backs of his hands. A foghorn sounded somewhere in the mists.

Something Midas Crook senior once wrote a paper concerning, something he had discussed with Carl in his cluttered office, was the wearing of time on a person. He had written the image of a person's life like a day's clothing. Beginning with the pulling on of layers on a cold morning, then adjusted to dress and leave the house for work. The change back to casual clothes in the evening, the final stripping away as night came. Crook said each garment was one of many characters a person held in their lifetime.

Carl had argued that the parable worked better if the clothes were those worn across a year, because personalities were not accrued and covered up throughout life, but shed and changed, bought and sold, many times over.

He walked off the ferry with his suitcase clattering behind him and sat in a poky tearoom overlooking the harbour, among used cups and crumb-covered plates the staff were too idle to clear up.

Now he worried that Crook had been right. Carl had always thought of himself as a being changed many times over by life, exchanged and bettered for more agreeable personalities. Just as his body had replaced every cell, he had replaced and rebuilt his entire personality to make it something robustly his own, owing nothing to Freya.

Yet now he felt himself as a man in the mould of Crook's parable: a man whose working clothes were wearing through, exposing the hidden cloth of the past beneath.

Booking a taxi on the island could leave you with a lengthy wait. Having finished reading *The Odyssey* for the umpteenth time while still on the ferry, the only way to kill time was with a tepid cup of tea (too sweet before adding sugar) and a two-day-old local rag blotted with coffee stains. He chased shades out of his head for thirty minutes, until a taxi honked and he left his teacup with the other dirty crockery and headed outside.

He vaguely recognized the driver as the man who'd taken him to the harbour when he left the island. The driver recognized him too, asking how the trip had been while they drove. Carl deflected the driver's conversation with monosyllabic answers. Bare fields passed like chessboards set with white trees and black crows. If you stared up at the low clouds you couldn't tell whether the fizz you saw was dust on your eyeballs or brewing snowfall.

They pulled up outside the cottage. He unloaded his suitcase, paid, then stood for a minute before the blue door and its ridiculous lucky horseshoe (Freya had given him that). He laid his palm on the dewy paintwork, rolled his neck from side to side so it clicked in a satisfying fashion. He broadened his shoulders, puffed into his hand to check the mint on his breath, then seized the knocker and struck it three times hard against his own front door.

Ida greeted him, leaning with one hand on the wall and the other on a wooden crutch. He recognized that crutch in an instant: he had made it himself. She had no doubt found it leaning on his sitting-room wall and thought nothing of helping herself to it.

She moved to hug him. He stepped timidly into her embrace and he felt her grip on his sides, as if there were a yawning drop beneath her. When in his frenzy to leave the cottage he had remarked on the walking stick she'd been using, she had blurted out an explanation, a broken bone nearly healed, that he had no time to doubt. Now he noticed her enforced stillness and doubted whether she was being honest with him.

Entering the cottage behind her he saw the sink full of popping washing-up bubbles. The washing had barely begun and steam still rose from the sink. There were two dishes, two sets of cutlery, two coffee mugs.

'You've had a guest,' he said flatly. He was surprised to feel riled at that.

She shrugged. 'You just missed him.'

He raised his eyebrows. She hit him with the tea towel.

'Sorry, Ida. Just sticking my nose in.'

'Snap out of it, Carl. We didn't do anything.'

He held up his hands and forced an amicable smile. 'It's none of my business if you did. He's a local lad?'

'Yes, of course. I met him in Ettinsford. He's a photographer.'

Then not a successful man. There was no room for a successful photographer on St Hauda's Land. 'Does he have a name?'

'Of course.'

Carl kept beaming. 'You're not going to tell me what it is?'

She wrung the tea towel.

'It doesn't matter,' he said.

'No. It's funny. I think you'll know him. His name's Midas.'

He should have known it was the boy at once, but it was the father he thought of first.

'You knew his father, didn't you? There's a picture of him on your bookshelf.'

'Yes.'

'Well then.'

They'd got the doctorates in a gale. The photographer had to keep retaking the shot, since every time he took it the wind buffeted Midas Crook and he staggered out of shot.

He saw them all jumbled up in his mind's eye. Freya and Midas Crook. Ida and himself. Ida and his younger self. Ida and Crook. He snorted and shook his head.

'What's up, Carl?'

94

He had played carpenter. Chopped the wood and tasted sawdust in the air when he made the crutch Ida now leant on. Knocked in the nails. Tested it with his whole weight. Then driven at breakneck speed to the hospital where Freya lay laughing in Casualty with fractured ribs and a broken leg from an abseiling accident. She had recovered with her body weight on that crutch. Then, one summer morning rich with blossom scent, he had answered the door to a sneezing postman and a narrow parcel. No explanation beyond the return of the gift itself and a saccharine card from Freya Maclaird, where she'd always signed herself plain Freya before. He'd unpacked the crutch and inhaled hard along the length of the wood, hoping for a whiff of her. All he'd smelt was the blossom in the air.

'Nothing,' he said. 'I . . . greatly admired him. He was something of a mentor to me. How is his boy?'

She laughed. 'He's a bit of a weirdo. But I think he's sweet. He didn't like his father.'

'That's no surprise. Only a few of us did.'

CHAPTER 12

As a small boy, sitting on the bottom step in the shadows in the house of his parents, Midas admired it. He'd have thought it would ooze or pour, but it blazed and was gone in the blink of an eye. Really it migrated. At six million miles an hour. And if you shut it out . . .

He closed the heavy curtains and drew the blinds behind them. The photos on the walls became sheets of paper again, their tones reduced by darkness to an average of grey. He could just as easily have been sitting on a rock in the murk of a cave. But then he plugged the wire into his flashgun.

And there it was, dashing itself on the curtains. Picking out the criss-cross of their navy threads, then vanishing as dramatically as it had appeared. Everything was darker after the flash. He waited in awe for dim traces of light to worm their way back into the hall. When darkness had reverted to near-darkness, he plugged the wire in again. The flashgun purred.

The photos on the walls changed from grey nothings to streets and stiff figures in formal dress, then back to nothings. The blue imprint of light on his eyelids faded and he was ready to press the button for more flash when the front door sprang open and the hall filled with colour and noise.

He squinted to see his mother limp inside, a cardboard box held to her chest by her freckled arms. Muggy air followed her, along with the rumble of traffic and the chirrup of a songbird. She wiped her feet briskly on the mat, then jumped with fright.

'Oh,' she whispered, relaxing, 'it's you. I didn't see you, it's that gloomy.'

The front door swung shut behind her, restoring the soft gloom. She smiled at Midas and pushed open the dining-room door with her backside. It was dark in there too. He plugged the wire into the flashgun and she shrieked and nearly dropped the box. She held it closer to her breasts, stroking it protectively with one hand.

'Son, you shouldn't surprise me like that.'

She limped into the dining room. He stood up and walked in after her. She placed the box on the table and clapped her hands.

'Your father's not in? Your father's not in, is he?'

He shook his head.

She grinned and clapped her hands again, then spun around and tore open the dining-room curtains so that sunlight poured through the windowpanes. She pulled a clip from her hair and shook out her crimped locks. The light shone through them and brightened the beige fabric of her dress. Humming like a music-box, she tore a strip of tape from the parcel. Dust particles panicked and swarmed in the light.

The parcel was full of polystyrene figure-of-eights that she pulled out in eager handfuls that flew through the air, turning the dining room into a kind of snow globe. Then she stopped and lifted a smaller box from the first. She took a craft knife and made a tender incision through its tape. Inside were a few more figure-of-eights and something wrapped in tissue paper that scratched and scrunched as it came undone in her fingers.

A deep frame with a glass front. When she turned it to show him he saw five insects pinned inside. They were dragonflies, each the size of his fist and each the purest white. Their milky wings were stretched and pinned. Their ghostly, unpigmented eyes were the size of pearls. There was an inscription accompanying them, but Midas couldn't read it.

Midas's mother closed her eyes and started to tremble. She swallowed loud lungfuls of air to steady herself.

'Now, son,' she said when her eyes reopened, 'run the box and all these bits of packaging down to the tip. I'll give you some money. You can get some sweets on the way back.'

He looked warily at the sun on the lawn, all sickly green. 'Can't you take it? You can drive.'

'Be a good boy.'

'I don't want to go outside.'

'Listen . . . I have to . . . hide these. Before your

father returns. He won't understand. Be a good boy, son.'

They gathered up the polystyrene and stuffed it back into the parcel. Then his mother gave him some coins and he grudgingly carried the box out of the house. But he went no farther, creeping back inside to spy on her.

He watched her strutting about in the hallway with an imaginary dancing partner, her bad leg making her moves lopsided. Without hesitation he sneaked to the cupboard where his parents kept their Polaroid and tiptoed back to use his mother as subject, taking photos one by one, loving the whirr as they slid out undeveloped. He laid them on the kitchen floor while she hummed a ballroom tune in the hallway. They emerged from the white like explorers returning from a blizzard. He was so engrossed by this enchantment that he didn't hear his mother's humming stop. She caught him poring over the photographs.

'Son!' she hissed, bustling over to the photos he'd taken. She put a hand to her forehead when she saw them and moaned.

'Mother?'

There was a noise at the front door. She turned to Midas, suddenly alarmed. He watched her eyes widen. 'Quick!' she hissed, but the noise was only the afternoon paper dropping through the letterbox. She held a hand to her heart. Then she became agitated again. 'I must hide the dragonflies,' she said to herself as much as to him. She picked up the pile of photos. 'And now I must hide these. But Midas, please deliver this box to the tip as you said you would. I beg you: do that for me.'

He shrugged and went back outside, picking up the box to carry it a few paces down the street before turning into a leafy alley. The hot sun drew sweat beneath his jumper. Birds screeched and fled as he passed. A black-and-yellow caterpillar dangled from a stalk, building a cocoon to melt itself into something else. Searing light was everywhere and blinding, and he jogged to get the trip to the dump over with. Soon he could smell rot. The alley took a right turn into a ring of skips and growling machines. Muscular workers in neon jackets frowned at him as he scampered up the steps of a skip and tossed the box on to a bed of litter. When he climbed down, one of the workers said something about his haircut. He hurried back up the shady alley towards the house.

Just as he was opening the front garden gate, somebody called, 'Midas!'

His father, walking down the street, a burgundy sweater over a cream shirt and black tie. Not a drop of sweat on him. The light gleamed on his glasses and bald head and buried itself in his dense moustache. He nodded to Midas at the gate.

'You've been playing in the street?'

'No. I . . . went to buy a film for my camera.'

His father shook his head and pushed through the gate. 'You should spend your pocket money on books. You know that? *Books*, Midas.' He paused, twitched his fingers and crouched down by the verge of the lawn. 'Ah . . . What have we here?'

He held up a polystyrene figure-of-eight as if it were a rare gem. He turned it round and round, rubbing his moustache. 'Hmm. Well now.'

Dinginess had returned to the house. Midas's mother, having redrawn the curtains and blinds, stood in the hallway as his father wiped his shoes on the mat and crouched to slowly unfasten his laces.

'Good afternoon, dear,' he said sweetly.

'Good afternoon. Hello, dear.'

She hovered closer, restless. He slid off his shoes and passed them to Midas, who put them on the rack and handed back his father's slippers. These his father pulled over his argyle-patterned socks. Then he took her hand, turned it over and pressed the figure-of-eight into her palm.

'Litter. Cast by some troublemaker, no doubt, into our front garden.'

The colour – what there had been of it in the gloom – drained from her face. She shot a desperate, sideways glance at Midas. But what could he do?

'Litter,' repeated his father, 'unless, of course, one of your parcels was delivered today.'

She bit her trembling lip into stillness. Her eyes flicked from left to right.

'Listen,' he said, rubbing his moustache, 'I don't want to go through this routine again. But you promised me no more parcels.'

She tried to stammer something but gave up.

'I appreciate, darling, that there's nothing you can do to prevent these parcels being *sent* to you. And though you've raised our objections, still the Post Office retains these packages for you. Naturally the staff there are rushed off their feet, they forget that you want these items returned to sender.'

'Th-there's no item, dear. It was just, j-just a normal parcel.'

'Containing what?'

'A . . . a . . .'

He sighed. 'Where did you hide it? I don't want to turn the house over. I'd hoped to finish my Pliny before suppertime.'

'I . . . I've not . . . Hidden . . .'

He shrugged and wearily turned to climb the stairs. Midas's mother followed him up to their bedroom. Midas watched from the doorway as his father went one by one through their drawers, turning on a lamp to see better. The bottom drawer housed underwear and night things. He plucked each item out individually. Simple grey briefs and, deeper down, frayed lace knickers and a bra bearing crumpled fabric flowers.

'*Ahh,*' he said, long fingers closing on the framed dragonflies. Her shoulders sank. He beamed up at her and popped the back off the frame, plucking the pins so the dead insects fell on the bed.

'Fascinating,' he said, 'if a little macabre.'

'You . . . They're pretty. Please don't destroy them.'

'My dear Evaline, the validation of their beauty is irrelevant. My question remains: who are they from?'

She was silent.

He nodded and carefully picked up the first dragonfly. 'The bin please, Midas.'

Midas skulked into the bedroom and lifted the bin up to his father, who didn't take it from him. The dragonfly crunched like tissue paper in his closing fist, and Midas's mother flinched at the noise. He opened his hand and wriggled his fingers. Bits of white wing and bent leg spiralled down to the bin on their last flight.

He ground the dragonflies one by one, with Midas's mother slumped heavily on the bed. Then he plodded back to his study. Midas loitered for a moment, then crept back to the bottom of the stairs where everything was pleasantly dark, to toy with his flashgun.

CHAPTER 13

An afternoon of snow lay deep in Gustav's garden. Denver (zipped, buttoned and toggled) scooped armfuls into a lump for a snowman's base. She was a mouse-haired seven-year-old with a grin full of disorganized teeth and a winter daisy in her hair. Gustav helped, doing donkey-work on his daughter's orders, while Midas provided the details: a carrot, a faded felt beret and a bag of nuts to make buttons.

He closed his eyes and felt bitter snow particles landing on his face. He sometimes felt like an impostor in these little family moments. Gustav had joked the other day that Midas was now Denver's surrogate mother. Then, seeing Midas worrying about that, he'd explained that this was no bad thing: he couldn't run the florist and look after Den if he didn't have an old friend to count on.

That made it worse because it was true. Of course Midas loved their company. It was just . . . If Catherine was here she'd be the one plugging in the snowman's eyes, not him, so with each nut pressed into the flaky snow he thought of what had happened to her up on Lomdendol Tor, and wished like crazy he could turn around and see her shaking a carrot or bringing out gloves for the snowman's twig-fingers.

A bittersweet afternoon with his friends was still better than sitting alone in his kitchen. For the past couple of days he'd suppressed the guilt he felt for hiding what he knew about Henry Fuwa from Ida. Now it had returned he worried whether his only release would be to own up to her. Then he wondered what good that would do, because although Fuwa's name had been familiar, he had no better clue than Ida as to which hiding hole on St Hauda's Land Fuwa called his own. He'd scoured his walls of photos for distraction, but photos churned up all manner of memories, sometimes creating new ones. He'd fled his kitchen, locked his front door and raced down slippery pavements to Gustav's house. He knew he was suppressing something else now. Although he didn't know Fuwa's whereabouts himself, he suspected he knew somebody who might.

'We're going to make mince pies tomorrow,' said Denver when they were back in the house and Gustav was forcing her to get changed into dry clothes. She was an earnest child with a whiz of ginger hair, eyes too big for her freckled face and newly grown adult teeth overlapping like a hand of cards. 'Dad's promised to find some cutters so we can make biscuits. Will you help?'

Midas was staring out at the whitening world.

'Midas!'

'Sorry, what was that, Den?'

Gustav butted in with a remark about her wet hair. He shooed her out of the kitchen. She left without complaint, looking back worriedly over her shoulder at Midas. Gustav closed the door after her. 'What's wrong?'

'It's Ida.'

'*Ah*. You want a beer?'

'I'm really not in the mood.'

'Midas . . . I know there are a hundred things you'd never tell me about and that's fine, but if you want to offload some of your melancholy, then muggins here is happy to help. What about a brandy? Some festive cheer?'

'Um. Gus, I don't mean romantic troubles. Just . . . You ever heard of this man called Henry Fuwa? He lives on the island.'

'Well . . . *pfff*. No. We could check the phone book, and the customer records at the florist.'

'I already have.'

'Has she *hired* you? Are you her private eye or something?'

'I, er, I . . . deleted him from the customer records.'

'Come again?'

The phone rang. Midas gestured for Gustav to go ahead and answer. Gustav looked at the caller's number on the phone's display. 'Catherine's mum again. She's really going through a phase about it.'

'You'd better answer.'

Gustav picked up and began another weary conversation with his mother-in-law about where they would spend Christmas. Gustav didn't want to travel to the mainland to see Catherine's parents, who'd moved there after her accident. Nor did Catherine's parents want to make the trip to St Hauda's Land, which they hadn't returned to since. It would end, many phone calls later, with stalemate, and then one or the other party would suggest they all got together the following year.

The door opened and Denver came back in. She grabbed Midas's hand and towed him into the sitting room.

'This game,' she said, kneeling behind a stack of shoeboxes on the carpet, 'is one I invented. I reckon it's pretty good.'

Behind them stood Gustav's freshly cut, undecorated Christmas tree. It had filled the room with the scent of pine needles.

'Right . . .' She lifted the lid off the first shoebox. Inside, folded in beige sugar paper, were baubles and delicate wooden decorations. Midas thought of last Christmas-time, when he had watched Gustav smash a snow globe with a hammer while he thought no one was watching. He had said it had reminded him of the air up on Lomdendol Tor.

'The rules are easy. What you have to do is decide what each decoration is before you hang it on the tree. Like this . . .' She reached into the shoebox and pulled out a blue metallic orb. 'This,' she said, 'is the world when God flooded it. And if you look super, super close,' she pressed the decoration to her eye, 'you can just about see the ark. And Noah.

Who's bald. And narwhals swimming.' She hooked the bauble's thread over a branch and held the shoebox towards Midas. 'Your turn.'

He reached into the shoebox and pulled out an orange bauble sparkling with rainbow glitter. 'This is a pumpkin coach,' he said after a while, 'but they've yet to find it wheels.'

Denver nodded her approval. 'Do you want me to put it on the tree for you?'

'No. I'm doing it.' He found a nice spot beneath where the star would go.

Denver picked another bauble from the shoebox. It was blood red, dusted with ruby glitter. 'This,' she proclaimed, 'is Father Christmas when he's had too much to eat.'

Midas scratched his head. 'I don't understand what the point of the game—'

'*Shh*!' She glanced back into the kitchen, where Gustav leant in resignation against the wall, rubbing his forehead with his free hand, tapping his foot on the floor. 'I was spying . . . The point of the game is to trick yourself for a moment. So things aren't what they are.'

'Uh?'

'It's *your go*.'

He pulled out a perfectly clear glass orb.

'Go on,' prompted Denver, 'you have to decide what it is.'

His palm distorted in its sphere. He shuddered. 'It's a crystal ball,' he said, seeing his reflection warping on the surface, made leaner and more bug-eyed: more like his mother. Then, when he rotated it, scrawny and sallow-cheeked: more like his father. He kept it revolving and watched himself oscillate between genetic codes. He could remember the smell of peat; his mother humming happier than she'd ever been; dragonflies from the bog; a bouquet of flowers crumpled in a bin; Nihongo inscriptions; water dripping from cut stalks; ink running illegible.

'Yes!' hissed Denver, her wild grin packed with teeth. 'I knew it would work!'

He gawped at her. 'What?'

'Because you were ignoring what was in the back of your head. And this is how I spend time in the back of *my* head, by doing things like this.'

He looked at her in admiration: 'How did you get to be so brave, Den?'

She shrugged. 'Shit happens, Dad says.' She stood up and adjusted a bauble on the tree. 'I don't think there is being brave, anyway. I used to not tread in puddles in case I fell in them and died like Mummy did. But then in the autumn when it flooded I got stuck and had to splash through one. It didn't feel safer or worser. I just had to splash through it or wait until the sun came up and it all dried out.'

He stood up. 'Den,' he said, 'you're right. At least, yeah, sometimes you have to scrap being brave and get on with things. I've got to go. Will you say goodbye to your dad for me?'

CHAPTER 14

The bridges from Gurm to Lomdendol Island always reminded Midas of toppled pylons. Old girders of steel coated with the sea's white tartar zigzagged between rocky islets across a space of chopping ocean. On the Lomdendol side of the crossing they plunged into a tunnel in a rock face. This was in fact the lowest reach of the tor. On the other side of the tunnel the road emerged uphill, strafing up snow-covered ledges. In summer the shadow of the hill falling across the island was starkly defined. The slopes would be grey, the sea between the bridges dark and deep even though, in the distance, the water would be bright blue where the sun shone unobstructed. Come autumn, it was as if the tor's shadow was unbound. It became like a gas in the air. Nothing on Lomdendol Island was free of the dark. The land responded with breeds of fungi and pebble-grey mushrooms. Slugs, snails and amphibians enjoyed the damp shade and could often be found crossing the pavements of Martyr's Pitfall, Lomdendol's principal village. Come winter, the shadow trapped the land in invisible coats of ice, made slides out of pavements and mirrors out of puddles.

In Midas's view, Martyr's Pitfall was old age's Death Row. Houses were built cannily out of sight from each other, to give the illusion that they were isolated homes in the countryside. Midas parked his car and tasted the tor's shadow on his tongue like a copper coin. He shivered. Somewhere up there on the foggy peak was the hidden pool that had swallowed Catherine.

Snow covered the front lawn and muted the chimes that hung in his mother's garden. Midas stomped about on the doorstep, rubbing his gloved hands together. A brass cherub gnawed the ring of a knocker, which he grabbed and banged again on the door. The house was only a few years old, the brick still characterless and the garden a square imposition on the landscape. Midas hated it: hated the tacky cherub knocker, hated the tacky garden fountain like a Grecian nymph, hated the tacky sundial inscribed with faux Latin. Granted, he wasn't the most adventurous man in the world, but his mother wasn't even sixty and he felt she should still have been busying herself with work, not consigning herself to a village that was little more than a dispersed care home. He always questioned why, when his father died, she seemed so incapable of unfettering herself of his ghost and living the life he had denied her. Instead she had checked in here, happy to skip her grey-haired days and cut straight to toothless ones.

He remembered his father's wake, picking at the drab food his aunt had bought and made. Tasteless pastries, sandwiches like something from a pond, little cakes with squashed glazed cherries in their icing. Dead man food. He had put slices of cucumber and an oatcake on to a paper plate and looked around for a corner where he could avoid the guests. His mother had found the best one. He could still picture her on the windowsill in her black lace dress, the net curtains stirring behind her in the draught, letting in the smell of rain on tarmac. Her fingers had tapped against a glass of untouched water. She hadn't moved all afternoon. Nor had she drunk any of her water or eaten any food. None of the scant few guests in attendance spoke to her. *He* didn't speak to her. But he remembered wailing at her, inside his head, to begin again.

He knocked a second time. A vacuum cleaner was whirring inside. Nobody answered. The wind gusted through the spindly plants in his mother's garden. They were rosebushes but he could tell from working at Catherine's that these were too unhealthy to bloom. His mother had given up tending white roses some years ago. He pressed his ear to the door and heard the vacuum cleaner's murmur.

He remembered, after his father's first suicide attempt, his mother redoubling her efforts to bind the three of them together as a family. Sitting inside on a drizzling afternoon, at the opposite end of the sofa to his father, he had fiddled with his camera while the old man pored over a huge book with yellowing pages. Then his mother tiptoed up to his father, bent stealthily over his shoulder, and kissed his cheek.

His father shrieked and leapt off the sofa, clutching his chest above the heart. '*Evaline!*'

She giggled. She held a bouquet of white roses, wrapped unprofessionally. She'd been tending them in the garden since the previous summer and had now picked the best ones as a gift. While Midas's father looked on in horror she stammered a corny and rehearsed poem, stumbling over the rhymes.

'Happy anniversary.'

She thrust the roses into his arms but he twisted away, cutting one palm on a thorn. She flinched and offered the roses again. He snatched them, hauled open a drawer and found a pair of scissors to snip and slash until shreds of white petal were all over the carpet and the room smelt of their perfume. He sulked out of the door, sucking his palm where the thorn had scratched it, and locked himself in his study.

Puberty was the thing incapacitating Midas in those days, leaving his courage as devastated as his father's. He couldn't comfort his mother. She sat down on the sofa and bawled.

Then her hands reached for him, grabbed his hair, slithered around his back, pulling him to her. He felt her dry hair on his face, heard her ugly sobbing in his ear and smelt her *breath*. He shrieked, but her grip was too tight. He had to shove her away to escape. He leapt away and stood there panting while she nodded violently as if in a fit. She clenched her fists and beat them on her knees. He felt guilt for not comforting her, but the horror of her touch was insurmountable. Her skin was so papery, her tears so warm. He simply stood there immobile, clutching his hands to his heart like his father.

Suddenly the door of his mother's house in Martyr's Pitfall opened a crack and a young woman peered out. Midas was cold, and on the doorstep, and grown up again.

'Hello,' she said slowly, examining his features.

'Hello. I've come to see my mother.'

Recognition spread across her face. 'Why, Mr Crook! I knew it was you! A pleasure to see you. I'm afraid your mother's gone out, to walk in the snow. I'll let her know you called.'

She clung to the door, pushing it a little further closed.

Midas placed his foot on the threshold as politely as he could. 'Um . . .' he said, 'I'm coming in.'

'But . . .'

'We both know she's at home.' He squeezed inside apologetically, took off his shoes and placed them on the mat.

The young woman looked annoyed. 'Well then . . . Let me go and tell her you've come. I'll see if she's available.'

He shook his head and walked down the sparse hallway, stepping over the vacuum cleaner and opening the door to the back room. The girl clapped her hands to her head in frustration. She was the maid his mother employed to look after her, doing her shopping and cooking, sometimes bathing her, mopping her up.

His mother sat on a chair pulled up to a bay window. The room was devoid of any other furniture save a tea-set on a table beside her. Outside, the white lawn and bare trees were as black and white as a photo. Icicles hung from a bird table.

His mother's hair still kept a bone-yellow tint of its old colour. She wore drooping pearl earrings and a salmon-pink shawl that couldn't disguise her skeletal shoulder-blades.

'Good afternoon, Christiana,' she said, in a croak of a voice, reaching to her tea table with willowy fingers. She selected a brown sugar cube from a pot. Her fingernails were the beigest of pinks. The sugar cube plopped into a cup on her lap.

For a moment he weighed up turning around and leaving. Coming here made his skin too tight for his body. But then he thought of what he owed Ida.

'I'm not Christiana,' he said.

Something in her neck clicked as she turned.

'Hello. Mother.'

She put her tea on the table shakily, spilling a little into her lap. She didn't notice: dried tea stains already marred her dress.

'You . . . you should have phoned. Given me time to prepare.'

'You would have made sure you weren't around.'

'I would never have. We would have gone to the beach. Had a nice day out. My goodness, you are like your father.'

She turned back to stare at the window. Not, he felt, at the snowy world outside, nor even her reflection, but at the glass pane itself.

'So,' she said, 'why have you come?'

'I brought your Christmas presents.' He opened his satchel and drew out a carrier bag of gifts he'd wrapped in black-and-white paper.

'Oh. Of course. It's that time of year already. I'm afraid I haven't done Christmas shopping this year.'

'That doesn't matter. I'll put these here shall I?'

'Yes. Christiana will deal with them when you're gone.'

He placed them carefully on the carpet. 'I'm going to Gustav's this Christmas. Denver's getting bigger. You're invited.'

'Didn't you go last year?'

'I go every year. It's fun.'

'Yes, well.' She looked down at her lap. 'I'll think about it.'

'Okay. Do that.'

'So . . . Was there anything else?'

'Yes, as a matter of fact.'

'Mm?'

He steadied himself. He had planned out his line of questioning to come gently to his main enquiry,

116

in the hope she would weather it better. They had never talked about Henry Fuwa, or the occasional presents he had sent her while Midas was a child. Midas had been happy to leave the topic with all the others. Until now.

'When I was a child, parcels arrived for you. Gifts. One time there was a frame of white dragonflies, another time some photographs. Father destroyed them. But you tried to hide them from him.'

She sat up, wary like a rabbit.

'Why did you try to hide them, Mother?'

She plopped another sugar cube into her tea and stirred it determinedly. The sugar didn't melt because the tea was tepid.

'Please tell me.'

'What's it to you? These things happened so long ago. Why stir them up?'

'Someone's in trouble.'

'What does that mean? What do you mean by that?'

'Please just tell me who they were from.'

She set down the teaspoon and slurped the tea. 'They were pleasant, weren't they?'

'Please, Mother.'

'From your father.'

'No. He hated them. He tore them up.'

'He was a contradictory man. He did worse things, things you don't know about. He stole my wedding dress, did I ever tell you that?'

'No.'

'One day it had vanished. He denied it of course, but I know it went the way of the dragonflies.'

Midas heard the moistness of his tongue click in his mouth. 'So . . . why are you pretending the gifts were from him?'

She fiddled with the spotted lap of her dress. He might as well have been pulling out her hair, for all the joy this visit was bringing her.

Her breath sounded like wind through dead wood. 'Have you ever hoped for something? And held out for it against all the odds? Until everything you did was ridiculous?'

He didn't answer.

'They were chosen for me. They were what *I* wanted. They were hand-picked for me.' She shook herself and tugged on the strands of her shawl. 'Forget it. Let's forget all of it. If they weren't from your father they can't have been intended for me. That would have been inappropriate.'

In the polished window their reflections were translucent doppelgängers. She looked him up and down. 'Your father,' she mouthed. 'My word, you are like your father.'

He licked his dried-out lips. 'Mother . . . You . . . I know you were having an affair.'

She nodded almost imperceptibly.

She broke down in tears and clenched her fists and hammered them on her knees. He looked away from the sight of her so wretched. With no second chair, he folded himself cross-legged on the carpet. He remembered his mother crying like this when

118

he was a schoolboy: when his father had snipped up the roses she'd grown for him. And here Midas Crook the younger sat, still as helpless to comfort her as he'd been all those years ago.

His mother sobbed. Tears traced the cracked skin of her palms.

He knew the father test would have him be the opposite of what he was being, but it was impotent to compel him, it only condemned him.

And then to his surprise he thought of Ida, and wondered what she might do.

He forced himself to his feet and moved stiffly to his mother's side. He placed a palm on her bony shoulder and her head, like an old statue crumbling down, lolled to the side. Thinning hair draped his skin.

'He was in love with me,' she gulped.

Midas fought a surprise distraction: anger. He had never met Fuwa, but he suddenly felt outraged at the man. Standing in this stale little room, it was clear why his mother had confined herself to Martyr's Pitfall. When his father had died he had cleared the way for her to be unguardedly in love with Fuwa but after eighteen years of strength-sapping marriage she didn't have anything left in her. All she could do was wait for Fuwa to come and rescue her. Nothing happened.

'It's okay, Mother. I just . . .'

'Of course you're appalled at my affair. You have every right to be, every right. But you don't know the half of it like I do. Marriage is *long*.'

'I'm not appalled. I understand entirely. In fact I was . . . glad for you.'

'Listen, have you . . . ever had a girlfriend?'

He nodded.

'What was her name?'

'Natasha.'

'You never introduced me.'

'We weren't going out for long.'

'And did you . . . feel anything for her?'

'Yes.'

She cowered back in her chair. 'Good. Your father . . . was never much cut out for love. Or perhaps love wasn't cut out for him. But Henry was cut out for love. I'm sure he was.'

'Do you know where he is now?'

'Shh!' She held up both her hands. 'It didn't last, son.'

'Where did he live, then?'

'In the mere.'

'Where? Precisely.'

'Why on earth do you want to know all this? Why do you come here after *nothing* and insist on knowing all this?'

He felt an overbearing urge to leave, to flee the suffocating house and its dweller, but there were Ida's feet in the back of his thoughts, giving him a need to stay.

'I . . .' he croaked, '. . . am trying to help.'

Her head wobbled as if it would spin off her neck. She looked up at him searchingly. There was so much white in her eyes. 'Help? It's late for that.'

'Not you,' he said, feeling callous, 'I'm trying to help someone else.'

At this she seemed to relax. 'There's a place I once watched him fishing. Under an old bridge the road doesn't lead to any more. Bog ivy hanging off the stone like curtains in the theatre. And him in his cagoule fishing in the shallow water with his bare hands. Amazing man. He pulled the fish out by their tails. They stopped flapping because they trusted he'd put them back.'

'Why don't you go and knock on his door?'

'I've not spoken to him for a very long time.'

He shoved his hands in his pockets and stayed in silence near her.

In the garden a white cat sprinted across the lawn, leaving dimpled footprints in the snow. Midas's heart was beating hard. 'It's a shame,' he said, 'that's all.'

She nodded. 'It's all a shame, Midas. Nothing good ever came from my marriage to your father.'

CHAPTER 15

His father left only a pile of boxes when he died. After his funeral, Midas and his mother tucked them away unopened, and when she moved house they travelled from a dark spot in her old attic to a dark spot in her new one. The boxes were thoroughly packed (his father had been a perfectionist, after all) and it was months before Midas or his mother stumbled upon the first of his oversights. Under the carpet they found a whalebone poker dice etched and inked with the suites of playing cards instead of numbered pips. Beneath the cooker, Midas's mother discovered a stained toothpick inscribed with her husband's initials in minuscule letters. When Midas tossed old books into the bin, a map slipped out from flapping pages.

His father's annotated map of the island: crammed with so many handwritten remarks on the aesthetics of the landscape that the terrain itself was confused with the words. Contours made trails between separate sentences. Midas could trace them with his little finger, following cross-sections of his father's thoughts:

splintered tree was hydra looking
coombe was memorable
frozen lake was coffin ice

Now grown up, Midas tried to keep his bearings with the map on his lap. Paper-clipped to it were the directions his mother had scribbled for him. It was odd seeing the two sets of handwriting together.

On the way out of Martyr's Pitfall the shadow of the tor had been loose, hanging in clusters around boulders and striping the roadside crags. A whole piece of shadow seemed to fill the interior of his car like black liquid. He expected it would gush out if he opened the door.

He drove down the slope and into the tunnel that left Lomdendol Island and crossed the girdered bridges to Gurm.

Across the bridges, Gurmton could be seen lazing along the coast to the south, before the road entered a different kind of tunnel: a dark shaft running uphill between pine trees. Inland, the dormant woods grew denser. Beeches stood aghast in pools of shed leaves. Silver poplars looked like moonbeams. These trees could be anything: he passed a crone, an elk and a hunting cat crouched in the undergrowth.

And then it was over the strait and on to Ferry Island, where the trees thinned out into expanding mere. He was in the bog, and the bog . . . Well, that always looked the same. He'd been brought here once or twice as a child, to stare into glutinous water. He'd always hated seeing his reflection made unwashed by the brown pools. For days after a visit he'd wake with the breath of the bog on his lips and rising itches from gnat bites all over his skin.

There were many paths through the bog, but slush and snow-thatched reed banks concealed the routes. At one point he passed a rusting car caught vertical in a pit of black mud. No doubt the road had sprung a pit trap, where bog had congealed to look like tarmac. Eventually the mere's mastication would swallow it under the surface for ever. Midas wondered what had befallen the driver.

A mist hung heavy and soon, when his bearings were gone entirely, he got out and gagged at the foul air. A skin of fluid on the dented road clung to his shoes with each step. He watched a bird the size and colour of a penny fly across the road and disappear between tall canes.

He looked at his father's old map. He hoped it was old enough to mark roads now hidden by slush. He got back in and started to drive.

A pattern of reeds and pitted peat grottoes continued for some time. Then the road came to a halt. A brook splashed across it. Midas checked the map as best he could and was certain that a road had progressed here, back when the map was new.

His mother had described a bridge that no roads now crossed, and up ahead was a peculiar mound of moss and slime. Midas got out of the car and hopped along a bank of the brook to get closer to it. Reeds and mud gauzed its sides, so he used a stick to poke them back. Beneath the mosses and lichens the mound was made of cracked old bricks. He kept clearing the brickwork until he saw the very top of a tide marker. *This* was the last of the bridge. He jumped back into his car and revved through the brook, sheets of parting water flashing through the air.

He had to drive carefully from there, for the track kept dropping down into sluggish rivulets. He came to a ford, drove through it and had been going only a few minutes more when he saw the silhouette of a lonely house ahead. Covered in ivy so dense and old its vines were thick as wrists, the house's bent chimney was a neck throttled by the creepers. The ivy had been hacked roughly back around the windows and a low door had been painted newt green.

The plants in the garden were strangling things with thread-like stalks. At the end of a plot that could loosely be described as a lawn the fence cut straight through a quagmire bordered with flints and made into a kind of pond. On one of the flints stood a curious bird with a long, curving bill like a straw. Midas watched it break the water's surface and suck up green fluid. Toads watched him from blinkless eyeballs. At the end of the garden was an old slate outbuilding with a padlocked, mossy door.

It had not been so hard to find his way here, and he envisaged it being a lot easier to make his way back. The whole journey had taken little over an hour, which again made him angry at Fuwa, for

125

never finding an hour of his own to go to Martyr's Pitfall and the house of his mother. Right now, however, there was something more pressing. He resolved to knock on the door and greet Fuwa solely in his capacity as the man to help Ida.

He knocked.

Henry Fuwa sat at his bedroom desk, changing the bedding hay in an old brass lantern. When he had finished he poured fresh water into a saucer, gently placed this in the lantern, then turned around and whistled to the moth-winged cow who was flying slow circles over the bed, her belly fat as a grape. At his whistle she veered and floated down to Henry's desk, landing softly and folding her lapis lazuli moth-wings. She plodded up to the lantern door, the weight of her full belly swaying from side to side with each hoof step. Henry smiled proudly and lightly stroked the curls of fur on her shoulders.

Getting the cattle to breed was a constant struggle. They were a species set against survival, he often felt. They took mates for life, but the bulls still sometimes grew fickle and harassed the younger heifers, distressing those with calf. Back when he started caring for them, Henry had often found mothers crooning over thimblefuls of miscarried matter and crumpled, half-formed wings.

Now he brought pregnant cows inside. Reintroducing her and her calf to the herd would be a tough job, but better the calf were born here than never at all.

126

He looked up to see a black-haired stranger leaping the stepping-stones towards his cottage. He gasped and swung backwards in his chair, nearly knocking the lantern off the desk as he did so. The pregnant cow lowed in alarm.

He took up post at the window, concealing himself with a curtain. He'd been shocked to see someone appear at his hideaway.

He'd been even more shocked to see a dead man.

Could this be happening? He had been to Crook's grave in Tinterl churchyard!

Wait . . . Of course, it was the boy.

Henry bit his fingertips. If he let him in, would the boy shake his hand, and what would that feel like? It had been a long time since he had touched another human being. This alone was nearly enough to dissuade him from going down to the door. In the past, he had let himself imagine this first encounter. It would be a welcoming occasion, in a room of warmth. The boy's mother would make the introduction and pour the three of them a glass of gin. Henry combed his beard with his fingernails. He had never imagined *this*. He had made great efforts, moving to the middle of nowhere, letting bog flood roads and unruly mere paint over milestones.

It was so unthinkable and ridiculous that he should be discovered here he felt like laughing. Only (his heartbeat speeding up) the boy really *was* here. Looking at him was like looking at a drawing whose sketch work had not been rubbed out. There were dark finalized lines, unmistakably that of a young man, but there were fainter shades from pencils, dupes of his mother that hung about him in movements and the scared look in his eyes. To keep life simple the Crook boy should remain ignored.

The boy was already knocking on the door. *Knock knock knock*. It thudded through the cottage. Should he pretend to be out?

He had cupped furred bodies against the winter wind, dozed with a heifer curled against his forehead on a pillow, her wings trembling in his breath, but the thought of such proximity to a human being was as terrifying as a trip into space. It was true he had felt alien around every one he had ever met, except for Evaline Crook. When he had seen her for the first time he couldn't believe the attraction that impaled him. He was shocked not only that he would want to be with a married woman, but that he would want to be with another human being at all.

After seeing her, he remembered returning to tend a grizzled moth-winged bull without a partner, the odd digit at the end of the headcount, who had grown old, rheumatic and despondent without a mate.

So absorbed was he in these thoughts as he tiptoed down the stairs, that he left the pregnant cow's brass lantern open. He loped through the hall and leant against the wall, letting Midas's knocking pass through him as an amendment to the beat of his heart.

Fourteen years back now, Evaline had smiled at him. He had sat with her, talked, and there had been an understanding. Like insects they had engaged on frequencies without the need for words or body language.

He rushed forward and opened the door.

He had no idea what to say. He was too tall for the door frame. He held out his hand.

'Um,' said Midas, not taking it. 'Um.'

Henry looked him up and down, wagging his head as he did so.

'I,' said Midas, 'um . . . I'm Midas Crook. I . . . believe you, um, knew my parents once.'

'Um,' said Henry.

'Um.'

'*Ahk.*'

'*Err* . . . May I come in?'

Henry puffed out his cheeks, then stepped aside to let Midas enter. His hallway had a low ceiling and creaking wooden floor, on which his ancient box files and bundles of paper tied with string were stacked untidily. He noticed Midas noticing the framed sketches of insects, dissected or in flight, hanging on the hallway walls, and this concept of a stranger noticing these things that he had seen every day for years made his skin tingle uneasily.

He ushered Midas into a sitting room decorated with more thoraxes, wings and multifaceted eyes. Preserved butterflies were pinned to a board in a cabinet. In a glass tank, ribbed leaves crawled with ants. Two thick candles made wavering flames

129

in paper lanterns, moving the room's shadows in stop-motion. There was a low, antique table, with four padded stools.

Henry tugged anxiously at his beard. 'So . . . I'm . . . Henry.' The words as he spoke them sounded strange. He did not often use his voice. His tonsils were mothballs and his tongue a creaking door.

'I know.'

'Oh.'

He held out his hand again but received only a queasy look in return. Was this an insult, this refusal to shake the offered hand, or was he himself being offensive? Henry couldn't be sure.

'So,' he said, trawling his memory for niceties, 'tea?'

'Do you . . . um, have coffee?'

'Sorry, only tea. Green tea.'

'Then yes. Please.'

Henry hesitated, then hurried off to the kitchen.

Midas got up, surprised at how simply the exchange had been navigated. The house smelt of dry parchment, but under that was the odour of the mere. He examined some photos on display in wooden frames. They showed the sea from the air. There was some kind of solar flare, but when he looked closer he saw this was no effect playing across a lens, but something tangible in the water, just beneath its surface. Alongside this photo stood a framed sketch of a jellyfish, tendrils labelled in Latin. Midas thought of his father chuckling to himself, reading books in the dead language.

Henry came back with green tea in delicate china cups, red petals painted along their rims. He caught Midas looking at the jellyfish sketch as he set down the tea.

'They chopped it into slivers, but they still couldn't find its lights.'

'. . . Is that so?'

'It's a local specimen. Drawn at dissection. These jellyfish glow . . . But you know about that, of course.'

Midas nodded. He knew all about the wintering invertebrates that swarmed the coves in December, catching the sun in their bloated bodies and setting it a-sparkle in an electric light show. Even so, even though they could glean every ingot from light and turn it into a glimmer of pink or a flare of yellow, he had a thing about them that kept him away from the spectacle.

'When I first came to St Hauda's Land, part of my work was to study them. I had seen smaller jellyfish in my father's kitchen in Osaka, little white creatures like puffball mushrooms that he'd cut into strips to batter. But the species that comes to St Hauda's Land is entirely different. Entirely.'

'What exactly is your work?'

Henry blushed.

'You're a biologist?'

'I have a certain level of . . . insight that keeps me in funds. The jellyfish, for example, were thought to gravitate towards the islands to breed, until my research showed they excrete light when they die.'

131

The idea of it took a moment to sink in, but then Midas was excited, turning back to the framed photos he'd picked out earlier.

'Then . . . St Hauda's Land is a sort of elephant graveyard for jellyfish?'

'They dissolve and leave only a shimmer.'

'So these lights in the water . . .'

'The deceased and the dying of the shoal at night. The matter of their bodies breaks down, dissolves and releases light. Each particle becomes like stardust, until all that's left are these vapours slowly dimming into the sea.'

Midas pointed to a glowing ring of dandelion yellow in one of the pictures. 'This one must have been enormous.'

'The size of a rowing boat. And I've seen bigger. I had, in my naïvety, originally intended to swim with them to take their photograph. But of course their poison can be lethal. Not as lethal as some species, but quite potent in a concentrated area. It can make a person limp for . . . Ah, but you know all this.'

'My mother was stung by a jelly.'

Henry shifted from foot to foot. 'Here,' he said after an awkward pause. He opened a drawer and took out a photograph album. He flicked through more and more pictures of the jellyfish alight. Then he came to some shots of a pebble beach. Among the mottled stones were shoals of washed up, shiny fish.

'They're not dead,' said Henry, 'or at least not

until they suffocate in the air. They're paralysed by the jellyfish, then washed-up like driftwood.'

They stood side by side, drinking the green tea Henry had made and looking at the photos for some minutes, until Midas, so easily lost in the image, again remembered his mother's limp. He realized how uncomfortably close Henry stood to him.

The issue of his mother was floating between them as unfathomably as one of those jellyfish. He watched a blue-winged insect of some sort drift along the underside of the ceiling and touch down out of sight behind a stack of journals with curling covers.

His tea was cooling quickly in its diminutive cup. 'Does the name Ida Maclaird mean anything to you? Blonde girl? Very . . . monochrome? Very, um, you know . . . pretty? She bought you a drink in Gurmton.'

Henry suddenly looked alarmed. 'She's not here, is she?'

'Yes. She's come to St Hauda's Land looking for your help.'

Henry's eyes were wide, the streaks in his irises sharpening into copper daggers. 'She told you?'

'Told me what?'

'What did she say?'

'She's . . . unwell.'

Henry frowned. He chewed the fronds of his moustache. 'Unwell? That's it?'

'Yes.'

'She's come to see me about that? She didn't tell you anything about . . . secret things?'

'Well . . . yes. Something deeply secret, yes.'

Midas watched Henry's fingers. There was peat under their nails. Henry wiped his forehead, blurted, 'Please excuse me, Mr Crook,' then hurried out of sight. Midas heard him hammering up the stairs. Frogs droned outside. He turned his teacup in his hands, leaves orbiting at the bottom of the china.

Henry had to go upstairs to get a moment's perspective. He sat on his bed and pulled the blanket up over his shoulders, wrapping himself in it like a child. The Crook boy's heritage was hard enough to bear, but this mention of Ida Maclaird . . . what did she want? She had to have come back about the moth-winged cattle. The bog was supposed to keep him safe from this kind of prying. He had swapped society for the simple life he had painstakingly constructed here. That of the entomologist: he who cups a cricket in his hands in a field, feels it sidle about looking for escape, then sets it free, to bounce bewildered through the long grass. That was to say, he didn't want the cricket to knock on his door looking for an explanation for its experience. Yet . . . Yet . . . At one time in his life he had wanted more than this detachment from the things he had a hand in. He had an acute memory of lying on his back in the bog one night last summer, just days after his encounter with Ida. The marsh gases had risen all day in the heat until they mingled with the atmosphere, marbling the blue sky with bottle-glass greens and browns. He would have admired the effect in awe had he not reached sideways, without thinking, to take Evaline's hand. He had grabbed a dry handful of toad, which beat its legs against his forearm until it squeezed free. He was the only human being for miles. Swamp gurgled into every distance, coughing up newborn flies. It had taken hours to get over his loneliness.

Henry reluctantly relaid the blanket on his bed and took deep, steadying breaths. Ida . . . She knew about the moth-winged cattle, and all he could think was that she had come here to threaten them. He looked at the brass lantern on his desk and stifled a cry when he saw its door hanging open and its insides empty.

Midas had decided to look again at the photos of jellyfish burning out in the sapphire ocean, but before he had a chance he was distracted by the blue-winged insect he'd seen land behind the stack of books. It whirred up through the air and drifted past his face. He blinked hard, snapped his head around to follow it, hands instinctively pawing for his camera.

It was a little cow, its fur blowing slightly in the breeze made by its whirring wings. Its hoofed legs hung relaxed beneath a plump stomach and a dozy-eyed head.

He wrenched open his satchel and swung out

his camera. The movement made the creature jerk away and fly higher, so Midas froze with the camera at his face. It drifted down to one of the paper lanterns, within which candle flames trembled. Midas took its photo silhouetted against the paper shade. The cow landed beside the lantern and fanned its wings, showing pearly-white markings on their insides.

A dismayed shout from the doorway.

Henry staggered into the room, gaping at Midas's camera.

'Y-you,' he spluttered, 'must give me the film. It must be destroyed.'

'There is no film,' said Midas, warily clinging to his camera. 'It's a digital.'

'Then delete it.'

He shook his head.

Henry squared his narrow shoulders, unpractised at intimidation. Midas, slowly, as if handling a bomb, put away his camera and zipped it tight in his satchel. The cow kneeled down on the counter and licked her muzzle.

'Please.'

'You have to help Ida.'

Henry nodded. 'What does she want from me?'

'I'm not sure. You have to see her. She thinks you know something about what's happening to her.'

'What is happening to her?'

Midas patted his satchel. 'I'll keep this secret, if you keep what I'm about to tell you secret too. You don't even tell Ida it was me who told you.'

'Y-you didn't know about the moth-winged cattle? She's not come because of them?'

The cow closed her eyes, her swollen flanks rising and falling with every heavy breath.

'She's come because her feet are turning into glass.'

Henry leant back against the door frame.

'You keep it secret,' said Midas, 'you promise.'

Henry nodded dismissively. 'How else would I keep it? Can we delete the photo now?'

'All right.' He looked at it for a second, glowing on the screen. It wasn't a great photo anyway. He deleted it.

'Okay, Midas. Ah . . . it's hard to know where to start.'

'Start wherever you like.'

'You've been to the mainland?'

'Yes.'

'How many times?'

'Five or six.'

Henry nodded cautiously. 'Maybe you noticed something different. When you returned to St Hauda's Land. A taste on the air. A mannerism the birds have. A peculiar snowfall, making almost mathematical patterns. A white animal that's not an albino.'

Midas shook his head. 'I suppose it's normal to me.'

'Yes, yes it probably is.' Henry sighed. 'For the most part, people are either born here and are used to these things, or they move away. There aren't many people who *come* here.'

137

'You came here.'

'Ye-es. But I had an ear to the ground. I heard a story about a certain animal who could turn a thing white with one look from its eyes. After I saw it I . . . had already found reasons to stay. But I digress, because you want to know about Ida.' He gazed out of the window at the sepia landscape of meres and muddy pools. He looked worn out, as if a hard day had passed since Midas stepped through the door. 'You had better come with me. I have something to show you in the bog.'

Soon the boots and waterproof trousers he lent Midas were glossy with slime. They tramped over endless marshland where soil was spotted with snow. Frosted mud squelched as it split underfoot. Slugs watched from the shade with stalk-eyes and secret expressions. At one point they saw a heron with a shaggy beard catching a fish, but it took off as they drew near and flew away with heavy wing-beats into the clouded sky. Midas waited nervously whenever Henry stopped to check his compass or consult the landmarks of the marsh: this rock with a crown of spikes, this log in the form of a stegosaur.

Then he found the spot. He explained how he'd marked it previously by tying a neon-yellow band to a nearby shrub. Now he recognized it by the dirtied label. 'This is the place,' he said, pointing a shaking finger at the inky pool before him.

'Okay. What . . . what am I looking for?'

Henry crept around the edge of the pool. The only thing visible within was a floating snail shell. He found a long branch, curved like a scythe. The water belched as he dipped it gently under the surface and combed the pool until it snagged on something. Steadying himself, he used the stick to lever out his find, his feet skidding slightly on the slushy bank.

The waters parted and something smooth and shiny emerged for a moment before Henry grunted and the object submerged again.

'You'll have to help,' said Henry. 'Take the stick.'

Midas took the branch from Henry and could feel from a weight on its other end that it was hooked under something in the water.

Henry waded into the pool until water came up to his thighs. 'Now pull,' he said.

Midas struggled with the branch, straining to lever out the object in the water, while Henry grappled with its weight in the pool. Slowly they lifted it.

Midas gasped.

It was a man. The water drained off him and spattered into the pool. Yet still the light passed through his torso, through his elegant face and the intricate hatching of his chest hair. Light emerged broken from his body and scattered in a hundred rainbows across the pool. Every inch of him was made of glass. Snails stuck to his skin like warts and he wore a skullcap of green algae. Henry grimaced under the weight and eased the body back under the water. It submerged as in a baptism.

Midas sat down heavily on a rotten stump, not caring that it made his arse wet. He put his head in his hands, marking his cheeks with silt palm-prints.

Henry climbed out of the pool and watched the ripples settle. 'No words for it, are there?'

'Are you saying this will happen to Ida?'

Henry looked grave. 'You mean you hadn't thought of that already?'

Midas nodded feebly. He felt aches all over from the hard walk here. 'Why is this in the bog?'

Henry shrugged. 'As good a grave as any.'

'You put it here?'

'No. I stumbled upon it while collecting toad spawn. I don't know who he was or how long he's been here. Could be years, could be hundreds. I've found glass hands in the bog, and a glass shape like a model of a glacier that turned out to be the hind leg of a fox or a dog. This bog is a glass graveyard. Sift the sediment from the bottom of these pools and you'll see flecks sparkling in your pan.'

'When can I bring Ida to see you?'

He'd thought Henry would accept without hesitation. Instead he fidgeted with the toggles of his cagoule. 'The thing is, Midas . . . The reason I brought *you* here . . .'

Midas closed his eyes and tried to expunge the sulphuric stink from his insides. 'You can't cure her can you?'

Henry picked a bulrush and started tearing it into strips. 'No. No one can cure her, because she's not ill. This isn't a disease. The glass is now a part of her, if you will. Like fingernails or the hair on her head.'

'Then can't she just . . . cut it out?'

'It would do no good. It would only grow back.'

Henry scattered the pieces of torn bulrush into the pool. Midas thought he saw a fish rise to the surface to gulp at them.

Henry sighed. 'I'm sorry, Midas.'

Things moved in Midas's gut: tectonic feelings he had never known. He spluttered all of a sudden at the idea of losing Ida before the two of them had even . . .

He glared at the caged black of the water. For a second time he saw widening gums break the surface.

'You *can* find a way to help. You said yourself you had unique insights.'

Henry shrugged. 'I would only be wasting your time and giving her hope where really there's none.'

Midas clasped his muddy hands together. 'My mother,' he said, 'what about my mother? I know all about it! I know she wants to be with you and I'll help you be with her. But you have to help Ida.'

Henry hung his head. 'I can't, Midas, don't you see? It's simply not possible. In fact, it's the perfect analogy. I can no more do one thing than I can the other.'

'*Why* didn't you go to her, after my father died?'

Henry looked pale. 'Where was she, Midas?'

'In our house! And now in Martyr's Pitfall.'

Henry shook his head. 'She had already left before your father died.'

In a flash of anger, Midas grabbed a sod of earth and hurled it at the water, which broke into a hundred chained circles. Picturing Ida like the body in the bog made his heart seem to wilt and blow away. His face screwed through expressions. He turned to Henry and for a bleary-eyed moment saw him as that other lonely academic. How could he shirk the idea of helping Ida? Had he considered it even for a millisecond?

'So what now?' he demanded.

'There isn't anything we can do now, except console ourselves that there never was.'

'Never was? You're just going to give up? Even now, when we've seen here what's to become of her?'

Birds laughed elsewhere in the bog. Midas's anger left him abruptly like electric earthing in the glade around the pool. He was left feeling cold and inanimate. Insects buzzed and reeds quivered.

They walked back to Henry's cottage and Midas's car without speaking and with a stone's throw distance between them. Henry stood in his cottage doorway. Midas left the borrowed wellington boots to weep mud on the path, got into his car and drove away.

CHAPTER 16

Midas's father sat in his study, bent over a heavy book. He licked his fingers before turning each thick page. Midas knocked on the open door, waited, then knocked again. He was a small boy and the door handle was at head height.

Slowly, his father's eyelids closed. He drew a long breath. His shoulders sagged. A weary expression seeped across his face.

When he acknowledged Midas with a protracted, '*Hmm?*' it sounded like the groan of a branch in a forest.

'Mother's crying.'

He sighed. 'What do you mean?'

'Mother's crying. In your bedroom.'

'Oh *God*, Midas . . .'

'Sorry . . . Have I done something wrong?'

'Did you ask her what the trouble was?'

'You said I wasn't to enter the bedroom. You said I wasn't . . .'

'Yes, yes. Oh, Midas, I was reading.'

He rubbed his moustache with one long, clean

finger, then looked longingly down at the pages on his lap. 'Didn't she see you?'

'The door's closed.'

'Mm. Why were you listening?'

'She . . . She was crying quite loudly.'

There was a photograph in his father's book. Midas moved to try and glimpse it, but his father pulled it shut, his thumbs wedged between the pages.

'You didn't knock?'

'I did. I got no answer.'

His father stared down at the closed book. It was a different sort of book to the ones he normally read. A large anatomy book with a diagram of a cross-sectioned ribcage on its cover.

'Midas?'

'Yes.'

'Tell her . . . Tell her I've got six pages. Then I'll go up and comfort her.'

Nodding, Midas left him alone and went upstairs. The door to his parents' bedroom was taller than the other doors in the house. It looked like a stone door, with slate-blue paint, dented and chipped.

'Mother?'

He heard a sob and pushed open the door. Light fell through a chink in the heavy net curtains, drawing a dazzling white bar down his mother. She sat facing a full-length mirror on the other side of the bed. She wore her hair loose, fine ivory locks hanging to the shoulders of a cardigan.

In the mirror, her reflection held a photo to her

stomach and stared at it. Her. As a young woman, not so thin or slouched. Posing on a river-bank, one hand in her hair, tangled branches above and behind her. A reflection (not hers) broken on the water. In the foreground white blurs, although they couldn't be snow for this was a summer scene. Blossom perhaps. Midas fancied they were fairy-shaped.

'Son,' she sniffed when she saw him, 'these photos are your mother. When she was younger. Would you like to look?'

She picked up more prints from the bed. There were five in all, each a slightly different pose behind a different configuration of white blurs. Midas took one from her.

'Careful,' she said, 'these were all that were sent to me. I don't have the negatives.'

Even so young, he'd begun to think of negatives as light snares: the light burns in a negative as a physical remnant of the past. Memories made of light. A print was a wonderful thing, but it was the negative that should be treasured. Without them you held only a simulacrum; with them he would have held a fragment of his mother's past, as real as a piece of recovered hair or nail.

'Midas!' she hissed.

She was wild-eyed. He quickly realized what was wrong: footfalls coming up the stairs. Before she could do anything his father was in the bedroom and for a moment all three of them were frozen and white-faced. Then his father darted forward and snatched the photos from his mother's lap.

His eyes roved over them, back and forth, as if they were words. Then he made a choking noise. He hadn't noticed the photo Midas held because the boy had slipped it under his shirt.

'Out, please, Midas.' He tugged the door shut behind him. But Midas listened.

'Darling . . .' said his father, 'what are these? What can these be? You told me you'd destroyed these. You made assurances.'

'But . . . darling, it's not that *he* took them. It's not that at all. It's me. These photos are *me*.'

Midas heard the tearing of paper. Again. Over and over again. When the door swung open he pressed himself to the wall. His father swept past, cupping a pile of white shreds in his hands. When he'd gone downstairs, Midas peered around the door frame.

She held a thumbnail-sized scrap in her palm. Midas watched her shoulders shaking, then tapped gingerly on the door until she looked up. He offered her the photo he'd hidden up his shirt.

Her mouth twitched at the corners and she stifled a noise. He watched her pupils widen as she saw herself in the image, their lenses adjusting like the lens of his camera.

'Keep it, Midas,' she said. 'So your father never finds it.'

And he did.

CHAPTER 17

A wind was coming from the north, blowing rain clouds like dust until they coated the sky grey. Henry sat on his cottage doorstep, the wind filling his mouth and nostrils, blowing the compost smells of the bog into his stomach.

He couldn't help Ida. He knew it in the same guts squeezed tight by the frustration it caused. He couldn't help her, and the Crook boy's demand that he should had been unfair. Of all the sacrifices he'd made to earn his privacy, the biggest was turning his back on the woman he had loved. So it was also unfair that her son had emerged fully grown from the sealing bog mists, demanding help and answers Henry didn't have.

In the distance the rain was a grey woollen join between the land and the sky. He couldn't help Ida, but . . . He covered his face with his hands. He hadn't been entirely straight with Midas.

As a boy, Henry had sold his bicycle for a chemistry set. It had seemed like a sensible idea at the time, putting childish things behind him in the name of mature study. Then he saw the boy who bought his bicycle pedalling gleefully in the evenings, while *he* poked crystals between Petri dishes with a spatula. It seemed that there were two Henry Fuwas inside him. Henry Fuwa the scientist, living in his head and aspiring to read biology and anatomy, and another Henry Fuwa sheltering somewhere beneath his ribcage, curling up remorsefully at the sight of that bicycle ridden by another boy, longing only for the push and give of pedals circling in time with feet.

Years later he had left Osaka with only a small pack and a feel for lifting the right stone to find an undiscovered bug. The Henry Fuwa who had pined for the bicycle feared leaving, but the other Henry Fuwa had always known there was no future in living above his parents' restaurant near Dotonbori, where he woke every day to the smell of steamed rice and felt his lungs starched. He knew he was making no mistake by leaving, that an isolated life among reeds and swamp lilies, where he could study in peace and diligence, was the right life for him. Only, when news filtered through of his mother's death, he was amazed at how peaceful he remained. He'd looked then for that boyish Henry Fuwa curled up in his chest, hoping he could help choke out some grief at her passing, but he couldn't find him. In truth, he had not been able to find him for some time. Perhaps in the course of the great journey over the oceans he had been lost or forgotten, in an airport terminal among unclaimed suitcases or misdirected airmail. And so Henry felt nothing at the death of the woman who had raised him in Osaka. He couldn't even remember what it had been like being her son. Bog life continued its cycles: mustard flowers made a yellow cosmos across marsh soil in spring, summer heat made viscous skins on pools, autumn birthed a million insects and sticky beetles.

But one afternoon, after many such cycles, that other Henry Fuwa came back, and he was now fully grown, and he had become something insatiable. He had ambushed him. Taken revenge. Overpowered him.

He had set eyes on Evaline Crook.

That summer's day he had been catching eels upriver, enjoying the way they slithered and thrashed in his bucket. Once caught he photographed them, took notes on coloration and size, then poured them back into the water, where they shimmered away like living liquids.

The day was pleasant and he walked aimlessly along the river-bank. Newly winged gnats and crane-flies in their thousands hopped out of the grass and bumbled around his ankles. In the river, dark dashes flickered: newborn fish ready to be gobbled by scaled pike and greedy toads. He sauntered along beside the water and was led, by meanders and turns, into deep woodland.

And then he saw her up ahead, sitting cross-legged on the bank in a beige summer dress and Panama hat with a fabric rose stitched to its brim. She sprang up when she saw him, but didn't say anything. She had a fine skeleton, lean limbs and hair floating around her head as if underwater. Her fingers toyed nervously with the lap of her dress, scrunched it into handfuls then let go, scrunched handfuls again, let go. He watched her repeat the action and repeat it until he remembered it wasn't acceptable to admire women as you would an excitable gnat or a mercurial eel. He bowed his head and apologized for his rudeness.

She laughed and introduced herself. He knew he would never forget her name. He asked her what brought her into the woods. Just wandering, she said. Her family were somewhere nearby, snoozing in a glade. 'Parents?' he enquired with hope. No. Son and husband, both dressed in long sleeves and trousers as a precaution against wasps and nettles.

She laughed sadly, then returned the question. 'What brings you here?'

He shook the bucket of eels as explanation.

When she asked him if he'd mind her company he nearly burst. He kept admiring the way dapples of sunlight through the leaves caught her hat and thin forearms. Her fingers couldn't keep still, whether illustrating a point or fidgeting in silences. They walked along the river-bank. She walked with a limp.

Suddenly he turned abruptly one hundred and eighty degrees. He shot out an arm and yanked her hat down over her face. She shrieked and leapt fearfully away from him.

He dared a glance over his shoulder.

It had vanished.

It had been kneeling to lap water from the stream. A coarse white coat and a domed head with a flat face pressed against the water's surface. Its large eyes, thank heavens, had been closed as it drank. What surprised him only slightly less than the sight of it had been its size: barely bigger than a lamb.

He asked Evaline if she had seen it too. She admitted (setting her hat back firmly on her head) seeing something. But had she met its eyes? How could she, with its head bowed? He hopped across the stream to the point where the creature had knelt. Green stalks poking out of the water were laddered with dragonfly nymphs, fully developed and clinging to the greenery. They were all as white as snowflakes. He sat down hard on the bank and bit his lip. He explained to her that the nymphs should be a sooty colour, ideal camouflage in the waters from which they had climbed. Now that they were white they would be easy targets for birds, their legs locking their motionless bodies in place on the stalks while their skin dried out in preparation for transformation into adults.

'Then we'll guard them,' said Evaline, sitting down on the bank opposite, kicking off her shoes and dangling her toes in the cool water. He did the same. His heart beat like crazy because she wanted to do this with him. She told him he was funny, but she liked that about him. They sat in comfortable quiet and watched the white exoskeletons of the nymphs split slowly open, starting behind their eyes. Chalk-coloured heads and thoraxes forced themselves out of the cracks in the skin and dangled half-emerged from their old bodies.

'If you concentrate,' said Henry, 'you can see them breathing. The air swells them up while the sunlight dries them out. Then they're ready to push clear.'

As if to demonstrate, one of the hatching dragonflies suddenly bent back on its nymph shell and tugged its tail and legs free. Its wings stuck to its back like shrivelled paper. It hung there hugging its wrinkled old body in stillness while other nymphs on other stalks did the same.

Henry and Evaline looked on in amazed silence while pairs of wings dried out and slowly expanded among the stalks like blooming petals.

The sun was hot on the back of Henry's neck. From the corner of his eye he watched Evaline enrapt. Light dappled the water. A white newt plopped up for breath between lily pads. Evaline was beautiful, he thought, more beautiful than any of this.

The expanded wings of the nearest dragonfly suddenly fanned out and were held stretched to their limit. The light picked out their crizzled facets. Other dragonflies did the same. The plant stalks were hung with glossy flakes.

A few minutes later the first one took off. It shot up vertically, then zigzagged around their heads. Evaline gasped and covered her mouth. Henry watched her. More dragonflies flung themselves free of their petrified former selves, fizzing into the air like white sparks.

Balls of hard rain dropped through the air around him, bringing him back to the swamp and the present. He closed his eyes while the raindrops squelched against the muddy grass. He adored and feared that memory's occurrence because although it had been a moment of promise, and the first time in his life he'd been in love, it had turned over the years into the aptest metaphor because he did not know where the Evaline of that day had gone. All that remained of her in Martyr's Pitfall was a dragonfly's abandoned nymph skin.

And here he was, standing sodden in the rain, feeling guilty that he'd not been entirely straight with her boy, as if the whole truth could do anyone any good.

He was suddenly outraged. A garden rock was acting as a summit for a meeting of slugs, and he clawed it out of the caked mud and cast it into a puddle. Lurking beneath, among the scrambling pill bugs and lice, was a beetle like a dot of jade. He drew air into his lungs and stamped on it.

He dropped immediately to his knees beside its pulped remains, choking and scratching his beard so hard that when he regained self-control he saw blood on his fingernails. Getting to his feet he felt monstrously tall. His shoes looked like a giant's, his hands gnarled and cumbersome.

Nothing was as it should be, because of the Crook boy's appearance.

'All right!' he yelled into the bog, 'I'll tell you!' At once his lungs felt bruised for the shouting, it had been so long since he had raised his voice. He held his sides as he stomped indoors and boiled water in a bubbling saucepan. Then he carried the pan outside where the cold air showed up the steam. Frozen worms of rainwater cracked under his wellington boots as he carried it into the swamp, hot water spilling over its sides and pattering to the ground to fizz in the mud. When he came to a pool the length and shape of a sarcophagus, he used the hot underside of the pan to melt a circle through the ice on its surface, then tipped the hot water on the weeds and dunked the pan into the pond as a kind of fishing net, scraping it along the slushy bottom. Water numbed his fingers. He could feel ice closing up around his wrist. He pulled the pan out of the pool. It was filled with dirty water and a hard lump swaddled in slime.

He carried pan and lump back to the cottage and, inside, drained the water. Then he plugged the sink and ran the hot tap, adding a long squirt of washing-up liquid. He put on his Marigold gloves, took a deep breath and reached into the sink for the mass now hidden under bubbles. He scrubbed it with a brush until the bubbles cleared and he could lift it spotless from the water.

Back when he had unearthed it from Midas Crook's grave, the stench had made bile leap into his throat. Now Midas Crook's glass heart shone multifaceted like a giant diamond. For the last few years pond snails had lived in its transparent atriums and toad spawn had stuffed its see-through ventricles. Clean and sterile again, it filled Henry with shame and terror at what he had done. He had plucked it like a ripe fruit from Midas Crook's chest, then sped home and scrubbed it clean of its film of dried blood. Examining it on the following nights he had learnt some of its secrets. The glass acted like the nails or hair of a person. It grew on after death for a time, even in the grave, but after that it came to a standstill just like the rest of the human body. He had dwelt on these things, on the enormity of what he had done, every day since he had smuggled it back with him into the bog.

He had heard back then that Crook had died from a growth in his chest, one that defied the understanding of doctors. Around that time he had also discovered, while crabbing in the bogs, the man turned to glass. While he crouched by the poolside staring through the glass man's chest, he had wondered *what if*.

He had bought and drunk a whole bottle of gin on that night when he shovelled topsoil off Crook's grave and prised back the rotten wood within. The flowers in the graveyard of Tinterl Church had caught the moon and were white even in the small hours. Lean muscles he'd had then were taut in his arms as he gripped the spade. Tinterl Church stood on an isolated ridge where wind swept away the thinner soil, leaving the earth gritty as a beach. Only once did he catch sight of living company, when he saw a pair of headlights approaching from a distance and cast himself on the earth, panicked by the bright beams as they flashed across the church wall and billowed the shadows of the headstones like black drapes. A cold sweat had covered him by the time the headlights vanished down the Gurmton road. He knew there was a dead man stretched out parallel beneath him and though he hadn't had time to check which headstone he'd hidden behind, he sensed whose grave it was through the hard soil. He sprung up and fought the cap off the gin to slurp alcohol from the bottle, smacking his lips before seizing the shovel and tearing the weak-rooted grass from the grave.

He remembered the bare plate of wood he'd unearthed in the autumnal starlight. He'd splintered off the coffin lid and gagged at what rested rotten inside. In the bog, decomposition was complicated. Gases and fluids in the water could preserve a man for centuries, or strip his skin in days like paint. He'd hoped this sandy grave had done enough in seven years to open up its incumbent's torso. That was all he needed: a view beneath the ribcage to the lingering matter. To the centre of love.

It had done more than enough.

Now, in his cottage kitchen, he put the glass heart in a carrier bag and left it on the coffee table.

If you asked a psychiatrist why a man might kill himself you might receive a hundred reasons, but none of them would be the object in the carrier bag. Henry had thought long and hard about the particular suicide of Dr Crook. He'd contrasted the glass heart with the glass body he'd shown Midas in the bog. If the transformation to glass stopped not long after death, then Crook had cheated it with his suicide. It also followed that the bog man had somehow *not died*. Upon death the glass ground to a halt too soon. It was impossible for the bog man, in life, to have transformed so far into glass that the metamorphosis could have time to complete itself as utterly as it had in his death. If the man had drowned in that pool, the glass would have stopped too soon after the water filled his lungs (pumping lungs good enough to drown him) to complete the transformation. If he had been poisoned by a swamp berry and lain down to die on the banks of the mere, he would have had to have a living stomach, not a glass stomach, to ooze the enzymes needed to digest the berry's toxins. If he had been murdered (his body showed no signs of injury, but he could have been cracked over the head) he would have needed enough cranium and brain remaining for the murderer to kill him. And even if the glass itself had finished him, transformed him organ by organ to the crystalline state in which he now lay at rest, it surely would have defeated itself, because come the moment a vital organ turned to hard silica, his body would have shut down, and he would have been dead, and the glass would not be able to spread fast enough to claim him entirely.

To all this Henry could only provide two hypotheses.

One: somehow, even after transforming into glass, the sufferer was still alive. Dr Crook did not seem to believe this theory, or he would not have given up his own life so easily.

Two: that the speed of transformation was not fixed at the steady creep Henry had envisaged. That perhaps it could build momentum, overcome its victim in a sudden burst of alteration. It seemed more likely that Dr Crook had feared this as he laid plans for his suicide. That the bog man had feared it too, as he contemplated his own condition, however many years or centuries ago, until all of a sudden he was turning at breakneck speed into hard and empty mineral, without even the time to be amazed.

Puzzling over this had been of interest to Henry, until now. Now it was different. He barely knew Ida Maclaird, but he knew her well enough not to wish the glass conditions of Dr Midas Crook or the bog man on her.

The only thing he felt like doing with the rest of the afternoon was taking his mind off Ida. To that end he finished his supply of gin, concentrating on tipping back each diamond-clear drop. He thought of Evaline, and white dragonflies skimming by a river, and the husks of the larvae bodies they had left behind in the reeds and green stalks, and the way, back then, he'd thought love had been hatching.

CHAPTER 18

The evening twinkling out behind snow clouds. The roof of the woods a serrated threat to the sky. Snow melting as it fell, settling on the leafy road to be pulped by tyres.

Carl Maulsen drove.

Time, that was what he lacked. You didn't have to have years under your belt: you had to have unlived ones, yet to be stored. Because when you got older, things broke. He wished his first serious brush with death had been with someone, anyone else. It felt perverse that his mother and father were sticking to life far off in Arizona. It should have been one of them who went first, not Freya. Anybody but her, to make him realize he didn't have all the time in the world, didn't have the luxury of outlasting Charles Maclaird, strategizing and making his move in some perfect future.

He felt his gullet tighten and a burning wetness on his lower eyelids. Surprised, he choked it back. He was feeling old and sentimental. Maybe it was the charm of the woods bringing it out. Silver thistles were shivering on the roadside. His headlights turned a hare's eyeballs a startling white.

159

Tonight, vividly, he saw her dancing in her ball gown on the last night of university, her dress and waist-length hair shimmering like the hare's eyes. He remembered her acknowledgement across the dance floor, a wry smile on just one side of her mouth. But to go to her was to make memory a fantasy, since he hadn't done it. He'd played it cool, approaching her only later to find her in the arms of another man.

He cut back to the start of the memory and reshaped it. This time he stepped on to the dance floor and strode towards her, dazzled by the radiance of her hair in the blinking disco lights. He took her outstretched hand and felt the soft fingers lock through his.

He hit the brakes too late. There was a doe in his headlights.

The deer crunched at the impact, leaving a dent in the bonnet and snuffing out one lamp. It fell away, flashing pale undersides. Cursing, Carl jumped from the car and inspected the dent in the metalwork. One of the lights was punched out, and the bonnet was rippled. He let out a tirade at the doe's corpse, then opened the boot, grabbed the deer and slung it over his shoulder. If he had to pay for his car to be fixed, he and Ida would eat venison for a week.

Impact had snapped the doe's neck, but as he dumped it in the boot he saw one rear leg had snapped in several places so that broken bones hung bulging in the fur like the toys in a Christmas stocking.

He stood for a moment with his hands in his pockets. The surprise of the roadkill and the sparkling of ice on every leaf and every thistle spike, made his thoughts fanciful.

Thirty years previous, summer had parched neat grass in quads between college buildings. Yellowing lawns had looked like shredded parchments rotting into the earth. Carl stood in the shade of a sandstone university building, hands in his pockets, a frown on his forehead. He took out a comb and ran it several times through his jet-black hair. Other students skirted clear of him as they ascended the steps to the airless corridors behind.

How he loathed them: their lack of vision. Not one of them possessed drive or ambition. They rushed about in earnest coteries or sauntered along, blithely accepting their impending academic failure. Be they fanatical about their studies or indifferent, not one had drive, not one had passion like he had. They cared more for lounging in the insufferable sunlight than for learning. He snorted like a boar, frightening a plump student who pushed her glasses nervously up her nose and tottered away. He tucked the comb into his pocket and folded his arms.

A girl rode into the quad on a bicycle. She looked hurried, riding fast, but as she drove over a cracked paving slab her bike jolted, the chain came loose and the girl tipped on to the path, legs twisting up with her bike. Carl smirked as she untangled herself and rose to her feet.

He stopped smirking. She was beautiful.

The girl had cut her knees. Dark blood wriggled down her shins like misplaced stigmata. Trying to tidy her arctic blonde hair, she got ruby blood in it. She abandoned the bike and rushed up the steps into the university, leaving Carl with the bitter perfumes of her scent and blood.

She'd made something tense in his loins. He'd thought himself above that drive, here for academic devotion alone. But now . . . he was shocked to find himself trotting into the quad to rescue the girl's abandoned bike. She needed a new one, he realized as he propped it up and noticed the rust on its frame. He set it gently against the wall and laid the palm of his hand on the saddle, hoping for residual warmth. He felt none, although he remained there for some time.

Later he fantasized about applying plasters to her split knees.

'Freya,' he said, and the word seemed to lead him out of his memory and back to the mute trees, the icy road, and the dead doe in the boot of his car. He turned away and looked into the banked thistles and the silver woods behind them.

'Freya,' he said forlornly.

Her name was dead on the air. It was no longer the name of anything more than the nourishment for roots of grass in a mainland graveyard. He had felt a premonition of this when her maiden name became an antique, but he had not acted to stop it from happening. He would never have insisted she take the name Maulsen. He grabbed at his hair and pulled so hard it brought tears to his eyes. How he envied those roots that supped on her body, the filaments growing where her skin had been hot and soft.

He turned back and shut the boot on the roadkill doe. Ida Maclaird: a name that still meant something. It gave him the first smile for days to think how she had once emerged from the body that was now interned in grass. The sheer reality of Ida was delightful.

Which made it all the harder to bear that she was unwell. He had watched her around the house and his suspicions had quickly developed that hers was a serious illness.

He was no stranger to injuries. In his time he had broken a metatarsal in his right foot and cracked the shin-bone of his left leg. Ida's wasn't that kind of injury. She moved about the cottage so delicately that her feet could have been ceramics. That comparison had brought to mind Emiliana Stallows, wife of Hector, who with the help of her husband's fortune had run for a time a small alternative medicine business up in Enghem on the north coast of Gurm. As far as Carl was concerned that stuff was all gypsy remedies and superstitious trinkets, but he had humoured her while they had been seeing each other. Their affair had meant more to Emiliana than it ever could to him, but she had been beautiful in her day and he had wrongly speculated that if any woman could break his futile desire for Freya it would be someone as glamorous as her.

He racked his brains to remember what she had told him. Something she had said when he had only been half listening, that had put him in mind of her now. They had been lying together in bed one morning, and he had been relishing the first cigarette of the day while she nattered on about the current bores of her life. Emiliana was always feeling sorry for some patient or another of hers, but the story of one girl – the details of which eluded him right now – was unusual. Emiliana had said she felt out of her depth with it.

He would have to dust off her phone number or make the trip up to Enghem, since he hadn't made contact with her for several years.

First, though, he had another visit to make. The Crook boy had crossed his mind on one or two occasions since Dr Crook's death. Carl was as curious about how he had turned out as he was about whether he was suitable company for Ida. If there was one bad thing to inherit from Freya, and Ida had certainly managed it, it was her taste in men. Just the other day, Ida had told him about ex-boyfriends of hers, leaving him stupefied as to what she saw in them.

She needed a helping hand, and Carl was all too glad to reach out to her.

'You'll like him,' she'd said of Carl Maulsen. 'And he'll be interested in you.'

But the point was he didn't like people and they weren't interested in him. Midas, sitting alone at his kitchen table, put his head in his hands. That was the way things worked. For the best.

'I'm getting too involved with Ida,' he confessed to his camera on the table. 'I should bail out right now.'

He looked fondly around his kitchen, the cosy life he'd made for himself. He should phone her and call off seeing her again. What good was it doing?

He stood up. 'I like things undisturbed.'

He strode to the phone, grabbed the handset and punched in the first digits of her number (realizing he'd memorized it). He faltered, then dumped the handset back on the phone. She hadn't disturbed things too much. He thought of her feet. The glow of the light passing through them, making her crystallized blood sparkle. His promise to her to *hang around*. How heartless would he be to abandon her now?

'If,' he resolved, returning to the kettle, 'things get untidy, I'll jump ship just like that. And I won't feel bad about it.'

He shuddered. He'd never really got to grips with people, especially with women. The only relationship he'd ever had convinced him of that.

He gave Natasha the full studio treatment, even rented some wardrobe. She enjoyed posing, said it made her feel good about herself. Since he enjoyed the camerawork, it seemed a perfect match. She was stunning . . . but only in photos. It became hard for him to go out with her. He preferred to feign illness so he could stay at home and look through folders of pictures he'd taken. Her dense and glossy hair in photographs turned dry and stank of spray outside them. Her luscious eyes became burnt bits of wood when he closed the album. It took enormous courage to break up with her, to have to sit down and *explain* that he was only attracted to the version of her he'd caught on film.

He had felt bad about it for a few years, while she moved on to find someone who loved her for what she really was, not for what silver nitrate and slow light made her. She wrote him a letter he had read so many times he knew it word for word.

You always seemed happier with flat things, with two dimensions. I never managed to drag you away from that. I never made you see in three dimensions. To this day, I don't know that you've discovered depth, or distance, but I desperately wanted to be the one who showed you that. Be careful, Midas.

It made him feel terrible, partly because he'd hurt her, partly because she'd misunderstood him. So ludicrous to say he didn't know about depth and distance. Every photographer knew about depth and distance. He wasn't blinkered like his father had been; he'd made certain to develop a healthy perspective on his place in the world. Which was why he stuck with his camera.

It was time for Denver to arrive. He enjoyed the girl's company because she preferred to be quiet. She was perplexed by unnecessary chatter of any kind. The pair of them would sit for hours at the table while Midas worked through his photographs and Denver drew.

And yet, since the other day when she had shown him the Christmas baubles and spoken frankly about time spent in the back of her head, he'd been worrying about her. Gustav had taken pains to usher her into the external world of objects, violence and weather. He'd tricked her into walking on cracks in the pavement, to help her see that nothing bad would happen (afterwards she'd done a kind of penance, hopping for hours back and forth from slab to slab). He'd faked power cuts to help her cope with darkness (although since then she'd hoarded candles in a box beneath her bed). It had taken him ages to cure her fear of water. At school she'd stabbed her water-wings with a fountain pen. The teachers punished her with lines, but she wrote them with patient acceptance and the teachers reported the futility of the situation to Gustav. Midas didn't like water either, so had silently approved of that particular defiance, but since the other day, he had worried that he'd been subtly undoing all Gustav's

167

hard work. He'd encouraged her introversion as a part of her identity. He'd always thought that was a good thing. When had he stopped thinking that was a good thing?

Right now she was drawing a horn-nosed narwhal with golden fins, while he stuck new photos to the kitchen walls. A wet moor in bright sunlight, with soil like a million inky fingerprints on a white sheet. A snail with a shell like black marble and antennae straining at the sky. An albino cat with one eye that he'd photographed outside Catherine's. All these he would have been pleased with a week before. He could have spent an hour fascinated by their depth of shadow and brilliance of light, only now they seemed like a waste of the wall space he was tacking them to. Instead, the select photos he spread across the table were the only ones to pique his interest. They were the pictures of Ida's feet he'd taken as she slept. He selected one, pinned it up, and filed the others away. Then he stood with hands in pockets, regarding it on the wall.

In the last few years he had drifted out of using his old single lens reflex. He missed the long evenings in the darkroom, its smell of damp and developer fluid, the red light that made you feel you were looking at the room through your eyelids. Despite these pangs of nostalgia, he was in thrall to digital cameras these days. The lure of the next photo, coquettishly waiting, was too strong for him. Before digital cameras the end of a film had always been his temperance, leading him back to the darkroom to coax prints from silver nitrate. His eyes had adjusted and learnt to see the world in the half-light, the half-image forming in the basin.

Then there were the negatives. How he missed negatives. They were the actual rays of light, bounced straight off a landscape, an object, a person, and scarred on to the film. Photographic negatives were the hardest evidence you could get of your memories. They were the char left by the fire, the bruise left on your skin. The same light that carried to your eyes, on the day of your photograph, that image of your mother, or your father, or your close friend, had recorded itself on the film. And now, staring at the photo on the wall of Ida's transparent toes against the bed sheets, he thought how similar her feet were to negatives: both subjects of that half-world between memory and the present. These were not real, flexible, treading toes, but a play of light that showed where toes had been.

The doorbell rang and he looked at his watch. Gustav was half an hour early.

He was surprised to find not Gustav but Carl Maulsen standing at the door in a leather jacket, hands in his pockets and snow on his shoulders.

'Hello,' he said. 'We haven't met, but it's Midas, right? My name's Carl Maulsen. A friend of Ida's.'

Midas remembered well the photograph of his father and Carl with their doctorates. In real life, the man had something the camera hadn't captured:

presence. Some kind of magnetic field like the air around a generator.

'Yes, h-hello. She showed me your photo.'

'I thought I might stop in. It's funny, you see. I knew your father.' He tried to peer past Midas into the house. 'This a bad time?'

Which meant, Midas supposed, *Can I come in?*

Midas backed up the hall. Carl came in and closed the door, helped himself to a coat hook, then followed Midas into the kitchen.

'Denver, this is, um, Doctor Maulsen. Doctor Maulsen, this is my friend Denver.'

'Hello, Doctor Maulsen.'

'Don't call me Doctor,' said Carl, softly. 'It's self-important.'

Denver shrugged and returned to her drawing.

'Do sit down,' said Midas, pulling back a chair from the table. 'Would you like a drink?'

'I'll share a pot of coffee with you.'

'Right.' He clicked the kettle on.

Carl studied the drawing Denver was working on, her narwhal in the depths of the ocean, wearing a seaweed harness and towing a carriage made from a shell she was colouring pink. A woman rode within. He pointed to her, taking care not to touch the pencil work. 'Is this a mermaid?'

Denver shook her head and kept drawing.

He turned his attention to the walls of photographs. 'So, Midas . . . you've turned out to be quite the artist. What did your father think of all this?'

Midas set down the coffee pot and the smallest

pair of cups he owned. 'He didn't understand photography. He only thought a thing was beautiful if he read about it in a dead old book.'

Carl nodded, sipped his coffee and continued to look around at the photos. 'I had the pleasure of working with him for a time, up at Wretchall College.'

Midas slouched in his chair. 'Look,' he said, 'my father was an arsehole.'

Carl looked surprised. 'I'd disagree. I was very fond of him. Did he ever mention me?'

'No. Sorry. He wouldn't have. He never talked about people, or what was going on in his life. He just rattled on about archetypes and stuff.'

Carl smiled fondly. 'That sounds like the man I knew, yes. I didn't expect him to have spoken about me. But your father said some admirable things. He opened a lot of eyes.'

'Maybe.'

Denver yawned loudly. Her pencil scraped across the silence between the two men.

'I can see your father in you, you know that? You have the same . . . how shall I put it? Composure. I was sorry when he died. That whole mess with the boat. It was a great loss.'

Midas shrugged.

'You don't feel *anything* for him?'

Another shrug, less pronounced.

'Do you even have a photo of him?'

'There's one on the wall there. I got rid of the rest.'

'I understand,' said Carl, carefully looking at the photo, 'it's an unwelcome topic.'

Midas stared into the coffee rings on the table's surface as if they might become vortexes through which to escape this conversation. Under the table he was driving his fingernails into his kneecaps.

'Well, all I'm saying is it's a shame you hate him so.' Carl lounged back in his chair. 'And it's interesting, don't you think, that the two of you turned out to look so similar, but be so different? Anyway, I didn't come here to talk about him.'

'You said you were just stopping by,' said Denver.

He glanced sideways at her, clearly having forgotten she was there. 'Well,' he said, taking a deep breath. 'It's true I came about something more. I came about Ida.'

'Midas's new girlfriend.'

'Den!'

She shrugged.

Carl raised his eyebrows.

'No!' protested Midas. 'No, no no, we're just friends. Besides, we've only just met.'

There was a bent smirk on Carl's lips, as if Midas's behaviour was familiar to him. He looked almost nostalgic. 'Ida's ill, isn't she?' he asked.

Midas nodded dumbly.

'But you and I will help her, won't we? I'm glad she opened up to you.'

Midas supposed that he had just blurted out the same sort of embarrassed denial his father would have given. But he wasn't practised at talking about

172

feelings. He wanted to run upstairs and jump under a cold shower.

'Did she tell you,' said Carl, 'about the thing that was wrong with her feet?'

Denver coughed. She was eyeballing Midas, trying to transmit something.

'I, um,' he mumbled, 'I don't think Ida told me *specifically* what was wrong with her.'

'You don't think so?'

Denver tapped her pencil on the table. 'No,' she said, 'he doesn't think so.'

'Did she tell you how she and I know each other?'

'Erm . . .' He *could* remember, but Denver wagged her pencil, so he didn't say anything.

'I was her mother's best friend. That puts me in an interesting position, as your father's old colleague.'

'Everyone knows each other on St Hauda's Land,' said Denver.

'Not many people knew your father, Midas, and I'm the only one Ida knows on St Hauda's Land.'

'She knows Midas,' contradicted Denver, 'and my dad, and me.'

'But you've all only just met. Ida and I go way back. Which is why I'm in this peculiar position, having known both your families.'

'Midas isn't like the rest of his family. He's like . . . like God started again.'

Carl smiled sweetly. 'She'd be surprised, wouldn't she, Midas?'

Midas mumbled something.

Denver huffed and closed her sketchbook. 'I can't concentrate.'

Carl stood up. 'And I've finished my coffee.'

They tailed him into the hallway, where he put on his leather jacket and opened the door, to stand for a moment on the step, posed as if admiring the loosely falling snow.

'That's an interesting photograph,' he said, 'on your kitchen wall. About five photos up from the photo of your father.'

'Er,' he racked his brains. 'Is it?'

'Yeah.' Carl tossed his car keys in the air, caught them and sauntered down to where he had parked. He climbed inside and drove away without looking back.

'That was horrible,' said Midas.

Denver had her hands on her hips and was red-faced. 'Stupid!' she gasped. 'Why are you so stupid?'

'Wh-what do you mean?'

'He saw something. When he was testing you. Like a teacher does in a test.' She huffed and turned back to the kitchen. 'It must have been the photo you put up this morning.'

He scurried after her. His nerves were ahead of them both.

'That one,' she said, pointing to it on the kitchen wall, 'but I can't reach it.'

It was the photo of Ida's glass feet. About five photos up from the photo of his father.

Oh *God*. Surely . . . out of context like that . . .

174

just a pair of feet made from glass . . . nothing else . . . that wouldn't mean anything . . .

'That's just . . .' he stammered, 'just special effects. Computers can, you know . . .' He took the photo off the wall and put it face down on the table, as if that could make any difference. Denver went back to the front door and shoved it shut with both arms, keeping the cold out of the house.

CHAPTER 19

Waking in the night offered moments when she forgot what was happening to her feet, only for the moment to spoil with a fog of pins and needles in her veins and the mute responses of dead nerves when she tried to flex her toes. Tonight sleep was hard to come by. She knew it was perverse but Carl, having returned to his own cottage, felt like an impostor. She'd slept the other night through with Midas an arm's reach from her bedside and that had felt homely. The following morning with him, as the oil had spat in the pan, she'd felt something blissful.

She got up early, sick of lying still, and made herself some cereal that she watched turn to soggy blobs in the milk. She wasn't hungry. She watched clumpy snowflakes fall against the window. After a quarter of an hour she heard footsteps outside and felt herself tense up. The kitchen door rattled and swung open, and Carl stepped in wearing a grey coat and thick scarf. His nose and ears were purple and he had sparkles of snow in his hair. Ida flinched at the lick of the cold that filled the room before he shut the door.

Carl smiled blearily and took a seat. 'You couldn't sleep either?'

'No.'

'Sometimes I just can't stop thinking enough to turn off.'

She tried to look sympathetic. 'For me it's my feet.'

'Ah.' He fixed her in the eye and squared his shoulders. 'Listen to me, Ida, I'm worried about you.'

She shrugged, poked at her dissolved cereal with her spoon. 'There's nothing to . . .'

'Ida. I think I know a woman who can help you.'

'Help me find Henry Fuwa?'

'No. Help *cure* you.'

She narrowed her eyes, willed her hands not to do a telltale fidget. Without sleep, willpower was in short supply. Bits of snow blundered into the windowpane. 'Carl . . . Please . . . There's nothing . . .'

He slapped the table. It made her jump and the spoon rattle in the cereal bowl. 'Bullshit, Ida. I've been up all night thinking about you. The way you move. Your timid steps. The way your head hangs when you think no one's looking. I've never seen you this way.'

'What . . . well . . . what do you mean, Carl?'

Dawn was hours away, but she felt like they were about to draw pistols. She tried to fathom what he knew, what he was trying to confirm in her expression. He drew a deep breath. 'Your toes have turned to glass.'

She choked in surprise, felt the anger rushing into her. Her feet had been her tightly-kept secret for months. 'Have you been snooping on me? Sneaking into my room at night?'

He was waving a hand dismissively. 'I'm surprised you'd think me so wretched, Ida. I spoke to Midas Crook yesterday.'

It was impossible to bunch her fists tight enough. 'He told you?'

'Yes. And perhaps some good can come of it. A friend of mine lives in Enghem. She was involved with an . . . unusual case some years back. I went to visit her yesterday, and she's promised she'll do all she can to help you. I could drive you to her house.'

She slammed her fists down on the table. 'You've already told someone else?'

He rolled his eyes. 'Ida . . . this offer is something to take very seriously.'

'I'll *think* about it.'

'Do that. And do it fast. You may have very little time. Certainly not enough time to waste hunting for eccentrics or hanging about with loose-tongued boys. When I visited Midas he said himself he wasn't ready for romance.'

'He said that?'

'Yes! And frankly, Ida, it hardly takes a psychologist to tell that about him. If you . . .' He stopped. She'd covered her face in her hands. She screamed into her palms. After a minute she hobbled out of the room to run a bath.

Carl got up and stepped back outside, tying his scarf tighter. The woods were invisible in the dark, but the snow layering the fields emitted a faint blue glow. He looked up at the roof of the cottage, where tiles showed through their snowy coat like bite marks. The light came on at the bathroom window and he saw Ida's figure silhouetted as she drew the blind.

He had only one smoke left in his pocket, which he lit and puffed especially slowly. He felt a little triumph, but beyond that only apprehension. Charles Maclaird had denied him the knowledge of Freya's cancer. Carl didn't know what he would have done if he'd had that knowledge, but he'd fucking well have done something. And he would do something about Ida.

When she was a girl, Mum bought her a puppy against Dad's wishes. It was a scrappy spaniel and Mum, upon seeing its nose wrinkle at the sight of her, burst out laughing and fell in love with it, christening it Long John.

Long John grew one part at a time. First his tail lengthened so that, wagging it hard, his momentum rocked him over. Then his legs grew and he'd race off so quick he surprised himself and they found him yelping from a pothole or ditch. His ears got so big they became secondary eyelids and he wore himself out flapping them back off his face.

Her dad was the one who walked Long John when Ida wasn't there. His objection to owning a puppy had been the expense but now he studied the labels on tins and bought only the most nutritious dog food. As Long John became a panting thing who sniffed the arseholes of other canines, Ida's mum lost interest. Her dad took him to the vet when he got feverish, fussed over him with plastic bones, and converted a lobster pot into a dog basket.

One day thirteen-year-old Ida walked Long John, as she had a hundred times along the coastal path where the cliff tops were ravaged. Long gashes in the soil exposed networks of flinty crags descending to where the sea infiltrated the land. Sometimes she would lie with her head over a crag, her hair dangling in its pit trap, hearing the sea whispering her name.

This afternoon, walking Long John, she discovered a brand-new crag that had opened in the path like a split opens in a rope. She could have walked inland a little, hopped a fence and come back on the other side. She should have turned back and phoned the coastguard to close off the path. Instead of either, she decided to jump it. She paced out her run-up, turned and sprinted to the crag, her final step a bound that launched her into the air. For a second she felt the malice of the sea in the depths of the opened cliff beneath her. She landed safely on the other side, her laughter echoing faintly in the fissure.

Eager to join the fun, Long John yapped and raced towards her. His jump came short. His paws scratched at the soil on her side then he skidded backwards into the crag. She darted to the edge too late. He was out of sight. Only his confused noises remained. His yapping could have come from any one of the shadowy downward passageways. It was followed by a scuffling and whining, the sibilant sea, a bark (an earthworm wriggled from the earth and plopped after him into the dark), the clap of a hidden wave, more yapping, a puff of salt air cold as caves.

When she got back home, teenage make-up melting down her cheeks, she found her mum in the front garden, reading poetry in her hammock. She sprang up to try to hug her distressed daughter, but Ida twisted away and struggled to explain what had happened.

'Hush, hush Ida,' said Mum. 'His life force has gone back to nature. It's like what I told you about nirvana. It's the way of all things. Dust to dust. In a way we can be glad for him.'

Ida sobbed and ran inside, slamming the door behind her. Her dad met her in the hall and sat her on the bottom step of the stairs. She brushed his hands off her and explained falteringly what had happened.

'Shh,' he said, 'shh. God in heaven has a time and place for all things. It can be hard to comprehend . . . But if God calls a soul back to Him . . . rest assured He has a place in His kingdom prepared.'

Her sense of betrayal came as a sharp gasp. She squirmed loose and hammered up the stairs. Halfway along the corridor Carl Maulsen stepped out of the bathroom, zipping up his flies, the toilet flushing behind him.

He had come unannounced to visit the family the night before. Since he had driven a long way, Mum had insisted he stay in the guest bedroom. Dad had said nothing and gone to bed early. Ida hadn't been able to sleep. She'd crept downstairs and listened through a closed door to Carl and Mum's conversation. They talked about places they'd been to. Other countries, nights slept in the freezing wastes of deserts and days spent diving through the barnacled ruins of sunken cities.

On the landing she found herself blurting out the story all over again, adding the epilogue of how her parents had tried to comfort her. He listened carefully, then leant back against the wall with arms folded.

'And what do you think happened?' he asked.

'I don't know.' She started to cry again.

'I'll tell you. He fell a long way. Probably some bones broke. He would have been in great pain. Then the sea would take him. If he was lucky it would sweep him out quickly and dash him on rocks as it did so. More likely he drowned in slow increments in pitch dark. Now his body's either wedged down there or already floating to the seabed on the ocean current, to be nibbled by carrion fish or torn to scraps by sharks.'

She struggled to speak. 'And then?'

He shrugged. 'Then the parts of him rot, matter breaks down and disperses in the water. His bones build up a covering of sand.'

182

'But his . . . his spirit?'

He shrugged again. 'Sorry, Ida. We don't know about that. Anything I could say would be fiction. Maybe his skull will shelter crabs from predators.'

She lunged forwards and hugged him tightly, pressing her face into his shirt and the hard width of his stomach beneath it.

Now grown up and leaving Carl's bath, watching the blue morning's reluctant transition to day, she compared his indifference then to what he had offered her now.

She opened the window to let the steam out. Her movement disturbed an owl that wheeled out of the trees then swerved silently back into them. She sat down on the toilet seat to dry, and thought of Midas, who had wanted to watch owls with her. That was the sort of thing she supposed she had no time for, in Carl's view of things. But she was incensed that Midas had told Carl about her feet.

Midas could go back to that horrible gadget hanging around his neck, the one that bent his posture into that of an old man. Except . . . Midas might seem as grey as his landscape, but she couldn't remember any guy who'd appeared in her thoughts unprompted as many times as he had over these last few days. She wasn't sure she'd have the will to take Carl's advice if it meant losing the one thing on St Hauda's Land that seemed vivid to her.

The bath was an antique old tub, raised from the floor on legs with feet shaped like lion paws.

Studying her own bare feet, she saw a ghastly similarity in their ornamental neatness. Only, she could imagine those cat paws padding through a far-off desert, could picture more movement in their leaden claws than she could in her own toes. She looked at each glass digit in turn, then at the condensation slowly lifting from their enamelled surfaces. She tried not to check them like this too often because they always looked worse. They had become noticeably so since last she checked. They were a mirage on the bathroom floor. Her left little toe twinkled in the dawn light from the window. Her metatarsals, encased in the forepart of her feet, were as fine as the nibs of quill pens, but they seemed a half-inch shorter than last time she had looked. The skin around her heel had turned a gummy white, preparing for the transformation. She mopped her feet quickly with her towel and pulled on her first pair of socks in a hurry. It didn't matter if her toes were still damp. Her socks would sponge up the moisture, and she'd never know they weren't as dry as bone.

CHAPTER 20

Sleet fell in a rain of white arrows over Ettinsford. A sneaking wind stole at pedestrians' umbrellas and pulled back their hoods in the High Street where Midas sat in his car, waiting for a red light to switch to green. The sleet could turn direction at will, one moment lashing the car from the left, then spearing sharply from the right. He could see the despairing look on a young woman's face as she swung her umbrella this way and that like a shield.

The light turned green and he drove. Downhill past the old church, past Catherine's, past the park beside the icy strait. Across the bridge, past where Ettinsford ended. One unfinished house stood on the far bank of the strait, half built since Midas could remember. He'd watched it change from a promise of red brick to a broken ring of rubble. He didn't know why work had been abandoned, but he knew he shouldn't like to live under the first branches of the wood.

The canopy of Gurm's woodland reminded Midas of a beetle he had found curled up dead on his doorstep that morning. The endless tiers of angular branches were like manifold legs. The light-starved shrubs of the undergrowth had thin, veined leaves like bug wings.

He sped on, concentrating on remembering the route he and Ida had driven before. He didn't want to take a wrong turn and become lost in insectile groves.

Then he found it. The cottage with its newt-green door, horseshoe hanging above the letterbox. The trees thinned out to make glades for its front and back gardens, which were spotted with snow.

She opened the door before he reached it and stood in the door frame, leaning on the wall with her arms folded.

'Are we, um, going inside?' he asked.

She shook her head.

'Oh. Is Carl at home?'

'No, Midas, he's driven down to Glamsgallow on work.'

'So . . .'

'We're not going inside because you're not one hundred per cent welcome.'

He took a step back and scratched his head.

'Don't be coy, Midas. You told Carl about my feet.'

There was a controlled resentment in her voice. It frightened him. He wanted to run back to his car and drive away fast. He blinked a lump of snow off an eyelash. 'Er, Ida, I . . . he came to my house and saw the photo. I didn't *tell* him.'

'You had that fucking photo on display? Jesus

Christ, Midas, that's one hell of a way to keep a secret. I expected you to delete it.'

'I . . . don't get visitors. Normally. Um . . .' He wrung his hands.

'Fucking pathetic,' she muttered, and slammed the door.

He stood with the wind buffeting his hair, slapping snow against his cheeks (inside, Ida leant with her back against the door). He supposed she was right, he should have deleted that photo like all the others. Still he felt in part the victim, hoodwinked somehow by Carl (she felt all her anger puff away, doubting he had intended to betray her trust). And he hadn't managed to tell her that he'd found Henry Fuwa. He knocked on the door again, hoping she'd open it and he could at least give her the address in the bog (she very nearly answered, doubting he even understood how he'd hurt her), but she didn't open the door. He trudged back to his car (she decided that anger was pointless when he was the closest thing to a friend she had on St Hauda's Land. She opened the door). Dots of snow streaked through the empty garden. Midas and his car were gone.

CHAPTER 21

Midas was washing up with his eyes closed. Often it was best to do it this way, cleaning the knives and the coffee cups by touch. He found it strange that among any number of unpleasant impressions of his father, the most vivid was of the man washing up. That was why he washed up blind, because his own arms dipping into the dishwater, the trails of bubbles on his skin, the purple the water turned his fingers, the involuntary mannerism he used to pull a plate from the bowl and hold it up to drain, all dug the memory up. Dishwater was a crystal ball on his childhood.

In the memory, Midas was small enough to spy through keyholes without crouching down. He'd watched his father wash the dishes, reciting something moribund under his breath, until his mother crept into the kitchen and touched the small of his back with her fingertips. Midas watched her touch flow into his father like wax setting in a mould. The plate he was holding dropped back into the bowl. His back went upright, his knees locked. She turned him around,

188

foam dripping off his hands to spot the floor. She dried them on her skirt, then pulled them apart and laid them on her hips as she pressed her body tight against his. His lips trembled and he stared over her shoulder.

'The, the . . .' he stammered after a while . . . 'the washing-up water will get cold, dear.'

She drew her hands away from him and stepped back. Midas ducked out of sight as she left the kitchen and climbed the stairs. Then he went in and stood beside his father, who removed the plate for a second time, watched the water run half-circles around it, and put it on the rack for hot bubbles to pop on its surface.

'Midas,' he said, dipping the next plate in the bowl.

'Yes?'

'Do you ever feel . . . No, let me think of an example. At school, if you do well in class, you feel elated, don't you?'

'What's elated?'

'Feeling good, really good. What do you *feel*, Midas? For example, when you do well at school.'

'Er . . . pleased? Proud?'

His father looked wistful. 'And you don't feel anticlimactic?'

'What's that?'

'Somewhat the opposite of elated.'

'What's elated again?'

'Good feelings. That is to say, very good. You

can feel, can't you? That's what I'm driving at. You don't ever wonder . . . where feeling went?'

While Midas did his dishes, Ida was huddled in a chair in the centre of Carl Maulsen's lawn, the cottage to her back and the woods beginning abruptly at the top of the slope where the garden ended. Carl had no flowerbeds, no tended bushes, just hacked growth and a glade of mowed turf in the summer. That was invisible now, buried under two inches of snow that had creaked like floorboards when she laboured across it with her crutch and the chair. The snow was as stiff as the rest of St Hauda's Land. The awkward bending of branches in the wind, the brittle leaves that broke like ancient parchments. Even a falcon she had watched fly without grace, with mechanical beats of its wings. As if that was the way of these islands, to seize things up, to weather away their vitality.

That was what the place was doing to her.

It was good to get outside. She would rather feel cold in her body than in her heart. She lifted hot tomato soup in a thermos mug to her lips, enjoying its sour steam inside her nostrils. She'd put on scarlet woollen mittens and scarf to fight the island's blacks and whites. But that was the story of this place and its people, as stilted and monochrome as sets and stars of pre-colour TV. Take Midas: what made a person rigid in every way? Years had made her mum rigid. Religion had done it to her dad. She remembered the only time she'd seen him cry, on the night before their relationship morphed from that of father and daughter to that of courteous housemates. He'd caught her in bed with Josiah, a South African exchange student staying in the house for a month (a tenure cut short by that incident), but the crying the night before came about when her dad, who'd been edgy for weeks leading up to Josiah's arrival, tried to address him in Afrikaans. He'd been learning Afrikaans for three years and she had no reason to believe him anything less than accomplished. Then when he cleared his throat at the dinner table to address Josiah he met a blank stare. He took it with blushing grace, although as she spied on him later (when he thought he was alone unnoticed in their garden of dusty dandelion clocks) she saw him cry. Slow-worm tears as he held a half-blown dandelion clock to his heart. That was rigidity like Midas's.

In a sudden flush of anger she dashed her tomato soup across the garden. She watched the red arc sink through the snow like a healing burn. A flash again of Dad. His craggy face turned childishly awestruck while he took communion. And seeing him pray with the stain of the budget sacrament wine on his bottom lip, crossing himself over and over. When he opened his eyes the first thing they had tearfully fixed on was her.

Midas had said he hoped his father would be in hell. He had described his character and told her about recollections from his childhood. From everything she heard, Ida got the clear impression that Midas Crook senior was vindictive, fickle, manipulative. She pictured him as a kind of goblin, and Midas's childhood home as a storm-racked cave in the mountains, like one she had once sheltered in with her mother when a dust storm blew up on a trip to the Middle East. All the same, there was something about the accounts of him that resonated. It was strange, but she fancied she would have understood him better than Midas had. Yet she doubted she would ever understand her own father, whose behaviour was far less severe than that of Mr Crook's.

Without her soup to warm her and feeling the bite of the snow in the air (remembering the hot dust storm blowing into that cave and flapping the tails of her multicoloured headscarf), she began the laborious retreat to the confines of Carl's cottage.

At the end of a street of town houses painted in crisp blues, stood Ettinsford Public Library. In contrast to the smart town houses, the little library's plaster walls sagged in on themselves. Buckled window frames looked like driftwood. Panes were tarnished with sooty dirt. It was an overcast evening and the windows threw orange projections on to wet pavements. Seagulls bickered, perched in lines along gutters, squawking at Ida as she toiled up the steps to the front door, gripping a slippery handrail and leaning all her weight on her crutch.

The smell inside reminded her of a school

classroom: a chalky smell mixed with disinfectants and something bubblegum sweet. The bookshelves were chrome, the walls beige and undecorated save in a kids' corner piled with stained beanbags. There the wall was covered in children's drawings of fictional characters, clothes brightly coloured and hands too cumbersome for their bodies.

She approached the librarian at a counter, a man in a bright shirt and novelty tie, with a ruddy double chin and blond centre parting. When she asked where the newspaper archive was he didn't answer, only raised his arm to point with an expression of pained ennui.

It shouldn't have taken long to sort through the tiny archive. Carl had given her what he assured her was an accurate estimate of the date when the suicide had occurred. Unfortunately the issues of the local paper were out of order and the system had been maintained with the same lethargy that the librarian betrayed at reception. Ida had little choice but to organize the issues anew, beginning by putting August through to October into their correct order. As she filed a newspaper from late September (too late a date to keep company with Carl's estimates) she saw a picture she recognized on the cover.

It was the same image Carl had framed in the cottage, only this time it had been reproduced from what would have been archive footage at the time. The accompanying article concerned only Midas's father. The headline read: SUICIDE

PROFESSOR EXHUMED BY VANDALS and made her put down the paper and cover her mouth. The grave, the article explained, had been spoilt and the coffin tampered with. She searched impatiently through the editions for the rest of September, and combed the October issues again. Several follow-up stories reported no progress with the investigation. Then the story vanished. She looked through the jumbled issues from November onward but realized that the story could resurface at any time in the years since the event had occurred. Asking the librarian for assistance would surely get her nowhere, so she decided to give Carl a call. Then she realized that he would have *known*.

He had been eager to impart the failings of Midas's family but he'd elected not to mention an event as dramatic as this.

She returned the newspapers to their correct shelves and quietly left the library. There was only one person she could safely ask about the news story.

That person's father and namesake, the person the story concerned, sat at his oak desk many years previous, resting his head on its scratched surface, smelling ink and pencil shavings.

After a long while he sat upright with great effort, exhaled a sigh and reached for a clean sheet of lined paper, smoothing it out on the desk. He unscrewed the lid of his fountain pen, laid it perpendicular to his paper, and began to write.

Often he compared his writing to white water. He had only to leap in to be dragged away on its rapids, thrown this way and that with his own will rendered impotent. While writing he found the words came from the muscles in his hands, the feel of the shaft of his pen, the locked joint of his elbow, the scratching noise of the nib marking paper and, underneath all that, some coordinating impulse in his guts. Certainly not from his mind. And, *God*, what blessed relief to lose one's turgid thoughts and anxieties in a gush of imagery and symbols. He was a man of words first and foremost: a man of flesh and blood second. Indeed (he massaged the ribs on the left side of his chest, easing the deep burn there with slow, circular strokes), the flesh had always failed him. In physical feats he'd always fallen short, be it racing laps of painted grass tracks on school sports days; be it the shameful way he'd fainted at the birth of his wriggling son, battled the swoon and lost, the ceiling blurring upwards and blacking out; the way he came to with an infant's weeping in his ears and was convinced for a second it was his own.

He rubbed his pained chest, his body's final failure, and wrote.

After an hour he set down his pen. His fingers flickered over his files, pinched out the manila envelope in which the X-rays were kept.

Years old, the doctor had concluded, of the growth between his diaphragm and his heart. The doctor was also keen to stress how hard it was to be certain, since he had never seen anything like it before.

Midas Crook ceremoniously opened the envelope and drew out the first X-ray. The bulb of his heart and the half-inch shoot of something crystalline. It looked like a mark on the print and sometimes, possessed by fanatical hope, he tried to scratch it off the paper and prove that the whole thing was a silly joke. Prove that he would be better soon and would have feelings again: base emotion long derided and now lost. That he would take his boy under the arms and lift him up, spinning him around until they both collapsed dizzy and laughing under bright skies.

CHAPTER 22

Midas was sixteen when his father, turning a black, leather-bound book in his hands, asked, 'Do you want this?'

Midas told him he did, although he didn't.

It was a humid night, later to become a hated night, played over in his thoughts until he could watch it like theatre, retrospect's dramatic irony making him scream at his younger self to see sense, see what his father had planned. Grey clouds had hung like dead petals in a spider web. In the far distance a lighthouse had pulsed. A haze of moonlight covered everything.

His father stroked his palm across the cover then handed the leather-bound book to Midas. 'It's my first draft. Handwritten. Pathetic to be sentimental about it really but . . . Look after it. Never bend the spine, always use a bookmark. There, you have it. Now, help me get these other things into the boat.'

Together they lifted each box over the shallow sides of the vessel. The boxes mostly contained the books, papers and pamphlets that had filled the shelves and covered the floor of Midas's father's study for years. The clear-out he'd been having had left a bare room and empty desk, bleached diligently clean of pencil marks and ink stains.

'Last one,' he said, as between them they lifted the biggest box on to the boat. It was far lighter than Midas had expected, and taped up. He thought he caught a whiff of paraffin.

'What's in that one?'

His father's eyes skirted down to the sea, which was as still as the sky. The tide had already brought feeble breakers within inches of the boat.

'What's in that big box?'

He shrugged. 'Junk. Nothing.'

'But . . .'

'Firelighters, son.'

Midas frowned. It was high summer. He supposed the firelighters were a stash to see his father through the winter.

The two of them had spent the day on the islet where his father had bought a cabin. It was only reachable by boat, so the two of them had crossed that morning with the first cargo of furniture: some shelves, a chair and a small wooden desk from an antique dealer in Gurmton. Midas was there to help transform the simple wooden hut into an isolated study, although while he had tried to fix one of the table's legs and put up the shelves his father had sat in the doorway staring out at the channel of water and the clefts in the cliffs.

He had remained distant like that as he rowed them back to collect the boxes of papers and books that would complete the study. It wasn't unusual for him to be sullen, but it was strange to see him so indifferent he forgot to be spiteful.

'Help me push the boat out, Midas.'

Midas couldn't help but sneak another look at his father's thin white feet. He'd seen so little of his body: he always wore long-sleeved shirts with tight cuffs and collars up to his neck. He'd never seen his knees. The sight of his toes, long as a monkey's, their fine black hairs and neatly trimmed nails, had felt astonishingly intimate all day.

There were so many books and papers in the boat that it was almost too heavy to push, but as they heaved it into deeper water the going got easier. Soon they stood with water up to their chests and the boat bobbing beside them. The sea was getting colder now because the sun was going down. Midas wished his father had picked an islet near a jetty. He had never been as deep in the sea as he was this day. The spreading expanse of water and the power of its weight terrified him, but his father's unusually assured manner had soothed that. His father took a deep breath and grabbed the side of the boat to haul himself, thrashing with his feet, up its side. When he was nearly over, his grip failed and he slid with a shout back into the water. A splash of white drops rose in the air as he submerged. Midas lurched after him, swaying in the currents.

His father surfaced spluttering, his glasses halfway down his nose, his moustache wet and slick against his lip. He grabbed the side of the boat again and stood for a minute with his head leaning against it, dribbling seawater.

'Help me up, Midas.'

'How?'

'Cup your hands beneath the water. Give me a leg-up.'

'What if I slip? I could drown.'

'You won't drown. It's not deep enough here.'

He nodded, reassured, and made a cup of his hands. His father scowled at the water.

'Where are they? It's too dark.'

'Right here in front of me.'

His father lifted his leg and his foot came through the water like a white fish. He misjudged the distance and his toes pushed against Midas's chest. Midas's heart drummed as the toes wriggled over his ribcage and found his palms. The white foot pushed hard on his hands, making him shudder so violently from cold and excitement he thought he couldn't hold on. Then, showering drops, his father launched out of the water and scrabbled over the side of the boat. After a moment he tossed a piece of seaweed back into the water and it landed with a slap. Midas held his arms up to his father. He could feel the sea chilling by the minute.

'Help me in.'

'No, no. The boat's already too heavy with only me aboard. My *God*, Midas, you're shivering. Get back to the beach. I've packed you a towel and a change of clothes. The car keys are on the dashboard. And you know how to work the heater?'

Midas nodded. 'But I want to go to the cabin with you!'

His father took off his glasses and wiped the water from them with his thumbs. 'Some other time, perhaps. I will be alone tonight, thank you. Now get back to the beach before you're too numb to move.'

Grudgingly, Midas turned and waded back to the beach. It seemed to take for ever, and when he splashed back on to the sand, shirt and trousers stuck to cold flesh, his father had rowed the boat a long way out.

'Midas!' he yelled through the dusk, 'Are you safe?'

'Of course,' he yelled back, wrapping his arms around himself and trying to control his chattering teeth. For a moment there in the sea he'd actually thought he'd made some connection with the old man. The boat drifted towards the islet, where a glow singled out the cabin.

'Midas! Are you safe?'

Perhaps he hadn't heard the first reply. 'I'm fine! I'm safe!'

Midas was halfway towards the car when the first lick of yellow flame sprang up on the water. He spun around and gasped. The boat was on fire. His stomach came loose and he sprinted back across the sand terrified, splashing through the shallows, already understanding everything. The flames formed a dancing teardrop. Smoke rolled through the air.

'Father!' Midas yelled, throwing himself into the water. The flames shuddered and split. He saw his father leap into the sea, wrapped in fire. The hiss of his submergence carried over the noise of the waves.

CHAPTER 23

That afternoon Ida took a taxi to Midas's house and rang his doorbell. He was surprised to see her.

'Hi. If you think you owe me an apology . . . then I think I owe you one too.'

'Um, um. I mean . . . I'm sorry.'

'Snap.' She smiled disarmingly at him. 'So are you going to invite me in, or play the same trick I did on you? It's chilly out here.'

He slapped a hand to his head. 'Yes, of course, how stupid of me.'

In the kitchen she looked around, daunted by the walls of photographs. 'So,' she said, 'this is where you live.'

'Um, yes. Would you like, um, a cup of coffee?'

'Please.'

Ida took a seat, looking at the crowded photos. He was good, she realized. Really talented. She always knew he would be, even though she'd not seen his pictures until now. They embodied that peculiar vision that had attracted her to him in the first place. Funny how much better she felt, being around him.

She laughed when he set the coffee in front of her.

'What?'

'It's black as sin, that's what.'

He sprang up, ran to the sink, poured out an inch then topped it up with hot water to set it neatly before her again. She laughed at the unintentional butler's bow he gave.

He flashed a sheepish grin. 'I've just remembered.' He went to the cupboard and returned with a plate of mince pies topped with stars of pastry. 'Denver baked them for me. We can eat them.'

The spicy juices and crumbly pastry reminded her of indulgent Christmas-times from years ago, when she used to go for long hikes through snowy dales. Winters when she used to *ski*.

'Have you ever been skiing, Midas?'

'Me? No. I've never even been swimming.'

'You're joking.'

He shook his head. 'Can't swim. Absolutely forbidden as a child.'

'Why?'

'My father thought it wasn't safe.'

'You didn't think to learn, now that you're an adult?'

He shook his head. 'I don't like large bodies of water.'

She burst out laughing. 'Jesus! You live on the tiniest island!'

He blushed. 'Well . . . I suppose that is stupid. But . . . it's the weight of it. I can't help thinking how heavy a body of water is. Being *in* it, lowering yourself into its airlessness.'

She could tell there was more to it than that. 'What about boating? Can you cope with that?'

His frown deepened. 'I can just about bear the mainland ferry. If I sit at its dead centre. Smaller boats I'm not so good with.'

'I'll take you boating some time. Show you how much fun it can be.' She'd been thinking about it for a while, although only now that she voiced it did she think how difficult it would be. A non-swimmer and a girl with dead weights for feet, stranded in the chopping ocean. She supposed that neither was it likely she'd sit some day in a cable car with him, gliding up a mountain, awestruck by an endless view of snow-capped giants.

The photos on the kitchen walls felt warmly reassuring: this was Midas's peculiar but homely hiding hole. She imagined spending mornings here in this sanctum, drinking black coffee in silence with him.

He was picking at the remains of his mince pie. 'Ida, I've got to ask you a question.'

'Go ahead.'

'It's about you and me.'

She tensed hopefully.

'Could I . . . um . . . Would it be possible for you and I to . . . um, I mean, if it's all the same with you . . . Would it be possible for me to photograph you?'

'Oh, Midas, I thought you were going to ask me

something quite different. I don't know. I'm not comfortable with it. I look so haggard these days. Perhaps when I'm better.'

She wished he hadn't asked. She had reservations about photography. She didn't want to be part of the ghostly chorus of the photographed.

'Sorry. Sorry, Ida.'

'It's okay. That's what I've come here to talk about. My official reason, anyway.'

'Er . . . ?'

She sighed. 'Getting better. Carl thinks he knows someone who can help. She lives on the north coast. We're going to go and stay with her. Me and Carl. For a few days, to see if there's anything she can do for me. I wondered if you'd like to come with me? Us. I'll have to clear it with Carl, of course, but I'm sure this person will have room at her house – she's Emiliana Stallows.'

The surprise formed on his face. '*Mrs* Stallows?' The husband owned most of the island's north coast, but he knew little about the wife. 'How can she help?'

'Carl told me . . . that there was a case once before, of a girl who went through something like this. Emiliana helped her.'

It was difficult to convey the story Carl had told her, here in the shelter of Midas's kitchen. Only the cold interiors of her boots reminded her that it was all real. She shrugged and saved it for later. 'I might as well hope that Emiliana can help me too, since looking for Henry has been so unproductive.'

206

'Um . . . It's good that, isn't it? I'd love to come with you. I mean, I don't love it that we have to go, but since we must – or at least think we should – I'd love to. But—'

'Don't say you can't come.' Suddenly she was desperate for him to accompany her. In truth, the trip to Emiliana Stallows felt like an appointment at a hospice.

'No, I can definitely come. I will. Only there's something else. I found Henry Fuwa. I have his address. I . . . hope you're not angry.'

She clapped her hands. 'Midas! How perfect! Why would I be angry?'

'Because I . . . Although I didn't tell him outright I think he guessed . . . Guessed what was happening to your feet.' He clutched his hands to his camera and prepared a wince on his face.

'But Midas, that couldn't be better! Don't you see? If Henry *guessed,* he must know what's happening to me!'

'He said he couldn't do anything.'

She frowned. 'Bollocks to that. Where's he hiding?'

CHAPTER 24

The lights were out in Henry Fuwa's cottage. Nobody answered when Ida rapped on the door with the handle of her crutch. She returned sulkily to Midas's car and waited with him for an impatient hour before throwing her hands in the air. 'Enough! Let's get out of this stupid bog.'

They drove on marsh roads that dipped in and out of opaque puddles. The tarmac, prised open by roots, made the car jostle them about in their seats. At one point she thought she saw a figure, standing in the bog, in a long coat buttoned up to its throat. But the coat was the colour of tall grass and the arms were just the shifting of reeds. They drove on by. Heavy snow, and rain all through the preceding autumn, had flooded the low-lying land where the mere became the fringe of the woods. Here the trees rose from the water like the coils of sea monsters, covered in the same scaly leaves that floated on the flood's surface and speckled the sheets of frozen mud that held hostage bulrushes. The ice lacquered tree stumps and half-rinds of striated bark.

'Stop,' urged Ida, seeing one of the stumps moving. This was no broken tree, but a man in waterproof trousers and cagoule: hood turned up, fishing net sieving the water. 'Stay in the car.' She got out carefully and called from the road, 'Hi! Hello there?'

The man jumped in surprise. It was obvious from the sheen on his glasses and the beard sprouting from the open hood that this was Henry Fuwa.

'Ida Maclaird!' he exclaimed, giving her an awkward salute.

'You remember me!'

He splashed towards her, careful not to tip his net, and she saw he'd caught some twenty crabs, pincers flapping, carapaces the grey of oyster shells.

Henry noticed Midas's car with Midas inside. 'I had already been reminded of you by your friend there.'

'We've just been to your cottage, Henry. I'd hoped we might catch up.'

He was still looking warily at the car. 'I'm not so sure that's a good idea. And my poky cottage isn't hospitable enough for three.'

She read him with disappointment. Was this the general suspicion among islanders, or had something happened between the two of them?

'Well, I expect Midas will want to wait outside.'

'Ida,' he said quietly, 'didn't he tell you?'

'Tell me what?'

Henry looked with frustration at the car. 'Perhaps *I* could drive you back to my cottage. My own car's nearby. That way I can drop you back at wherever it is you're staying. Then poor old Midas won't have to wait around.'

Henry glanced upward in admiration as a swan called its bass *horrnk* and took to the air nearby, the beat of its wings rocking the algae leaves into swarms. In a quiet voice nearly carried away on the breeze Ida asked, 'What should Midas have told me?'

'It . . . It'll take some explaining.'

She shrugged and made her way up to the car. 'I'm safe with him,' she whispered to Midas, 'you can go back and enjoy your afternoon. Look out for me in a couple of hours.'

'I want to help . . .'

'You are helping. Only, Henry says he'd rather see me alone.'

'We fell out.'

'I gathered.'

'He said he couldn't help you.'

She nodded. 'Go on. I'll come and see you when we're done.'

He looked worried, but drove away like she'd asked.

'I planned to take these back and cook them,' said Henry, tipping the crabs he'd caught into a pot in the boot of his car. 'I've got plenty of tuna cans, so that's no trouble. And anchovies, plenty of those. Wait . . . you're not . . .'

'Vegetarian? No. Crabs would be lovely.'

She got into his car and they drove through the flooded bogscape, Henry's headlights glowing off puddles all the way back to his cottage.

'So,' asked Henry, when he was taking off his

210

shoes in the hallway (he didn't ask Ida to take off hers, even though they were cusped with mud). 'Are we going to get straight down to talking business, or have a . . . a . . . chit-chat first?'

'A chit-chat, I think.'

'Ida, this is going to be hard.'

'I want to apologize. I tried to catch up with you after I offended you in the pub in Gurmton. I couldn't find you then, but now I realize . . . Those things you told me about . . . You weren't drunk, were you?'

He closed his eyes. 'Gin does tend to go to my head. But if I was drunk I wasn't lying. I told you about the moth-winged cattle after you saw that poor bull. I think I told you they eat and shit and die like everything else. You see, just because something's . . . unfamiliar, doesn't mean it isn't bound by all that stuff.'

She shivered. 'There's something unfamiliar happening to me.'

'Yes. Midas let on.'

She stared at the framed diagram of the jellyfish on the wall. She sighed. 'How are the moth-winged cattle?'

'Well . . .' he hesitated. 'Do you know, this is the first time in my life I've been asked that question? They're in fine health.' He leant on his chin, scratching his beard ruminatively. 'Would you, um, care to see them?'

The moss-covered door swung open. He led her into a musty kind of airlock and took an excited breath as he opened the inner door on to the pen proper.

A heater hummed quietly in the centre of a floor smattered by dung. Birdcages and gutted lanterns of all sizes swung from rafters on the ceiling. The herd of moth-winged cattle lapped the pen in a figure-of-eight, swooping and turning sharp angles like a flock of autumn swallows. The blur of so many wings wrapped them in a shimmer. They tossed their heads and kicked their forelegs as they flew. Some of the larger bulls had curving horns and flew with heads bowed as if charging impish matadors. Thread-like tails flowed behind them in a breeze created by their flight. Ida felt it as a faint blowing on her cheeks and laughed in involuntary delight.

Afterwards, in the house, Henry fussed as he helped her into a comfy armchair, 'Can I offer you some tea? I've only green, I'm afraid.'

'That'd be a refreshing change. Being with Midas all I get is coffee.'

'So you're . . . with . . . the Crook boy, are you?'

'The *Crook boy*? Who would that be? Don't tell me you're like that about him.'

Henry's smile had a knowing twinge to it. 'I meant no offence. I merely called him that to distinguish him. What happened was tragic.'

'Concerning his father?'

'And the way his mother took it.'

She scowled. 'I don't see why any of that should impinge on how people treat Midas. He's been so sweet to me.'

'You're young, though, Ida. That's what you have to remember. People look for patterns in their existences, and one of the patterns they see on these islands is that of families making the same mistakes through generations.'

She huffed and folded her arms. 'That only happens because the community here's so tiny. People don't have the imagination to see Midas as his own man. They file him neatly in the spot his dead dad vacated.'

'Quite, quite. I couldn't agree with you more.'

'Yet you still don't want him in your house. The two of you fell out, he said.'

'He hasn't told you why?'

'No.'

'Did he tell you . . . anything at all?'

'Only that he'd found you. He said the two of you talked about his mother. He said you knew her once.'

'I . . . That is, I . . .' He scratched his beard. 'Did he tell you what I showed him in the bog?'

'No. What did you show him?'

'Just . . . Well it was a bright day. I showed him the light on the meres.'

They were briefly quiet. She knew there was something more, but decided to press Midas for it later. 'I'll make the tea,' he said, forcing a smile and leaving her at the table while he went through to the adjacent kitchen.

He poured simmering water on to the tea leaves. It wouldn't help to tell Ida what lay in the murky

213

bog pool, which he assumed was also Midas's reasoning. The poor girl was here because he was her last resort, and he didn't know how to convince her there was nothing he could do. He had certainly done a bad job with Midas. He watched the tea leaves flex and expand in the water.

Ida hobbled into the kitchen behind him.

'Forgive me . . .' he said. 'I fear you've terribly misunderstood me. I don't feel any aversion to Midas because of his father. It's his mother . . . that's . . . what . . . I must be honest with you.'

'You mentioned her earlier.'

'Yes. You must understand that I'm telling you this in the strictest confidence.'

He stared into the steam rising from the pan. She had this power (he recalled feeling it now at their first meeting that summer) to prise open your carapace and get in amongst the gooey mess beneath.

'You're in love with her,' she said.

He hung his head. 'Yes. And no. Not any more, I think.' He hoped his honesty would help her accept what he had to say about the glass.

'Did you have an affair with her?'

'Not everyone can speak as . . . freely as you can, Ida.'

'Sorry, I thought you wanted to discuss it.'

'I wanted to explain that . . . Midas offered a route to Evaline. But as a kind of bargaining chip to get me to help you. And you see I could not accept his offer, not only because Evaline . . . Evaline is something different now . . . but because I have nothing to bargain with in turn.'

'I'm turning into glass,' she said softly.

He wiped sweat from his brow and set the teapot down with a clunk. He felt so hot inside that the thought of drinking it made him swoon. 'I fancy a glass of something,' he declared, then covered his mouth shamefaced. 'I mean, of course, a drink. A . . . tumbler of something.'

'It's all right. It's everywhere, isn't it?'

He gave an awkward kind of bow, then went to a cupboard for a bottle of gin. He poured them both a shot, leaving the tea in the saucepan. 'I don't really drink. I've found myself doing . . . things while drunk. Yet under pressure . . . I am weak-willed.'

She nodded.

'Her husband was an obstacle that nervous people such as she and I could never hope to overcome.'

'He's been dead for a decade.'

'That makes no difference now.'

'It makes all the difference. Move away. The two of you.'

'And leave the cattle behind?'

'Then defy what people think. People here don't even know you. Bring her here to you.'

He bit his lip. 'How selfish. Forgive me, Ida, for bringing this up.'

'Don't be stupid. You must be so lonely you barely notice any more.'

He shook his head. 'You're too young to understand.'

'Don't patronize me.'

'Ahh . . . I didn't mean to. I just mean . . . it's too late for me and Evaline.'

She looked into her gin. 'It's never too late.'

He watched her closely as she said it. 'See,' he said sadly, 'you were surprised by the doubt in your own voice.' He put his glass down and wiped his palms on his trouser legs. 'Thank you for your optimism, but it was too late long before Midas Crook died. One day the Evaline I knew was simply . . . gone. If I had done more back when she was still with us perhaps she would have stayed. But who knows where that woman is now?'

There was silence, broken by one or the other of them slurping gin.

'Henry,' she said quietly, 'if I show you my feet, what are you going to say?'

He held up his hands. 'I don't want to see them. Thank you, Ida. I can picture them perfectly.'

She nodded.

'And as far as talking about them goes . . . I've told you everything there is to tell.'

She put her gin down heavily. 'But you haven't told me why. Or how. I've always been a really normal person, Henry. How the hell does a person go from a normal life one second to a life like this the next, walking on a stick with no feeling in my toes?' She had screwed up her fists. Her eyes were bulging. 'What did I do, to bring this on myself? Just tell me what I did, where I stepped, who I crossed . . . Something.'

'You came all this way, to find me, to ask me that?'

'Because of the moth-winged cattle. And the creature you said can turn a thing white with one look. You know how these islands work.'

He shrugged meekly. 'I don't know anything.'

'What . . . what does that mean?'

'There's no why. No how. Things happen, and all we can do is try to live with them.'

'How am I supposed to live with a body made of glass? I can't accept it.'

'It doesn't matter,' he said softly, 'what you accept and what you don't. The glass is there regardless.'

'You think there's no hope for me.' She puffed out a long breath. 'Well, then. You should know that my friend Carl is taking me to Enghem Stead, Hector Stallows's house. He says Hector's wife can help me. So you see, it's not as hopeless as all that. He says she's seen something like my feet before.'

Henry looked suspicious. 'Why don't we cook those crabs while we talk?'

He began to boil water in a large green cooking pot. He put the bucket of crabs on the counter, their claws tapping inside.

'Look, Ida . . . I couldn't sleep after Midas visited. I so terribly hoped I could help you.'

She shrugged despondently. 'It's not your fault. I can't feel them, Henry, but sometimes I can feel the dead ends in my ankles. If you're . . . if it turns out there's no . . . no cure or anything, what will I still be able to feel at the end?'

'I don't know.'

'Will it be painful?'

He stirred the crabs. 'I don't know.'

'So what are you saying I should do in the meantime? I've come all this way to find you.'

'It'll sound crass.'

'Go on.'

'Carry on with things. Living your life. Don't indulge in any mumbo-jumbo.'

She looked angry for a split second, but reined it back in. 'I've *had* wild nights. Partied. Done all that thrill-seeking stuff. That was all bullshit. I thought those experiences would be vivid and life-changing. They were just in the mind. Here I am bungee jumping. Here I am sky diving. Beneath all the adrenalin there's the same old sense of self-awareness.'

'I didn't mean go on a parachute jump. I didn't mean anything of the sort.' He sighed. 'I've never done those things, Ida, so I can only conjecture. But I've been thrilled in my own way. I've been mobbed by moth-winged cattle. When I first found them they swarmed all over me, with their wings humming so hard I thought for a moment I'd be lifted from the ground. I remember the hot musk of the herd more startlingly than I remember my mother's smile, but you *see* . . . The only time I've really felt alive in the gut . . . which is to say . . .' he patted his chest, level with his diaphragm . . . 'in the heart . . . was the time I spent with Evaline Crook.'

'Recently . . .' The boiling crabs screamed in the pan. 'Recently, with Midas . . .'

Henry hadn't been paying attention to the crabs. A claw had broken off and was floating in circles.

'Recently, with Midas, I've felt . . . I don't know what I've felt, but it's . . . different . . .'

'Exactly.'

She straightened her shoulders. 'But I have to go to see Emiliana Stallows. It's my only shot.'

He had never been as frank as this, but he owed it to her. 'You have only a short while left, Ida. Maybe less than that. It depends when the point comes where your body can't cope with what's turned to glass. It could happen in an instant! You could simply cave in.'

Her lip trembled. 'How long is a short while?'

'It's impossible to say.'

'How long, Henry? Tell me that at least.'

He thought of the glass bog body and his hypothesis that its transformation could have accelerated in an instant to leave it as a statue, but he had no clear evidence for that, and didn't want to alarm her any more than was necessary. He compromised. 'Months,' he said, 'if you're lucky. Probably more like weeks.'

There was an iron kitchen chair behind her. She lowered herself into it.

'Wow,' she said, 'that was a bolt from the blue.'

'I don't mean to discredit what your friend and Emiliana have found out up there in Enghem, but anything they put you through will only be a . . . a false promise.'

They sat down to eat at the table, over which

he threw a cloth patterned with brown butterflies. Henry served the crabs, and Ida thought they tasted of the swamp.

Eventually she booked a taxi back to Ettinsford. When Henry objected that he should be the one to drive her, as promised, she pointed politely to his emptying bottle of gin.

The trees on the journey back were the bowed white heads of old women. Snow came down at a lazy pace and coated the hackles of a tomcat Ida saw dragging a blackbird along the road. Her taxi drove down Shale Lane, coming into the town via a bridge over frozen water. People plodded the streets in wellington boots, their hoods and umbrellas all gone white with snow. Outside the church, someone had wrapped a lilac scarf around the neck of the statue of Saint Hauda.

The taxi dropped her off outside Midas's house and she moved so slowly through his gate and yard that a laughing kid yelled in passing, 'Cheer up Granny!' then saw her youthful face and looked confused.

Midas wanted to know how things had gone with Henry, but she didn't feel like talking about it.

'He didn't say anything new, let's put it that way. I want to forget about it for a bit. Can we do something? Can you take me somewhere?'

So he drove her out to Toalhem Head. It was the gorge where the Ettinsford strait opened on to the sea. There was a viewpoint atop a cliff here, near an old dead lighthouse whose paintwork the wind had stripped on one side only, replacing it with the white stains of salt deposits. They stood in the snow at arm's length, wrapped in scarves and bracing themselves against the air. On rocks in the cliff, and all the way down to the sea, puffins stood like skittles on their perches, occasionally honking and clacking their bills.

Midas had imagined he and Ida might look down into the water and see jellyfish turning into living lights, but there were different kinds of drifters in the water that afternoon. Icebergs the size of chapels, cloaked in a fizz of snowfall, were sailing into the warmer water flowing from the gorge, to melt into a hundred white chunks.

'Did I tell you I found out about your dad?' she asked.

'Found out what about him?'

'About what happened to his grave.'

He remained silent.

She watched an iceberg crash in on itself as it entered the currents surging out of the gorge. It cracked and dissolved like bubbles in a sink.

'You don't like to talk about what happened? I thought it was a terrible story, but I understood him better.'

Midas opened his mouth and a dry croak came out, wrapped around a word. 'Understood?'

'Him. Your father.'

'What do you want to understand him for?'

'I thought it might help me better understand y—' She forced her mouth shut too late.

'You thought knowing about him would make you know me better? You never even met him, and already you think I'm like him!'

'It's not like that, Midas. He's in your thoughts so often. I figured that . . . well . . .'

Plates of broken iceberg forced underwater by currents resurfaced further out to sea. The waves mashed around them. Truth was she felt some kind of empathy for Midas's father. It had always been that way with her. She found time for inhibited men, and in doing so found excuses for them. There must be some excuse for the way his father left an inheritance of inhibitions for his son.

'I'm sorry,' she said.

He shook his head. 'Don't be. You've forgiven *me* enough times since we met . . .'

She laughed. 'Is that how it works? We're even now?'

'No, no, I didn't mean . . . Oh God.'

'Midas, it's all right. It's good that we're even.'

'Good. Phew.'

'Yes . . .' She took a deep breath. She watched a puffin jump into the water down below, at once straining to swim against the current.

'So now I'm going to ask you a favour. Tell me what Henry showed you in the bog. The thing you've both been coy about.'

The puffin struggled back out of the water and rested with its head bowed on the rock it had come from.

He raised his eyebrows and puffed out his cheeks. 'I'm not sure . . .'

She rolled her eyes. 'Just tell me.'

He threw his hands in the air. 'A glass body. A man turned entirely to glass.'

'Oh,' she said.

He looked at her. She was nearly as white as the icebergs.

'Sorry,' he said.

She shook herself. He was amazed at how she took a moment to encounter the fear, then shouldered it and moved on. She stepped towards him. The space between them seemed to shrink by a mile, every snowflake falling around them looking large as a feather. The salt air made his lips feel chafed. She came even closer, her mouth slightly open.

He stepped backwards.

CHAPTER 25

With the tide out, the smooth sands were dotted with pebbles and shells.

'Here we are,' Midas's father said, dropping his bag on the white beach. 'And a fine day for it.'

Both father and son stank of sun protection cream and were dressed like members of an orthodox sect, while Midas's mother wore her old, beige summer dress. She crouched to unravel a faded towel. Midas rolled up his sleeves and undid a few shirt buttons. His father looked perfectly comfortable in a starched shirt tucked into his trousers. Bright reflections shone off his shoes, imitations of a million bright reflections on the turquoise sea.

Low, crumbling cliffs were full of cracks and the echoes of caves.

'You're not to go in those.'

The caves were like blast holes in the cliff's chalk fortress wall. Midas loved the way shadows cowered within. 'But, Father . . .'

'Too dangerous. You see those boulders, all along the beach? They're bits of cliff that fell suddenly, unannounced. It takes only an echo to bring them crashing down on your head.'

Midas folded his arms and looked back at the sea. 'May I go paddling?'

His father shook his head. 'You're not to take your shirt and trousers off because you'll burn. Your skin will fry up and turn red. And you're not to get your clothes wet because saltwater ruins fabric and your poor mother shan't cope. Your poor mother. Think about her.'

Midas looked at her. She lay face down on the beach towel, greying hair swept over her face. A dead crab lay not far from her, claws crossed in comic piety on its sun-bleached chest.

'What about that rock? May I climb on that rock?'

Midas's father followed his pointing finger. Among the gently breaking shallows stood a chunk of tall stone the height of a lamppost. His father rubbed his moustache.

'You'll have to give me your word – your word – that you shan't climb to the top. And you shall be extra careful.'

'I promise.'

He snorted and unfurled his blue beach towel, flapping it out then laying it gently on the sand some distance from his wife. Midas opened his satchel and pulled out his camera, the little silver compact one he'd got for Christmas. He wrapped the cord handle around his wrist and started to unlace his shoes.

'What are you doing?'

'I'm taking my shoes and socks off, to paddle out to the rock.'

His father laughed. 'Not yet. First you must read a book.'

'But look,' Midas said, pointing haplessly to the sky.

His father looked puzzled. 'Look at what?'

'The sun. It's right up. Above the sea.'

He wanted to explain that the light would change soon and shouldn't be missed. All he could do was point at the swollen sun.

His father pulled books out of his bag and lined them up on the sand. Book after book after book. On the first day of their seaside holiday near Gurmton they'd spent a whole morning in a bookshop while his father leafed through nearly every tome on every shelf, finding what he called the *most pertinent*.

When he'd lined up his selection on the beach he asked, 'Which takes your fancy?'

Midas pointed desperately out at the rock he longed to climb. A proud white gull had settled on its pinnacle, watching the water. Suddenly it took off, flew seaward for two wing-beats and dived. It surfaced in an arc of droplets.

'*Mermaids, Sirens and Capricorns*, that sounds appropriate.' His father turned it over and read from the back cover. '*A thought-provoking collection of essays examining the fantasies and nightmares of sailors*. Hm. What do you think?'

Midas's pointing arm sagged. He sat down and began to retie his laces.

'What about this one? More immediate, perhaps. *Below Her Midriff: Dogs!* This'll perk your interest, Midas. *This splendid book, complete with twelve full-colour plates, traces the coastlines of Greece in search of the mythical beast Scylla, whose legs were famously transformed into dogs by the sorceress Circe.* That sounds just your cup of tea.'

Midas sat and leafed through *Below Her Midriff: Dogs!* while his father watched proudly. He flicked past the dedications and contents pages.

'No, no, no!' said his father, waving his hands, 'Don't go straight to the colour plates, you'll spoil your enjoyment. You look at them when you *reach* them, savour them once you've a contextual understanding.'

Midas turned back to page one, a dense prologue, and stared at the words without reading them until his father stopped watching and took out his own book, which was a brick of a hardback. After a while Midas turned the page and stared at the next, occasionally glancing up, until his father settled into his own read. Then he took off his shoes and socks, stood up and crept away from him, past his inert mother and down the beach to the shallows. On his way he found a fabulous branch, crooked and taller than himself. This he carried like an adventurer's staff, dragging a line through the sand behind him. He paddled through the breakers towards the rock. Cool, crystal-clear water lapped back and forth over his feet. Stepping on a sharp shell made him stifle a hoot of pain, and something like hair stroked his ankles. He looked down to see loops of green weed coiled around his shins. They were heavier and slimier when he lifted them dangling from the water. The hush of breakers sifted the smell of bone-dry salt.

The rock's gnarled surface made an easy climb. He pulled up to a barnacled spot and sat with feet dangling towards his reflection in a rock pool. He wriggled his toes in the pool's warm water to clear out the sand and scraps of weed, but retracted his feet when he saw the many poppy-red arms of an anemone swaying between burgundy tendrils of seaweed.

He glanced back at the beach. His father hadn't budged, except to turn his book's pages. Nor had his mother, still lying face down precisely unmoved. He trained his camera on her and wondered whether she were happy. She looked at least content, basking in the sunbeams.

He waited on the rock spire, as immobile as his parents, for pictures to come. With only one spare film for the holiday, he had to bide his time. The sea lost some of its lustre. The sun moved across the sky. He kept waiting, and in the space of three hot hours he took only that many photographs. Then, when the light no longer glared, a movement on a rock further out to sea brought his camera to his eyes.

He thought it was some kind of seabird, but

its flight was too chaotic. It would flitter out from behind the rock then flitter back again. He suspected it had a perch obscured from sight and waited with his camera on his knee, ready for it to fly into his sights. When it did it was so fast he suspected all he'd capture was a blur. He prayed madly for God to enhance his frame rate.

When it whooshed into sight he realized it was a dragonfly, big as his fist and white as milk.

It was late afternoon when his father called to him from the beach. He stood on the edge of the shallows, using his book to shield his eyes from the sun. The tide had come in and was several feet deep around the rock. Midas started to take off his shirt and trousers, to tie them in a dry bundle around his camera then hang them on the end of his stick so he could carry it above his head and paddle with his free arm. He was about to knot his shirtsleeves around the wood when he saw something drifting below the water's surface, buoyed on each wave. Translucent, with a violet rim and flowing tentacles. He'd never seen anything like it. He climbed closer to the water . . .

'What are you doing, Midas?'

His father was pacing up and down. Midas reached into the sea with the stick and hooked out the floating thing. It sagged as it left the water: a gluey, deflated lump with droplets streaming from it.

'Look what I've caught!'

His father froze and gasped, 'Don't touch it,

Midas!' A creeping wave sloshed over his ankle and he hopped backwards on to the beach with a yelp.

It slid off Midas's stick and landed with a slap in the water, where it unfurled gracefully.

'Oh *God* . . . They'll paralyse you!'

There were others floating in the water now, violet haloes picked out by shimmering light.

'What are they?'

'Medusae! Jellyfish!'

Midas climbed a little higher up the rock, clinging tight now. He didn't dare look down at them.

'What happens if they see me, Father? Will I turn to stone?'

'Oh God, Midas! Good *God*!'

For a while there was only the sound of the waves and a pair of gulls swooping overhead. Then Midas's mother walked down to the sea with her dress fluttering in the breeze. She dragged a plank of blackened driftwood by a cord of rotting rope. She kept going when she got to the shallows, the tiny waves splashing up her bare legs. When she was close enough she broke a piece of wood from the corner of the plank and tossed it into the water. They watched it drift out to Midas's rock on the current. Having performed this test, she pushed the plank out. Midas climbed down the side of the stone and jabbed his stick through the loop in the rope as the plank passed. It was heavy and he clung hard to the rock face as he pulled it closer.

'Lie flat!' urged his mother, 'like a surfer!'

Midas hesitated. He couldn't take his clothes,

or the camera they were bundled around, back to the beach. With a gut-wrenching feeling, he placed them on a shelf of the rock.

He climbed on to the driftwood board. It lurched and nearly flipped over. Water frothed across its surface and a jellyfish bobbed dangerously close. He held tight as the breakers rushed him to shore. But just when he thought he was clear he heard the sea slurp beneath him and it hauled him back from the beach towards the open ocean. He screamed as he felt the board betray him, screwing up his eyes awaiting submersion and venomous death. But he didn't go under. When he dared open his eyes he was being lowered on to the beach, and his mother was lowering herself down beside him, her dress soaked through so he could see her scrawny body and ancient underwear. She bit her lip and covered her eyes with one hand while the other itched a swelling red mound on her calf. His father strutted about like a frightened hen nearby.

In the hospital they said the paralysis in her left leg would heal within a week. But it never quite left her, and from that day forth she walked with a limp.

CHAPTER 26

A black seabird dipped into the ocean like a nib dipping into an inkwell. A boat lurched horizon-bound with engines chugging, tearing frothy furrows into the water. The coast road had the cliff drop for its kerb, and Midas was so terrified of veering off it that he wouldn't take his eyes off the tarmac. When Ida looked out into the greyness and something horned poked its head through the sea's surface, she couldn't persuade him to look up at it. It kept the horn raised as if it were a finger testing the wind.

The road descended. Two gulls swept across, pecking each other in midair, and she caught a flash of their yellow eyes. Soon they had driven down to sea level, where breakers were up close and salt spray fogged their way. Further out the ocean surged over hooks of granite and drained through channels in flats of black rock.

In the rear-view mirror the gloomy silhouettes of hills rose like the shoulder-blades of giants. Through the windscreen the landscape, when not occluded by sea spray, was a plain of brown rock and water channels. One or two trees stood trailing branches on the ground. Knotted shrubs looked so black they could have been hauled from an oil slick.

There were all sorts of myths about Enghem, this territory of Hector Stallows's in the north of Gurm Island, circulated since the perfume man bought the land, and born out of resentment at a swathe of landscape suddenly privatized.

He had been a captain of industry, obliterating livelihoods in the name of competition. No wonder people said he always got what he wanted. Now as a retired man of leisure, he was said to be mercurial with his wealth. His reasons for once hanging the woodlands of inland Enghem with amber baubles were not understood, but locals knew those sap tombs of ancient insects were not dangling from the trees for *their* pleasure. There was an incident when a boy from Tinterl stole a bauble – a single specimen among hundreds – from the branches of a willow tree. The following night he woke up itching furiously and thinking something had got into an eardrum, because there was a dry hum in the air of his bedroom. He turned on the lamp and cried out for his mother (he was seventeen) because the walls, the ceiling and his bare arms and chest were speckled with mosquitoes. The drawer where he had hidden the bauble was open: the bauble was gone. Or so the story went.

After a time, fickle Hector Stallows got tired of the sight of golden orbs glowing warm in the woods at twilight, so cut them down, packed them away and sold them to a bidder in Shanghai. In their place he bought quartz (locals watched trucks carry iceberg-sized blocks through his gates, watched helicopters rattle overhead). It was said he had quartz spruces cut for the gardens of Enghem Stead, his home. Quartz walls were inlaid in his house, bookshelves chiselled with the names of authors. His mainlander guests ate from quartz plates clunking on quartz tables.

And then, it was held, the quartz had been seen leaving the estate: sold to a collector somewhere in Russia. As it moved in lorry-loads across St Hauda's Land towards the docks of Glamsgallow, smaller vehicles were seen travelling in the opposite direction and passing into Enghem. Soon rumours circulated that Hector had purchased birds of a hundred species, canaries and cockatoos and nightingales, but that every single one was silent. An aviary of mute birds. Those who had entered the gardens told of an eerie quiet, the opening and closing of a hundred beaks without a single warble or tweet on the air.

The road ran here through a stone archway, crumbling and ivy-covered. There was no wall, the archway standing all alone in a clump of trees. This land was full of deathtraps: Ida saw in the drive of the only cottage they passed a tree hung with both Christmas lights and dead moles. Beyond it the road turned in from the sea and climbed a series of zigzags back to higher ground where, at the very summit, Gurm Island's last headlands were laid out below to the north, like bones cast on the ground by a soothsayer. No defined shoreline separated land and sea at Enghem. Instead, shale beds, inlets, rock pools and saltwater creeks made up the ragged scenery between here and the coast. The tide poured into it and retreated like a gigantic grey comb. Somewhere in this landscape were built the four tidy houses of Enghem-on-the-Water, their destination.

That Midas was prepared to come all this way touched Ida. But did he want to be with her or was he just playing at being a photojournalist and tagging along until he got bored? Her conversation with Henry, and his verdict that she could withstand her condition for weeks or months, not years, had accelerated her thinking. So, while they drove in comfortable silence, Ida's brain ticked through what to do about her relationship with Midas Crook.

Midas drove carefully along the threatening wintry roads. A sudden skid on black ice would plunge them into a dark pool or crash them into a horned rock. The headlights swung across the green-grey corpse of a pike lying in the road, and launched a crow screeching and flapping into the air.

Midas had bought her a second crutch. Her balance had become awry and she needed one before she had an accident, but she'd joked he could make it her Christmas present to delay it for a few more weeks. Then that morning he'd presented her with a long package wrapped in silver crêpe paper. It was tied by florist's twine and had a fastening made from a sprig of star-shaped chincherinchee flowers. She unwrapped it and found a polished shaft of diamond willow, elegant where her other crutch was sturdy, patterned with brown rhombuses where Carl's was planed and even-textured.

She watched Midas fondly from the corner of her eye. Was there something embryonic between them, or had she simply misunderstood him?

He held the wheel tight when he drove, his knuckles and elbows all sharp angles. She loved the way his shirtsleeves were too short for him, the cuffs buttoned tight around his scrawny wrists, showing off the plastic schoolboy watch he wore. He chewed the inside of his cheek. His Adam's apple bulged in his throat. He had washed his hair that morning for the first time in days and it stood up in a black ruff.

She wondered what he would do if she reached out to touch him. He'd probably crash the car. Yet she had to hurry things along somehow. Not now, but at the first chance she had.

Suddenly the road rounded a bank of sandy soil, on to a snowy track at the end of which was Enghem-on-the-Water. Only the largest of the four houses had lights in its windows: this was Enghem Stead. Beyond it the sea shuffled in and out, and as they drove closer Ida saw that all the houses were built on sturdy wooden stilts that high tide could pass beneath. The houses were also made of wood, their slats painted pastel blue or white, although the paint had flaked to show greening timbers beneath. She knew from local say-so that only Enghem Stead was inhabited. Hector had bought the entire hamlet to guarantee privacy.

'It's . . . still quite a sweet place,' she said.

Carl was drawing on a cigarette while he waited for them on the wooden deck outside Enghem Stead's door. As soon as they'd parked he trotted down the steps of the deck to the car and helped Ida climb out. She'd hoped Midas would fight his instincts and do this, but instead he was left portering the luggage behind them. Back over her shoulder the vast sweep of the cove could be better appreciated. It was a colossal dent in the white hill-line, as if one night the sea had risen up and raged against the island until the coast cowered back for miles.

Jerky snow fell as they thumped up the steps of the deck, Ida's arm linked with Carl's to keep her steady, the other pressing the crutch Midas had given her hard into the damp wood. Slush dropped in lumps from the house's gutters and one end of Ida's scarf came loose and fluttered in the wind, so that she had to reel it back in and wrap it tighter around her neck. A robin flapped off the fence of the deck. She thought how brown its red breast looked.

The door opened after a short wait. Hot air rushed out to greet them. A glamorous woman followed.

Emiliana Stallows had black hair and a tan that

looked real enough, even in winter. Heavy mascara, a hip-hugging skirt and gracefully cut blouse all went some way to creating an impression of exoticism in the cold expanse of Enghem Cove. It was hard to judge her age, but she looked like she'd faded out of beauty and glamour not so long ago. Ida put her at the end of her forties. The whiteness of her scalp emphasized how her jet-black hair had thinned.

She clasped her fingers together, nails dark as bluebottles, and flashed them a girlish grin.

'You must be Ida,' she said. 'And you must be the photographer, is that correct?' She blinked dark eyelids. 'I shall have to look my best around you.'

Carl helped Ida up a step into a wide, whitewashed hall with a high wooden ceiling and bare light bulbs. From here they proceeded into a dining room with a rustic wooden table at its centre. The walls were off-white and grey rugs overlaid the floorboards. Midas jumped in alarm when he stepped on a board and a snoring creak echoed in the room.

Emiliana laughed. 'It wasn't you, silly. It's the house creaking in the wind. You get used to it.'

Ida closed her eyes and listened to another long creak coming out of the wall, like the lowest note of a cello, and smiled. It was a peaceful noise, in keeping with a house built at the ocean's mercy.

'I know Enghem Stead looks bare and Spartan,' apologized Emiliana. 'But it's the way Hector likes it. Through this door is my guest room. You'll be more comfortable in here.'

She took an iron key from her blouse pocket, unlocked and pushed open the door on to a cool room that smelled of Turkish delight. Giant azure and gold cushions were piled up on rugs. Complex North African patterns of topaz and diamonds tiled the walls. A fireplace made flaky ash from logs.

Only, thought Ida, it hadn't worked. The distance between this wall and that, and the loftiness of the ceiling, overpowered the restful space Emiliana had tried to create. This kind of room could only be filled with a hymn or a prayer.

Soon they were eating bowls of couscous made floral with herbs; plates of Parma ham and purple chorizo; pots full of olives; trays of peppers and aubergines stuffed with still-bubbling cheese; boards of bread drizzled with olive oil. The other three were surprised to learn that Midas had never tried any of it before.

'What do you normally eat?' asked Emiliana, as he chased an olive around his plate with his fork.

'Fish fingers,' he admitted. 'Can-o-Soup.'

He forked the olive and put it on his tongue.

'Like it?' asked Carl with a readied smirk.

His mouth felt so full of acid he might as well have kissed a snake. 'Mm,' he managed.

The others piled their plates up while Midas remained cautious, suspiciously analysing the stuffed peppers. Strands of cheese dribbled from the dish to his plate as he served himself one. It smelt of goat.

They chatted while they ate, or rather, the other three chatted and Midas sat in baffled silence, hearing Emiliana's views on an orchestra, or Carl's on a man called Hemingway. When they had finished eating, Carl ceremoniously laid down his knife and fork and said, 'I think everyone would appreciate getting straight to the point of this visit.'

Ida blushed and spoke very quietly. 'You're right. It's because of me we're here. To hell with it, perhaps I should just take my boots off.'

Emiliana leant forward among the cushions, stretching her long legs in front of her.

Fingers aflutter, Ida reached down to her boots. She untied the buckles, then the laces. Her boots slid off gently and she rolled off her socks.

There was a pattern on the rug beneath her like the map of a labyrinth. Her toes moved across it like magnifying glasses, warping the pattern into a three-dimensional maze. The glass had become worse in the week since Midas had first seen it. Ida's metatarsals, which he had witnessed half visible before, had now vanished in the crystal-clear bodies of her feet. Strands of blood tapered out like frayed cotton around her ankles. Her heel, which had still been made of skin before, was a hard lump with foggy white insides. Aside from these, her feet were now entirely transparent. Raised veins pulsed at the bottom of her shins and calves, as if the blood there were evacuating ahead of what was to come. Hairs on her lower leg trembled as if they were on the back of her neck.

Her inanimate feet, he realized, were no longer a part of her. All the foreign tastes of the night's meal came back and filled his gullet. Those blocks of glass, though gracefully shaped, were amputations.

Somewhere above him, another floor lowed and creaked.

The others hadn't moved or made a sound, apart from the noise of Emiliana's lips parting. She looked as if she'd heard news of a terrible bereavement. Astonishment paused her body and puzzled her eyes. He was surprised because Carl had said she'd seen something like this before. She couldn't speak until Ida broke the spell by pulling on her socks.

'Ida,' she said eventually, locking her fingers together, 'I'll . . . try my very best to help you.'

Carl nodded like a wise old judge. 'Get the film of Saffron Jeuck.'

Emiliana looked uncomfortable. 'Are you sure you wouldn't rather wait until morning, Carl? Do this bit by bit?'

'If you're worried about me,' said Ida, 'there's no need. I can cope.'

'It's just . . .'

Carl glowered at her and she held up her hands. 'I'll go and get the tapes.'

As Emiliana left the room, Ida sighed and ran a hand through her hair. Carl put a heavy hand on her shoulder and patted her while Midas watched sullenly. He supposed they were going to see something to make them think how awful it would be, should Ida transform entirely into glass.

Emiliana returned with two chunky old video-tapes, and didn't make eye contact as she plugged the first into a small television unit.

They all waited in awkward silence as the tape rewound. They could hear the faint squeal of the wheels whirring in the VCR. The house groaned a louder echo.

'Now,' said Emiliana, when the rewinding stopped with a clunk. A black screen danced with white bars, and then cut suddenly to a shaky picture.

A girl stood in a sepia field, squinting as she shielded her eyes from summer sunlight. The sky had probably been ultramarine when this was filmed on a doddery handheld recorder, but the age and quality of the film had saturated the colour to a greenish hue. Threads of dirt flickered across the footage.

'Okay, Saffron,' said Emiliana's voice on tape, from behind the camera, 'lift up your top.'

Saffron wore white shorts over chubby thighs. She was in her late teens, but her haircut indicated that this footage was filmed six or seven years back. She reached down and scrunched up the hem of her top, bunching it beneath her small breasts. Ida glanced warily at Carl, but at that point he sprang up and hit the Pause button, pointing at the screen. 'See?' he enthused. 'Look at her midriff.'

Across Saffron's belly ran what looked like an awful scar, but the details were lost in twitchy freeze-frame and horizons of interference descending the screen.

'It zooms in,' said Carl, pressing Play.

'Now hold it,' said Emiliana's voice from out of shot. The wobbling camera approached Saffron's belly.

This close, her entire stomach looked discoloured. It was hard to gauge depth on the video, but her abdomen, which was a blushed red, seemed to be set back an inch, as if she were holding her breath in. Midas realized suddenly that the surface of her belly had turned to glass. Her stomach was a glossy viewing screen on to the muscles and organs of her abdomen, although the details were hard to make out in the footage. Ida had covered her mouth with her hand. Midas wished suddenly that Carl had let Emiliana have her way and shown this in the morning, when daylight would comfort through the window.

Ida leant forward in her chair, fingers steepled and lips pursed, intent on the image. Saffron's shadow on the corn had distended into a yellow wash. A deathly static tinged the audio.

Carl stopped the video again and ejected the tape from the machine. 'Where's the second tape, Mil? The one you filmed after you treated her.'

She had it on her lap. Instead of handing it to Carl, she affected a yawn. 'I'm exhausted,' she said. 'Perhaps we should look in the morning?'

Midas liked her considerably for this.

'No,' said Carl, 'Ida wants to get this over and done with.'

For her part Ida was staring at the blank television, expression impenetrable.

Carl took the tape from Emiliana's lap and plugged it into the VCR. They waited again while it rewound, Carl's fingers tapping against the chrome surface of the player. There was a clunk, and the tape started playing. After the curtains of static had lifted the picture settled on an indoor scene, although an open window showed an autumn orchard deep with leaves. The light was weak, and Saffron Jeuck, who sat in a rocking chair by the window with a tartan blanket over her lap, was ill-defined against the walls of the room. It was impossible to say where her hair, tied in a fraught bun, ended and the shadow of her rocking chair began.

'Saffron,' said the off-camera Emiliana. 'Saffron, how are you feeling?'

Saffron took for ever to take her eyes off the loamy orchard and fix them on the camera. The footage was too grainy to define her pupils but Midas knew they were fixed on the lens. Other than to turn her head, she did not respond to the question. Midas chewed his fingernails while the others watched the video intently. He had always believed in a point where a photograph became like a headstone. The photos of the dead had a distant quality about them that the photos of the living didn't possess. He had a gut feeling that this was a film about a dead woman.

'Um,' he began timidly, 'Saffron is still with us, right?'

'Of course,' snapped Carl. 'Shh!'

The Emiliana behind the camera repeated her question. 'How are you feeling?'

Saffron opened her mouth. 'I feel awful.'

'Will you lift up your blouse?'

Slowly, Saffron's fingers emerged from the blanket that covered her lap, to undo the bottom buttons of her blouse. She parted the cloth slowly, and the camera zoomed in on her belly as it had before.

Midas noticed two things at once. First, that the glass did not appear to have spread any further or deeper into her belly than it had in the previous, summertime video. Second, that every inch of skin visible around the edge of the glass was a raw red that defied the dim light of the day and the quality of the footage. Her flesh was blistered, wealed and peeling ragged in places, as if she had been flogged.

'Is it any worse?' asked the on-film Emiliana.

'Not the glass,' said Saffron, and turned back to the orchard.

'You're ready for another poultice?'

Saffron took a long breath, but as she did so the wind blew in through the open window, placing dead curled leaves on the carpet and making it hard to tell whether what could be heard was the noise of the air entering Saffron's lungs, or merely the rustle of the weather. Either way, the filling up of her lungs could be seen through the glass plate of Saffron's stomach.

The video camera turned off.

Even after Carl took out the tape, Ida's eyes

remained on the screen. Midas recognized that distant look, seen so many times on his mother's face. An elsewhere look. Ida's thoughts would be in some other year, no doubt, before all this began.

The others waited on her. After a while, she asked, 'Poultices?'

Emiliana cleared her throat, but when she didn't speak Carl took it upon himself. 'Playing dead would be a more appropriate starting point. Mil, why don't you tell her what you did for Saffron?'

Emiliana looked miserably from Carl to Ida. 'We can go into the details tomorrow.'

Carl rolled his eyes. 'We can begin applying them tomorrow.'

'Okay.' She kept her eyes on the empty dishes and oily plates of their meal. 'To begin with, it came about at the suggestion of Saffron's father. He was a friend of a friend, but he came to me because at the time I was running a small business in alternative medicine. I had always been interested in it, and Hector enabled me to set up a small surgery of my own. Hay fever remedies were my speciality, and that was what drew Saffron and her family. They already had the idea, you see. They only wanted somebody to carry it out.'

Carl was tapping his foot. 'You need to explain about the bird in the jar.'

She nodded and cleared her throat a second time. 'Mr Jeuck brought with him a bird in a jar. It was long dead and quite horrible, quite badly preserved. But it had a tail of glass. A fan of beautifully etched feathers, where all its others had wilted and decayed. He had bought it at great expense from an old widow in Glamsgallow because it was evidence for his idea. The bird had died, she had told him, because it couldn't feed properly in its condition. What struck Mr Jeuck was this: the bird's final condition meant the spread of glass did not continue into death.'

Midas closed his eyes and thought of the pure glass body Henry had shown him in the bog.

'Well . . . My hay fever remedies were simple things. Honey based. Local bees help cure the fever from local pollen. So you see . . . Saffron and her family proposed a local remedy, although from the moment Saffron walked through my door, I knew there was something far worse than hay fever afflicting her.'

'Playing dead was the answer,' interrupted Carl. 'The proposed remedy was simple but probably the most brilliant idea a man like Jeuck would have in his lifetime. To paralyse the flesh around the glass, turn it into a state half dead. And the Jeuck family had already thought of the means.'

'What was the means?'

'St Hauda's Land jellyfish.'

'Jellyfish,' murmured Ida.

Midas thought of his mother's limp.

Carl clasped his hands enthusiastically. 'Emiliana prepared poultices of jellyfish matter, warmed them and applied them to Saffron's stomach. They treated her in this way all summer long, and as you can see,' he gestured theatrically to the screen, 'the results were successful. The treatment trapped the glass, beat it at its own game. And all thanks to Emiliana.'

Emiliana smiled wistfully.

Ida closed her eyes.

They waited.

'It looks painful.'

'Think about it overnight,' suggested Emiliana.

Ida shook her head. 'It doesn't matter if it's painful. It's worth a shot.'

'That's my girl,' said Carl. 'I'll let you turn in now. We should make a start in the morning.'

It took Midas several hours to fall asleep that night. In part this was due to the alien double bed in his guest room, so much larger and softer than his sturdy single mattress back home. In part it was the bass moans the house emitted in the wind, and the crunch of the sea mining the shingle of the cove. More than these, it was the thought of Ida sleeping mere rooms away, and the pain this esoteric remedy was likely to bring her. It filled his knees with a weak feeling, made his feet seem impossibly far from his legs.

He rolled on to his side and stared at the moonlight slanting under the heavy curtains. He knew he had finally got to sleep when a tapping on the door woke him. He sat up stiffly as it swung open and Ida hobbled in, wincing at each clunking placement of her crutch on the floor. Thankfully, Emiliana and

Carl were sleeping in bedrooms on the floor above, towards the other side of the house.

'I can't sleep,' she whispered.

'Nor me.' He rubbed his eyes. 'I mean, I was asleep just then, but before that, nothing . . .'

She went to the window. 'Have you seen what's going on outside?'

He shook his head.

'Get up.'

It was hot in the guest bedroom, so he had gone to bed in only his Y-fronts. He realized this now, and sat up holding the white duvet to his scrawny chest. She wasn't wearing night things, she was wearing her coat over a patterned woollen jersey.

'I'll look away,' she laughed, 'so you can preserve your decency.'

He crawled to the foot of the bed to get the clothes he'd left in a heap. He pulled them on while she opened the curtains, then joined her at the window. The moonlit sea glittered in the cove, and swaying under its subtle waves were dimly glowing lights. He pressed his face against the window. The lights were flickering like candle flames.

'Midas,' she said, 'do you remember when you stayed at Carl's cottage with me? We heard an owl hoot in the night.'

'I remember, yes.'

'You asked if I wanted to go out walking in the woods. To look for it. And I said I was too frightened of tripping. Well . . . I said that because I didn't know you well enough. I didn't know how safe I'd be in the woods with you. Now I know you'd look after me. Let's go outside and look at the lights.'

'What? Now?'

'*Yes*. Put your coat on.'

He pulled it on and followed her out of the room. They moved slowly, in part to make as little noise as possible, in part because Ida had no choice. She had to sit and bump herself carefully down the stairs while Midas cradled her crutches. They found their way out to the wooden deck and leant on the rail, overlooking the high tide that swilled between the stilted houses of Enghem-on-the Water, turning them into arks. The painted timbers reflected weakly on the surface, mingling with the dim, manifold lights that shone beneath it. An armada of jellyfish had floated in on the tide. One or two were large as sails, with bodies rippling just inches under the surface, flying pennants of tentacles. The tiniest ones were the size of thimbles, with crests of violet suckers. One giant orb glowed brighter than the others. Its body was full of a nebula of golden light, as if it had swallowed an angel.

Nearer by floated a swarm of about a hundred lantern-sized jellies. Ida gasped when a spark of electric yellow sputtered momentarily in the body of one. It had been a flash of light like a faulty light bulb. A second spark faltered in another jelly, this time a strobe of pink. Another lit up deeper down, red as a clot of blood. The tide gulped against the stilts of Enghem Stead.

Another jelly flashed, and this one stayed alight.

A yellow blaze bobbing in the water. Its emanation kindled the lights of its neighbours. Their bodies sparkled, and the sparkles turned to steady shines: yellow, pink, crimson and cyan. The effect slowly ricocheted across the cove until the water was a multicoloured brilliance. Refracted colour glittered up the walls of the houses.

Midas and Ida leant in silence over the rail of the deck. He noticed how close her hands were to his on the rail. He didn't move away.

'Imagine living in a place like this,' she said, 'where you could watch this every night.'

He did as he was told. Living in the middle of nowhere, just the two of them, and it made his mind settle, as if all the worry it normally contained could be buoyed away on the idea alone. He felt serene leaning on the railing with her, absorbing the sight of the incandescent sea. They remained like this, side by side, faces lit up by the glow from the water, for ten minutes more. Then the jellies darkened in quick succession, as if something were swimming through the water snuffing them out.

When he had been playing porter and bumping the luggage up the deck, Midas had been jealous of Carl's arm linked with Ida's. So when they returned inside after the last jellyfish had fizzled out, leaving only the moon to decorate the night, he whispered, 'I-I-I'll help you up the stairs.'

At first he was too busy enjoying her grateful smile

to let the enormity of what he had volunteered for sink in. He shifted his weight from foot to foot.

How would he get her upstairs without touching her?

She followed him to the foot of the staircase, then handed him her crutch.

'Right,' he said, longing for elevators, escalators, pulleys.

She took his arm and set her other hand on the banister. His joints stiffened. He got a whiff of her scent: something alpine (like vertigo). He felt as if his sleeve had starched involuntarily.

All the way up the stairs, his elbow poked her side and her skin. Her body's warmth made sweat beads roll down his arm. She didn't notice any of it, she looked so absorbed in her thoughts.

At the top of the stairs he abruptly tried to let go of her, but she clung on.

'We're up now,' he whispered.

'Help me to my room.'

He steadied himself. They found their way to her bedroom. Inside, when she finally let go of his arm, he sank back against the wall.

'Well . . . um . . .' Midas was dabbing his forehead with a handkerchief. 'I suppose we'll be seeing a lot more of the jellyfish now.'

She sighed. 'I think we should forget all about remedies tonight.'

That confused him: he had thought the beautiful spectacle, would excite her with the prospect of a cure. She cleared it up by placing her hand lightly on his chest. His heart started beating hard, like it was trying to drive her away. She tilted her head and leant it towards him. Her lips were parted an inch from his.

He jumped sideways, spluttering half-started excuses for why he'd best leave her to get much-needed sleep. She sat down on the bed and cast her eyes away. He wanted words to speak themselves. When nothing happened, he slipped from the room and closed the door behind him.

Halfway down the stairs he ground to a halt. He had wanted to kiss her but when the moment arose his head had been yanked away as if nerves were a bridle. Remembering his father battling away from his mother's embraces, he felt a sudden rush of hatred towards the man. He wondered how you could alter your gut reactions when your body overrode your control with the same power it used to jerk back your hand from a burning hot surface or throw you away from an onrushing crash. He clapped his hands to his head and screwed up his eyes.

For a moment, Ida considered returning to bed, but she knew it would only be to lie there wide awake. She decided to take a bath, instead. Back on the mainland she had used to enjoy a blistering hot bath in the middle of the night.

A spider hung in the corner of the bathroom ceiling, legs bundled around thin air as if clutching an invisible bead to its thorax. The thought of it scuttling over her naked body made Ida want to bruise it into the wall as she undressed and waited for the gushing water to fill the bath. She'd never been scared of spiders and she didn't plan to become so now. It was just the way the little creatures were so nimble while her feet were like anchors. *Nimble little Ida,* that's what Carl used to call her on the dives.

She was probably just jealous of that octet of legs.

She tested the water then climbed in. Steam clouded around her as she rubbed lather from fragrant soap across her belly. Her glass feet under the sudsy water were just blurs. The water lapping over her toes looked hotter than it really was, looked hissing hot like a volcanic pool. She thought of geysers whose spray had cloaked her when she'd hiked across Iceland. When she poked her toes out of the water, droplets wriggling down their surfaces, they belonged to a landscape of newborn rock and cloying mineral. Not here, on the end of her legs.

She raised her legs further out of the bath. Their skin was horribly pale, and on her shins it was already a pithy white. When Carl had been helping her into Enghem Stead she had caught her leg against the side of a door. She had not complained out loud, only yelped, unnoticed by Carl, and looked to Midas for reassurance (he had been looking at his shoelaces). It had been only the gentlest blow, but now on the outside of her knee where she had caught it was a fingerprint-sized bruise. There wasn't any blue in it, only a slate grey. She touched it and it was hard like a shell.

The spider stretched three limbs simultaneously. Relaxed.

Stupid, stupid Midas.

The bath was too hot. She twisted the cold tap on. The bathwater had cooled. Now it was too cold. She swore and slowly pulled herself out so she could sit on the side, suddenly determined to remain as dirty as possible. Sweat and dead skin were all that held her together, all that made her certain she had a body to inhabit. She enjoyed the tightening of her cold flesh and the raising of hairs on her arms. Droplets ran down her thighs and explored her knees. That was as far down her legs as she could feel them. The skin of her shins was already that glazy white that was the first stage of the transformation. Funny how grateful she'd become for goose pimples and itches, for burns and scratches. She wanted it all. She wanted bad backs and arthritis, she wanted to go deaf and barmy if it meant she could stay alive for however many years it took her to tick off those things.

She dried briskly and dabbed the water off her glass feet. She missed Midas even though he was probably nearby, agonizing about that failed kiss. He was an idiot, to puzzle his life away like that. She grabbed her crutches and used them to swing herself laboriously into the bedroom, where she dressed in her nightie.

They gleamed in the dim light.

She clicked off the lamp and went to bed. Dark was a fine thing: in the dark she couldn't tell what her feet were made of.

All she could feel was their absence.

She thought of Midas's lips coming closer then jerking away. She thought, suddenly of what she had invested in him. If soon she was immobile, half girl half ornament, then soon there could be no sex, perhaps no passion. She panicked that she had unwittingly picked him to be the last romance of her life, and that he would be too slow to trust her. She wanted to know him better and understand him, yes, but sleeping alone here in a strange bed, she wanted a warm body at her side and some recognition that she was alive. Could he ever give her that?

As her thoughts metamorphosed into half-dreams, she translated the night-time noises of the house and heaters into the huffing of moth-winged cattle.

CHAPTER 27

The fields and hillsides glowed white. Light dazzled off the windows of Emiliana's house, tinting Midas's cheek and waking him like a lover.

The thick duvet slid off his chest as he sat up and rubbed his temples. Still in last night's clothes, he felt sluggish and uncomfortable. His final memory of the evening was of swaying along the landing, gripping the banister tight, intoxicated by embarrassment as if it were wine. He groaned shamefully, rubbed his stubbly chin and got up. His room looked out over black rivulets evacuated by the tide. A concertina of icicles had formed above the window.

He crept out of his room and along the hallway to a front-facing window, which looked inland. Driving here the evening before, he'd been too bent on the road to absorb the landscape's changes. To the east and west were snow-brushed fields, and dead ahead a finger of woodland beckoning to the house. This was odd, because he couldn't remember a single tree from the final part of the drive. It was as if the woods had crept up to Enghem Stead under the cover of night.

A cup of water and a stretch later he was heading across the snow, adjusting his camera as he went. Faint clouds stealthily accumulated, urging him to make the most of the light before they abducted it. He picked his way into the woodland where plant quills poked up around interlocked trunks and branches. A crow rasped and sidled along its perch.

He had not met anyone as he left the house but he'd heard Emiliana talking on a phone in the kitchen and crept past the closed door. He couldn't miss this light, and he didn't think the others would understand. Better they thought he was having a lie-in.

He'd taken a wrong turn finding his way out of Enghem Stead and in doing so had stumbled into a room bare except for an ashy fireplace, an armchair and a coffee table on which a crumpled copy of a financial newspaper was strewn. Then, turning around, he came face-to-face with Hector Stallows. It was a twelve-foot painting on the wall. Hector Stallows, painted wearing a business suit and a frown, with a night-black beard and pitted cheeks. The paint had been applied with economic strokes and dated from nearly a decade before, but it was easy to imagine what time had done to its subject. Hector would have even steeper frown lines and imperial flashes of silver in his hair. By contrast the thin paint on the wall on which the picture hung had cracked, and the cracks had branched across the wall until the painting looked as if it were hanging on a tree.

Now, crunching across the snow and into the

woods, he was trying to forget his embarrassment. 'Ida tried to kiss me,' he said out loud, to try to understand. And he had failed to kiss her back. Among the trees, he hoped he could temporarily force both her and his embarrassment to the back of his mind with the distraction of prospective photographs.

A white leaf was caged in evergreen needles. It was a dainty composition, so he approached to take a photo. He jumped when the leaf flew to another branch, then realized it was only a bird, wren-sized with white plumage. He approached with camera ready, but a stick cracked under his shoe. The bird took off and darted through the air, cheeping and touching down on another branch. He waited for its nerves to calm and then slowly climbed a tree to get a better angle. Ignoring scratching twigs, he ascended a forking trunk and squeezed into a parting of boughs, the bark cold and wet with snow.

The bird glanced nervously this way and that. Midas looked around for anything to fear. There were only countless grey trunks. He licked his lips and lined up the shot, resting his camera against the tree. Another twig cracked. Snow pattered off vegetation.

This would be a fine picture, the subject's feathers unblemished against earthy bark. He judged the composition, zoomed a little closer, and had just taken the photo when he saw, segmented by the camera's crosshairs, that the bird had white eyes.

Something tapped his shoe.

He fell out of the tree with a shriek and scrabbled about terrified in the snow, clawing his camera protectively to his chest.

A tall, dishevelled man with a roughly cropped beard was leaning over him, propped up by a walking cane made from a polished narwhal tusk. He wore a creased charcoal suit, with patterns of mud dried up to its knees. Leaves caught in its creases and folds, as if he had slept burrowed under a pile of loam. His hair stood up in clumps, like immature antlers, and his face was leathery and as creased as his clothes.

He raised his narwhal cane by way of greeting and spoke in a gravelly voice. 'And what might you be doing in Enghem?'

Midas got to his feet and glanced back for the white bird. It had vanished. 'I'm . . . I'm . . . Midas Crook.'

'I said *what*, my boy, not *who*.'

Midas pulled himself together enough to feel freezing, wet and bruised from his fall. 'Um . . .' he said. 'Photography.'

The man raised his cane towards Midas and tapped its wavering point against his camera. 'That's a fine-looking thing you have there.'

Midas clung to it warily.

The tall man extended a hand. 'I am Hector Stallows.'

Midas thought he'd misunderstood him, though the man spoke with perfect diction. He remembered the oil painting in Enghem Stead and couldn't quite merge the businessman it had portrayed with this crumpled stranger. 'I'm sorry, what did you say your name was?'

Hector ignored the question. 'I used to be a keen photographer myself. But I let it go. I thought I would spend my retirement in Enghem photographing this and that, but cameras were something I became suspicious of. Digital cameras in particular. They were the most robotic and futile of things. A mechanical eye with a mechanical memory. It reminded me of . . . mistakes in the way I had seen the world.'

Midas, confused, swallowed the lump in his throat. Above them a crow croaked and hopped from branch to branch, wagging its tail.

'I am sorry,' said Hector, 'my mind flits from thought to thought. I get ahead of myself. I don't explain. The doctors say there's something wrong with me, but it feels like my mind is more correct than ever it was in my business years.'

He shook his head solemnly and rolled back his shoulders. 'Forgive me, Mr Crook. My rambling I don't have an excuse for.'

Midas looked over his shoulder. The crow's beak dangled open, a hungry triangle of pink inside. 'You seem very collected to me, Mr Stallows.'

'You're too kind.'

'So . . . it's, um, it's a fine day to be outside.'

Hector leant closer to Midas. 'There's a creature I intend to hunt down.'

'A creature?'

'They say it turns whatever it looks on pure white.'

Midas swallowed. He remembered the little white bird he'd caught with his camera.

Hector swished his cane through the air. 'Can you, as a photographer, imagine the world it leaves behind? Everything is in monochrome. Only the strength of the light can distinguish this thing from that.'

He imagined it, for a moment, in reverence. 'I saw a bird! With white eyes.' To prove it he raised his camera and showed off the photo.

Hector's eyes widened. 'Then the creature's nearby!' He stepped closer to the camera, the leaves in the folds of his suit crackling as he moved. 'It has a den,' he whispered, 'somewhere in Enghem.'

Midas became suddenly aware of Hector's height. He seemed to loom as much as any tree. 'And what, um, will you do if you find it?'

'*Blind* it.'

Midas couldn't stop himself from gasping.

'You think that's barbaric, of course you do. But you're young, and a photographer. When I first heard the stories of the creature, I was still a man of cameras. I wanted to trap it and have it make for me a black-and-white garden. I pictured myself strolling in the white woods, crushing the white grass underfoot. It would be like living and breathing in the monochrome photos a photographer loves so much. But those fantasies were a long time back, when I was young. I was just starting out on a long career, in which I had enormous success by anyone's standards. I thought back then that a person achieves success through incremental gains. You could work your way up. For many years I held this belief. But then, one day, I learnt that a single look can change everything. And since then I have seen it countless times. I have grappled to understand it and failed. For instance, all it took was a look from another man for my wife to fall out of love with me. It baffles me that a simple alignment of eyes can cause so much devastation. I learnt of this the hard way, and as I learnt it the existence of this creature, this devil who can turn anything white with a *look*, became a foul thing indeed.'

Midas thought it sounded unfair to blame all that on one animal. 'You've met my wife, no doubt,' continued Hector, scratching the tip of his cane across a tree trunk. 'Nobody visits Enghem unless she invites them.'

'Yes. She's very, um . . .'

'What? What did you think she was like?'

Hector's tone was demanding, but Midas couldn't tell what kind of answer he was looking for. He had the impression that Hector both loved and hated Emiliana in equal measure. 'She's very,' he faltered, 'er, charming.'

'Yes. She is charming. I miss her charm. Don't think I hold it against her that she has turned her charm away. Studying this creature has taught me that. There is an astrology of eyes at work in the world. Looks can align like planets and, in this instance, the resulting eclipse shaded out yours truly. It is the fault of *this* . . .'

Midas watched in alarm as Hector jabbed his cane accusatorily at his surroundings, but then he settled.

'Do you know what it's like to lose someone, Midas?'

'Yes.'

'Someone you were in love with?'

'No.'

'Have you ever *been* in love?'

'Erm . . .'

Hector's eyes narrowed. He grinned wolfishly. 'You are at this precise moment! It's written all over you.'

Midas looked down at himself, as if expecting this literally to be the case.

'If you are in love,' Hector said, and his voice seemed deeper and flintier, 'you should take her away from Enghem. You should take her away from St Hauda's Land. There's something in the very earth of this place.'

As if to prove it he drove his cane into the soil and flicked up a sod of earth. All that lay beneath was more damp soil, and a worm twisting over itself to escape the sudden light.

'I think . . .' said Midas slowly, 'I might be.'

'Might be what?'

Midas cleared his throat. 'In love.'

Hector threw his arms wide open. 'Then always make sure you *act* like it.'

With that he gave a kind of salute, turned, and marched away. Midas was left to find his way back to the house by getting lost in different directions. It was amazing how far the woods seemed to stretch, when there had appeared to be so few trees from the house. He wished he'd had a ball of twine, like in one of the half-remembered stories his father had told him.

The plants grew at different heights over the uneven ground, and the half-path he followed wavered between them. Heavy branches creaked like masts. Roots grew outstretched like the arms of beggars.

He was grateful when he saw an opening in the trees, and through it the house up ahead. He was almost at the front door when he heard his name called.

Carl Maulsen was smoking a cigarette by the steps to the deck. He beckoned to Midas. 'What were you doing out in the woods?'

'Walking.'

Carl nodded. 'We didn't know what had happened to you.'

'The light was too fine to stay in bed.'

He narrowed his eyes and dragged on his cigarette. 'You shouldn't have gone out like that, you've been gone for hours. We started the remedy while you were gone, even though Ida said she wanted you here.'

Midas kicked at the shingle. He hadn't realized he had been gone for so long. If he went to find Ida now he'd have to explain his disappearance as well as the failed kiss.

'Sorry,' he said.

'Don't apologize to *me*.' He stubbed the cigarette against one of the stilts of the house.

Suddenly something shot out from behind the house. Midas looked up in alarm as a hare weaved across the grass and sprinted into the wood.

'You scare easy, Midas.'

'It startled me, that's all.' He put his hands in his pockets. 'It's freezing out here. I'm going to go inside and get warm.'

Carl held out his packet of cigarettes. 'Help yourself.'

Midas shook his head.

'Don't be a sissy. We haven't finished talking.'

He offered the cigarette again and Midas took one with blue fingers. He held it awkwardly, trying to remember the last time he'd smoked. Probably as a kid when playground bullies called him a sissy if he refused. He put it between his lips. Carl took a match from a packet, struck it and reached over to light Midas's cigarette. Midas flinched at the proximity of the flame and the bigger man's hand.

Carl deftly tipped out a cigarette of his own and lit it before the match went out. 'I wanted to ask you something. Concerning your father.'

The cigarette smoke became a frost on Midas's tonsils. 'What about him?'

'See if I can jog your memory. His work. What do you think of it?'

'Do you mean what do I think of it now, or what did I think of it? When I was a very little boy I naturally thought he was a genius. My father was the cleverest scholar on the earth. Whereas now . . .'

'I understand that I'm being impertinent, but your father's thoughts have always exerted quite a hold over me.' He flicked ash from his cigarette. 'I credit them, in fact, with the birth of my own academic career. But your father could be . . . difficult.'

Midas swallowed hard. 'Well. It's easier to come across as eloquent when you only have to do it in writing.'

'I'm not criticizing him.' He puffed at his cigarette. 'I bring it up because that kind of difficulty is the last thing Ida needs.'

'I don't follow.'

'He had the finest academic brain I've known. He could dissect a thought like a physician dissecting a body. So I'm not saying he was lacking as a person. But I never even saw a glimmer of romance in him. In fact, even his studies, to which he devoted so much, didn't seem to move him or inspire him one jot. I don't know what kept him going, really.'

'He didn't *keep going*, did he?'

Carl raised his hands. 'Sure. Whatever. I can clearly see it's too raw for you.'

'Yes,' said Midas, 'it is.'

Carl shifted his position. 'He said once that the personalities of a person throughout their lifetime are like clothes worn over the course of a day, layered up to preserve dignity or weather the environment. He said it was possible for a person to be caught out this way. Imagine, if you will, the man who has put on a heavy coat, mittens, warm hat and scarf to brave a blizzard. His mind and body are attuned to the task ahead – that is, stepping out into the snowstorm. So if he doesn't hear through his earmuffs a whispered voice behind him pleading for him not to go, or feel a gentle tug at one of the layers of thick clothing he's put on, he can hardly be blamed. He has simply made one adaptation at the expense of another.'

'Look, I don't understand any of that stuff of my father's,' said Midas. His teeth were beginning to chatter.

Carl reached across and cuffed him playfully on the shoulder. 'Listen, about Ida . . . She needs to focus on getting better right now, that's all I'm saying. Not on anything else, okay? Don't feel bad about letting her down like you did this morning, just make sure she doesn't have to deal with your problems on top of hers.'

Midas felt like he'd swallowed a jug of ice. Fists clenched in his pockets, he told Carl as forcefully as he could manage that he was going inside.

CHAPTER 28

Midas would need to load the photograph on to his computer to zoom in on the white bird's eye in perfect detail, but he sat on the corner of his bed in the Stallowses' house and he already knew he hadn't been mistaken. The eye and the eyelid were white as the snow outside. It made him think about his run-in with Hector, which had felt strange, dream-like. And the strangest thing of all was what Hector had made him say. *I might be in love.*

He got up to look out of the window. He wanted to escape the house again. Earlier, at lunch with Carl and Emiliana, eating fresh white fish from the cove, Ida hadn't even looked at him and he couldn't manage a word to anyone. She had seemed worn out from the poultices Carl and Emiliana had spent the morning applying. When she had come to the table she had done so even more slowly than she normally would, as if both the crutch he had bought her and her old one together were no match for her body. Afterwards Emiliana disappeared and Carl took Ida aside to talk to her in serious tones.

Midas had washed up, thinking about his father's forearms covered in dishwater bubbles.

Now in his guest bedroom, with its whitewashed walls and sheer white sheets, he tried to remember that Ida had invited him here. As moral support. But as something else? Her lips had approached his, too delightful to meet. She would think he had shunned her, and now he wanted a second chance, to receive those lips and reach around her waist. He could fantasize about it, but he wasn't sure, given that chance, he would take it.

He heard a brittle knock on the bedroom door. He spun around, straightening his hair, terrified at once of Ida stepping in to confront him. If she were coming to tell him he had blown it and should make his way home, well . . . He suddenly realized he wanted to put off that moment for as long as he could. He kept quiet, not daring to make another movement, hoping she'd think he wasn't in.

After a second knock the door opened anyway. It was Emiliana.

'Oh,' she said, 'I'm sorry. You didn't answer so I didn't think you were here. May I come in?'

'Um. Of course. Yes.' He hung his head. So Ida's verdict would not even be delivered in person. It was Emiliana's house, so it made sense that she would be the one to tell him to leave. She pushed the bedroom door shut behind her.

'I brought you this.' She held out a scratched leather satchel covered with pouches and poppers.

He took it and guessed its contents at once from its weight.

'Um . . .' he said.

'It's for you.'

'Th-thank you.'

Emiliana sat down slowly on the bed, smoothing her skirt over her thighs.

'Open it, then.'

He unzipped the main compartment and took out the camera. It was the kind of old SLR that would have cost thousands of pounds in its day. The bag juggled with lenses and attachments. The camera's grip was made from worn snakeskin.

'It was Hector's. Photography was a hobby of his, once upon a time. He hasn't touched that camera in years. Nor will he. Don't worry, I've had it looked after, like so many of the other things he's abandoned. I'm a human broom, tidying things up in his wake. I took it to a specialist on the mainland, thinking I might play around with it, but I don't seem capable of finding the time. And it's such a terrible waste to have it lying around. Perhaps you'll make better use of it.'

A childish grin spread across his face. He turned it on and played with the aperture dial, using Emiliana's sharp profile and the black of her hair as his subject. It was so easy to forget the pleasures of older cameras: the trust you had to place in instinct instead of display screens. 'Stop photographing me,' she said, with mild irritation.

'I was just . . . experimenting.'

'I know. I just . . . don't like having my photo taken these days.'

He slung it over his neck so it hung side by side with his digital, the two lens caps nuzzling each other.

'So,' said Emiliana, 'you have time for a little chat?'

He swallowed, suddenly feeling the weight of both cameras tugging on his neck. *God*, this was it.

'Midas, why don't you sit with me?'

He did as he was told. The mattress was soft as he sat down beside her. He could smell her perfume, something shocking and alcoholic that ghosted through his lungs into his gut. He wondered what the SLR she'd given him would have done in the test shots he had just taken. It would have recorded truthfully the crow's feet she'd painted closed with her make-up.

'It's about Ida,' she said.

'You've started curing her.'

'Ye-es. It might not be as easy as that.'

He shook his head, becoming cautiously optimistic that he wasn't being told to leave the house, becoming anxious that he was being told something worse.

'It might be difficult.'

'Why? You cured Saffron Jeuck.'

'That was different.' She sighed. 'In my youth I was of course in better shape than I am now. I was approached several times by scouts who saw modelling potential in me. I'm only telling you this

272

because . . . I hope it'll help you understand, when you've heard it all.

'At this time I first met Carl. I had been married two years and was already realizing that, in Hector, I had a very different sort of husband to the one I had anticipated. I loved him, you must understand. And I still do. But it was a love born out of great comfort and not out of . . .' She sighed and threw her head back, her black hair tossing. He felt the mattress move beneath them. The cameras clinked on his chest.

'There was no sex, to put it bluntly. Because Hector, although he is a man of passions, is most peculiar. Amber in the trees. The quartz room. The aviary of birds born mute. As I say, I love him, Midas, as one might love one's brother. But for a young woman like I was at the time, who had been commended for her looks and who was hungry to . . . make the most of them . . .' She looked Midas dead in the eye. 'Well, I needed more than that. So. That was when I met Carl Maulsen. In those days the idea of an open relationship was still rather new. People were naïve about it, hadn't foreseen the inevitable emotional entanglements.'

Midas nodded to appear understanding, even though this frank talk of Emiliana's sex life was making his palms itch and his back sweat. Worse, he'd had no idea that she and Carl had once had . . . an involvement. What else had he been too naïve to pick up on? He wanted to bolt out of the door. Ten times already he had pictured himself crashing through the window and plunging to the snowy garden beneath. All the same he was rooted to the spot. He examined the topography of her as she talked, the wrinkles across her neck that traced its length into three equal segments. The contours from her collarbone, over her chest and then out over the tops of her breasts, the skin that would once have been tight now lax. Her scent lay heavy in his stomach like a sheet of iron.

'What I'm trying to say, Midas, is that when a person feels imprisoned by their circumstances, they make mistakes.'

'You . . . made a mistake with Carl?'

'No. Yes. The mistake wasn't being with Carl. It was trying too hard to hold on to his interest in me. The mistake was making myself seem . . . more interesting than I really ought. Do you understand what I'm saying?'

They sat side by side in silence, knees lined up. He couldn't see what this had to do with Ida, poultices and the rest of it. 'I just,' he said, fiddling with the SLR, 'I just don't. No. Uhhm . . . sorry.'

Emiliana was blushing hard. She took a deep breath. 'I have been very foolish, with my life, simply by never going out on a limb. I think about it every day. And I have been very naïve. Because I have always been comfortable, physically and circumstantially, you understand?'

To be polite, he refrained from shaking his head.

'I wonder whether I am transparent, sometimes. I feel . . . flimsy and insubstantial.'

She paused, studying his expression, which he tried to lend an air of compassion and wisdom.

She sighed and brushed her hair back off her shoulders. 'Let me put it another way. I feel like a half-exposed photograph. I can make out what it portrays, but it doesn't have any depth.'

This he understood.

'I don't feel I have much substance. I have struggled for substance. And once, a long time ago now, Carl appeared, and just one look from him felt like the last exposing light that photograph needed. It sounds pathetic recounting it now, but it filled in the details, created new depths I had not known existed. For that, I felt I owed him everything, and to *let him down* would mean to jeopardize everything I was. I still find it very hard to let Carl down. So . . . you're still wondering how this relates to poor Ida, and the poultices, and so forth.'

Midas was about to say yes when the door opened and Carl stepped in. 'Good morning,' he said, and waited, as if their presence here demanded an explanation.

'We were just chatting,' obliged Emiliana, 'and Midas was photographing me with his new camera.'

CHAPTER 29

Ida sat alone beside the log fireplace in Emiliana's sitting room, deep in an armchair with a book on her lap, flames clicking and snapping behind her. The parts of her legs that were still skin and bone below her knees – her calves and shins and the bastions in her ankles that weren't yet glass – were all as numb now as the glass itself. Above her knees, where the flesh wasn't paralysed but the venom had lanced, she could feel a pain like a burn near heat. She summoned the courage to peek again at her inflamed skin. Her lower thighs looked like joints in a butcher's shop. Her knees were puffed up, elephantine. To think it had *receded* since the treatment that morning, when she had hitched up her skirt and watched Emiliana tie with tight threads the poultices of warmed jellyfish matter. The pain had been fierce and instantaneous, like a needle in every skin cell. Her eyes had watered so fast that within a minute they had dried out and blinking felt like peeling them. She had screwed them up and wished that Midas had been there so she could clamp his hand in hers as the pain flared. That had been her plan the night before. The attempted kiss would have cleared the way for it.

The patterns on the walls swung in and out of focus at the whim of the firelight. The door creaked as it opened.

She picked up her book again when she saw Midas enter. He tiptoed over and sat on a cushion opposite.

'Is now a good time to talk?'

She kept quiet. Out of the corner of her eye she saw him lick his lips. He'd want to blurt out every excuse for his jumbled-up shock when she'd tried to kiss him. All that rubbish about an inherited phobia of touch.

'So, um . . .' he managed, 'what are you reading?'

She laid the book down open on her lap and laughed curtly. 'I don't know. I just picked it up the moment you came in to give you the cold shoulder.'

'Ah. Um.'

'So what are we, Midas? Close friends? Aspiring lovers? That kind of talk gets you jumpy, doesn't it?' She snapped the book shut. 'But you see, Midas, and I don't mean to be cruel, you've more time than me to give heed to your insecurities. I need to know where we stand.'

The fire crackled. She worried she'd said too much, defeated his droplet words with a river of her own. She carried on. 'Can't you just . . . write me a note or something? Or just . . . say it from the heart.'

His jaw wagged as he tried to eject something.

'Stop thinking so hard about what you'll say. Just spit it out.'

'I-I'm sorry.'

She thumped the arm of the chair. 'You're bloody well forgiven, Midas. That doesn't matter. What about *us*?'

'I wasn't to . . . I want to . . .' He was almost bent double. She noticed the second camera hanging from his neck, as if forcing his posture into a bow.

'Where did you get that camera?'

'Em-Emiliana. I was t-taking her photo.'

She felt a sudden clamminess in her gullet, an oyster swallowed wrong, dropping through her stomach and into her bowels, becoming a numbing absence beneath her knees. He just sat there looking concerned. He had said before that he wanted to take her own photograph and she had avoided the topic because she didn't want him to. She knew what photographs did to her these days and she hated the idea of being recorded in one. All the same she had been flattered that he *wanted* to take one. She had read it as a sign that he was interested in her. Idiot, she was an idiot. She looked away from him. Of course he had never made a promise to abstain from photographing someone else until she was ready, and yes, she was being irrational, but she was so exhausted and her legs were so sore.

'I-Ida?'

'For fuck's sake, Midas. If nothing's going to become of us, what are you even doing here?'

He got up. Ducking and bowing subserviently, he backed out of the room.

'Midas! Come back!' But he didn't. She heaved herself up and hurried after him, but the thick rug snared one of her crutches and she tripped forward. Her hands rushed out before her (she had rehearsed this fall a thousand times in her nightmares). She screwed up her face and had time to remember parachutes and bungee jumps (she had to hit the floor first with anything but her feet). The impact against her face was silenced by the rug, but she felt every inch of the hard floor hit her. Her neck twisted with a click. Her shoulder-blades and vertebrae jarred. She lowered her legs slowly and pressed her face hard into the rug, trying to hide the pain in its smell of carpet and the softness of tassels. Her body remained intact.

Lying still on the rug, hoping that Midas would return, she wondered what it would be like to lie on top of him. She wondered whether his hair would feel soft like the rug. She wondered whether when he made love his heartbeat was frantic like a shrew's and whether his skin became slippery like a fish. These were implausible thoughts, implausible enough to distract her from the hunch that he would not come back to help her to her feet.

Boys and their dashing about . . . made no sense to her. Midas laboriously working through his emotional gauntlet. Henry distant and non-committal. Carl somewhere else in this house, promising remedies and protection. The fire puffed out smoke. She could put her feet in that fire and not be harmed, should she wish, yet she couldn't do so little as jump on the spot . . . That morning the first thing she had done on waking up was to examine the bruise on her knee. It had turned from grey to transparent, like a little pool of clear water in the white geography of her leg.

She was being shut down, paralysed, physical avenues cordoned off. Thank goodness, she thought, she had done what she had when she had. She had waded in the Ganges, felt downy snow fill her mouth in the Alps, breathed deep to get the last of the oxygen from the high altitude of mountains. Swum. She had once swum.

How she wanted patiently to explore Midas's caution, make inch-by-inch gains on his emotions, but she lacked that kind of time. She might wait for ever for his return. She might wait for ever for his dithering affections.

And her feet . . . these fragile shackles she lugged around. She could feel their emptiness. If she tried to bunch up her toes in fury . . . nothing happened. Her nervous system fizzled out somewhere beyond her shins. She looked back at her boots stretched out behind her on the rug. Dad's old policeman's boots. She remembered her own shoes, her pretty dancing shoes and her mud-caked hiking boots. She had left them all on the mainland, neatly packed in tissue paper in boxes.

She was coming to terms with it now: that some things were behind her. Life now would be an adventure of the mind, and perhaps of some other part of her body as yet unaffected, something interior.

The door creaked slowly open.

She reached towards it involuntarily. 'Midas, thank goodness you came back . . . Oh.'

'Bloody hell, Ida, what's happened?'

Carl rushed across the carpet. She winced as his thick arms slid under her armpits and sat her slowly up. He crouched beside her, made her head rest against his chest. She heard his heartbeat speeding up beneath his shirt.

'I'm okay,' she said stiffly, trying to push him away.

He didn't let go or say anything. His grip tightened almost imperceptibly. The heat of his palms seared through her blouse.

She pushed him more forcefully. He let go, sprang up and stepped away from her, taking a deep breath.

'I'm okay,' she said steadily, forcing herself back up and into the armchair.

He nodded without looking at her.

'Actually, I'd like to be alone. Sorry, Carl.'

He nodded and headed out of the room. In the doorway he paused. 'Where is Midas going?'

'What?'

'I just watched him packing his bags. He's driven away.'

She held her head in her hands. It took all her effort to speak with any volume. 'Like I said, I want to be alone.'

He nodded and closed the door softly behind him.

CHAPTER 30

The air was filled with a million flakes, sinking slowly like ocean sediment. Snow flew across St Hauda's Land's roads and heaped on shrubs. A bird with broad wings coasted on the air currents above like a stingray. Midas was in no hurry to get home (he had a foreboding that home would remind him of Ida) so he drove back by a long scenic route.

He stopped in a car park at a viewpoint, looking out across low valleys cut into squares by drystone walls. A brook ran past the viewpoint, and after a while Midas took off his shoes and socks and dipped his toes into the cold current. Something stung him and he hopped out of the stream. A little leech hung from his big toe, sucking blood. He had a lighter in the car, so sat on the bonnet while he burnt the leech off. It shrivelled and smelt noxious. He held its burnt body in his hand and was going to take a photo, but the moment he touched the camera he felt nauseous. A sudden revulsion came over him and he pulled the bag off his shoulder and locked the camera in the boot. Then he stood over a bush, hands on his knees, feeling the need to vomit. Nothing came. He drove home listening to traffic reports and corny seventies love songs. The heater hummed as a creeping snowfall came down. Snowflakes stuck to his windscreen and shrivelled there like dying starfish.

Getting back at dusk he sat at the table with coffee in one hand and a glass of red wine in the other. He'd spent a perplexed half-hour in the off-licence trying to understand the differences between all the available bottles. The taste was as vile as he remembered, but he drank it anyway. On the radio, a distinguished actor was reading an adaptation of *The Wizard of Oz*. The Lion was drinking his courage, the Tin Man had his heart, and the Scarecrow's head was stuffed with what he took for brains.

Midas lashed out and knocked the radio off the table. It lay on the floor with its reception lost, the actor's voice slurred into an alien gargle.

He had known that mixing with people wouldn't work out. He'd told himself that when he first met Ida, repeated it like a mantra as he'd lain awake at night thinking about her. He was plainly incapable of social interaction. And what did he have instead? His eyes came to rest on his camera, which he must have pulled out of the bag without thinking because it sat, smug, lens cap dangling off, on the table. He imagined dying and being cut open and there were all his bones and muscles and his bared arteries and capillaries leading to a cavity in his chest where instead of a heart he had his camera.

He grabbed it by the strap and flung it after the radio. It hit the fridge and clunked on to the kitchen tiles. He drained the wine, topped up his glass and lowered his head on to the table. It was strong wine: at point-blank the table's coffee rings orbited through his vision. He managed to regain focus, but when he looked up it was like being on a roundabout with the walls swirling around. All those pictures he'd pinned up there, grubby fingerprints of the past, black-and-white memories. He groaned and closed his eyes, but the memories remained. His father crunching dragonfly carapaces in his fists, his mother crying with a bundle of tattered roses on her lap, a swarm of jellyfish floating in the sea around him, Ida entering the florist with wet hair stuck to her head.

Someone was knocking on the front door and the bell was ringing over and over. Midas blinked hard and stood up. He was in the doorway between the kitchen and the hall. The ringing and knocking continued. He stared back at the wine bottle on the kitchen table. Knock knock knock. Holding his head, he staggered to the door. Dazzling bright light came into the hallway. It took him a moment to adjust.

'Blimey, Midas. Heavy night?'

'Hello.'

'You had your girlfriend round again?'

He shook his head. Beside her father, Denver studied Midas, a scarf wrapped up to her nose.

She'd pulled her sleeve over her fingers to hold a prickly holly branch. A little arctic poppy was brightening up her hair.

'Ah,' said Gustav, peering inside, 'oh, I see. What happened? And what happened to you?' He stepped inside. 'You smell something rotten. You sure you're okay?'

'I . . . messed something up. Had an accident. Come inside. It's freezing today.'

Soon Midas sat holding an ice pack to his head while Gustav rooted through his cupboards and Denver sat opposite, watching with faint amusement.

Gustav closed the fridge door and put his hands on his hips. 'There's nothing green in your whole house. There's no fruit either. What are you living off?'

Midas gestured to his empty coffee mug.

'Right. I'm going to make you some lunch. Get your spirits up. I'll be ten minutes.'

Denver twisted in her chair. 'Where are you going?'

'To get some veg. Back soon.' He left, muttering under his breath. Denver sighed, then stretched her arm across the length of the table and took hold of one of Midas's fingers. Her skin was still cold from the chill outside. He tried to pull away but she squeezed. It was sometimes okay, being touched by Denver. She had spent so much time with him that he sometimes forgot she was a separate entity. He wondered miserably if he would ever have reached a state like that with Ida.

Denver squeezed harder.

'Ow. Ow, Den, ow.'

'Were you in love with her?'

He shook his head.

'Don't believe you.'

He tried to pull his finger away again. She gripped it hard and twisted it back.

'*Ow.*'

'Was she horrid to you? I hate her if she was horrid.'

He swallowed. 'Actually, I think I was horrid to her.'

'You said something nasty about her feet?'

'No.' He gulped. 'Denver, why do you—'

'I know, remember. I saw the same photo that nasty man saw.'

'That was . . . just a doctored photo.'

'I didn't tell anyone.'

'Thank you.'

She loosened her hold on his finger. He didn't pull it away.

'Your camera's on the floor.'

'I threw it there.'

'Why?'

'I was cross with it.'

She let go and for a second he wanted to feel her cold little hand around his finger again. She lifted the camera with both hands and put it on the table.

'You haven't shown me new pictures in ages. Show me some now.'

He shook his head. She started to play with the

287

digital's buttons. The two of them sat in silence as she flicked through its image bank.

'Not even one of Ida,' she said.

Midas rubbed his forehead. 'They were all too awful. I couldn't get them right.'

'And you got rid of them because they didn't look nice enough?'

'Precisely.'

'I think you *were* in love with her.'

'Love . . . is not something you understand when you're a grown-up, Den. It's just as if it's . . . a memory of something that should have been. From stories . . . and . . . I don't know whether you really can be in love.'

'You could be,' she said. 'You and a few other people. You're like me. You've got it.'

'Got what?'

She shrugged. 'A grip. On the bits in the back of your head. And here . . .' she touched her tummy. 'Somewhere in here.'

He wrapped his arms tight around his chest. He hardly thought he had a grip on anything.

Gustav came in and dumped bags on the kitchen counter. 'Lettuce, tomatoes, spuds, honey roast ham. I'm making you a salad and a jacket potato because you, well . . . Bloody hell, Midas, look at you.'

He didn't tell Gustav everything: that would have been too much. He only told him enough to make him understand the situation regarding his relationship with Ida: the failed kiss and abortive

288

explanation. Then his flight and the long drive back here. Denver sketched throughout the recounting, as if her mind were elsewhere. Midas waited for his friend's damning verdict.

Gustav sat back and looked impressed. 'I can't believe you went to Hector Stallows's house. Does he have as many cars as they say he does?'

'Gustav, this is a nightmare for me.' Of course he wouldn't see the urgency, when he hadn't told him about her feet.

'Sorry. Sorry, mate, but do you see my point? Um . . . listen. You're chicken. You know you are, I know you are. You hate confrontation and you'd rather bottle than fight. You're not even looking at me now.'

Midas's eyes flicked up then shirked away.

'You've got a bloody heart of gold, and I think Ida sees that in you. You need to get your arse back up there and fully, sincerely apologize for anything you did do wrong, which I suspect is a whole lot less than you've convinced yourself of. I think she'll see you mean it. I don't think she'll execute you, though you might do to be ready for some frank words.'

'I'll phone her in the morning.'

'No. Phone her now. If you think it's worth patching things up with her, you do it before she moves on. Time won't wait for you. You know exactly what I mean.'

He meant: Remember Catherine. Remember frozen lakes and paramedics. Remember no ice

289

where a floor of ice had been beneath her feet. Remember trying to sound like you meant it when you told a little girl about narwhals and water angels caring for her mother now.

Remember shins turning hard like enamel where they had been smooth and pink a week before.

'You're right,' he sighed, 'but I've not the heart for it.'

'You'll have to do better than that.'

'Listen, Gustav, I'm a knot of inhibitions. One, I can barely phrase my sentences. Two, I see my father in bloody well everything I do and I hate myself for it. Three, every time I touch someone my body feels like iron.'

'All right. In the order you put it. One, you phrased that little list of defects perfectly clearly. Two, your father's gone now. It's just you. Don't shake your head . . . we'll come back to that. Three, well, stand up.'

'I'm sorry?'

Gustav pushed back his chair and got to his feet, motioning Midas to do the same. 'Den, I need you to go out into the hall, or into another room, and shut the door. I'm sorry.'

She sulkily did as she was asked, while Gustav rolled up his sleeves. 'Come on, Midas. I should have done this years back. I'm going to fix you once and for all. Up.'

Midas dragged back his chair and rose to his feet.

'Put your camera back on the table.'

'Why?'

'Do it.'

Midas huffed and put down the camera. 'Now what?'

He shrieked when Gustav tackled him to the hard kitchen floor. His bones juddered and his head clunked against the tiles. He was still shrieking when Gustav climbed on top of him and punched him in the stomach. Midas's breath erupted but Gustav didn't stop. Straddling him, he grabbed his shoulders and pulled him off the ground, then slammed him down with full force. 'Fight me, you twat!' he puffed, slapping Midas's face.

Midas shoved pathetically but the weight was too much. Another slap stung his cheek and cuffed his nose. He could smell blood. He grabbed Gustav's wrist when it swung at him again and, when he was too puny to shove it away, dug his nails into the skin. Gustav roared in pain and sprang off him.

'You *girl*!' he bellowed and kicked him in the ribs. Midas rolled to avoid a second kick, grabbed Gustav's foot in both hands and twisted. Gustav dropped to the floor and thumped his head hard on the tiles, beads of blood swelling on his forehead.

Midas sat up beside him. 'Are you . . . are you okay, Gus?'

'Ugh . . .'

'Oh *God*, I'm sorry.'

Gustav swung wildly at him and caught him hard across the chest. Midas grappled with flailing arms and scrambled to block kicks along the floor with his knees. Then they were wrestling wildly, rolling over each other and knocking a chair on its side. One of Midas's hands was locked with Gustav's, the other was spread over Gustav's face while he tried to prise it free. Midas felt the rubbery skin of a nostril, puffing lips and bristles spiking his palm. With a final effort he wrenched free and threw his whole weight back at Gustav unguarded. The impact questioned every joint but Gustav fell back and Midas was on top of him, pinning portly stomach with scrawny knees, pressing for all he was worth to keep Gustav's arms on the floor.

Gustav laughed with a choke and licked his split top lip. 'Okay, okay,' he wheezed. 'Midas wins fair and square.'

Midas groaned as he climbed free. Gustav remained on his back panting and laughing. Midas examined his body fresh from scrapping, his flesh a peculiar ruddy tone, his clothes uneven and creased.

Gustav moaned and sat up. 'Jesus. The things I do for you.'

'Thank you. That really . . . it sounds silly, doesn't it? That really helped.'

'If you get to touch Ida, you'd better be gentler. You owe me, remember. And you can start by letting me use your shower and capping a cold beer or a cup of tea if you've got no booze.'

Gustav opened the kitchen door to Denver crouched at the keyhole biting her fingers to prevent herself from laughing. Midas blushed and felt his skull like a plastic bag full of blood.

Denver stood up the kitchen chair they'd knocked over, then climbed on it while Gustav thumped up the stairs and turned the shower on.

She opened her sketchbook on to another new drawing of a narwhal.

'You know,' Midas said, blowing traces of blood out of his nose, 'your father's a madman.'

She began to sketch. 'He's worried. You're all he talks about.'

'Since when?'

'Since you met Ida. He said . . .' she chewed her pencil end while she tried to remember, then did a vivid impression of her father. '"He's going to miss the best bit of luck in his life."'

'He said that?'

He watched her draw. She added bridles to the narwhal and reins leading back to an open-topped carriage in the shape of a shell. In the carriage she began the sea queen.

'Den . . . how's your daddy been? Since his trip to see your granny?'

She paused for a moment to chew the pencil. He heard her crunch the wood. 'He came back with a whole lot of Mummy's things. We went through some of them together.' She pulled a piece of pencil wood off her tongue.

'I know what that's like. My father left boxes and boxes.'

She left the queen half finished and absent-mindedly dotted bubbles and grains of sand on the seabed. 'I wasn't sad. I was happy in a funny way.

In the boxes were things Mummy had when she was a little girl. Beautiful dolls and stuff. They're on my bed now with my own. I go to sleep with the one she gave me and the one she had when she was little. That's weird, isn't it? Her doll isn't older than mine.'

She'd mauled half an inch from the pencil (she wasn't allowed pencils with rubber tops). 'Midas?'

'Yes.'

'My mummy's watching me now. Is your daddy watching you?'

He shuddered at the thought of it. 'I used to think he was. All the time.'

Midas packed his bag as soon as they had left. After about half an hour Denver briefly returned with a vase full of red roses that Gustav had hand-picked to take to Ida.

When she had gone again he sat down and enjoyed the smell of the petals as he poured himself the remains of yesterday's wine. It would accompany a plate of the lettuce and ham Gustav had brought him, and although he still felt bruised and unwell from the previous night's drinking, he needed something to fire his courage.

The wine made his heart flutter. Bravery did not become him and nor would it ever (his DNA guaranteed that). He tried to decide on the bravest thing his father ever did. Kill himself (the waves sloshing quietly while the flames burned)? Or conceive a son? That was a thought. His mother desperate for love, and his father who flinched at the briefest contact (he remembered giving him a leg-up into the boat) coupling together in bed, and all the stickiness *that* entailed.

He stared accusingly at the red wine, then knocked it back and went to the phone. He had been rethinking the time he had spent at Enghem, and the thing that stuck in his mind now was Emiliana: how she had behaved in the guest bedroom when she came to give him the SLR. It had been as if she were trying to confess to something about the remedy. He had been too dimwitted to notice at the time.

He dialled Ida's number and she picked up in seconds.

'Ida! It's me.'

Brief silence on the other end of the line, then a man's voice, 'I'm sorry. This isn't Ida.'

'Oh. Carl?'

'Yes. And I don't think Ida wants to speak to you.'

'Carl, I . . . I don't know whether this remedy is a good thing.'

'You've already made that quite clear.'

'Will you pass me to Ida?'

'I don't think so.'

'Please.'

'No. I don't think so.'

Carl hung up. Midas tried ringing again, but no one answered and the tone cut to a voicemail service.

He sulked back to the kitchen feeling rejected.

That was that, then. She didn't want to speak with him.

On the table lay Denver's sketch of the shell carriage, complete apart from its half-drawn passenger. He thought grimly of Catherine's frozen body when they pulled it from the murderous water.

He couldn't give up.

He badly wished there was some wine left.

He had to see Ida again, to tell her things straight.

He took up the phone and called Emiliana Stallows, praying that Carl wouldn't answer. After a long time ringing, Emiliana picked up.

'Who's this?' she asked.

He was too scared to say his name, in case she hung up abruptly. 'I understand now,' he said instead, 'what you were trying to tell me when you gave me the SLR.'

'Oh,' she said.

'It's not going to work, is it? There's more to the story of Saffron Jeuck than you told us.'

He thought he could hear Enghem Stead creaking in the time that passed before she answered.

'It's not going to work,' she admitted. 'It's only going to delay things.'

'Delay for how long?'

'I don't know.'

'How long did it delay them for Saffron?'

'Midas . . . you have to understand that when Saffron left me, we all thought it was working.'

He was winding the cord of the phone so tight

around his fingers it was cutting off the blood supply. 'How long?'

'Not long.'

'I'm coming to get her.'

He put down the phone, grabbed his bag and car keys, and was off. Only halfway to Enghem did it strike him that he'd left the roses in their vase on the kitchen table.

CHAPTER 31

Carl was smoking a cigarette on Enghem Stead's wooden deck when Emiliana tiptoed out to join him. A mist cottoned the hills inland. Earlier in the day it had been a low cloud bank, but inexorably it had sunk on to the hilltops. Later it would roll down over Enghem-on-the-Water and spread north across the quiet ocean.

Emiliana came closer and leant her elbows on the railing beside him, watching the smoke from his cigarette hang in the cold air like a thread, as if the cigarette would float there if he let go.

'Carl.'

He flicked ash on to the pebbles beneath the deck. 'What's up, Mil?'

She took a deep breath. 'You know . . . it's been so busy since you all arrived, I feel like we've barely had a chance to catch up.'

'We stayed up chatting last night.'

'We did. But . . .'

He drew a long, snorting breath and stabbed the cigarette out on the railing. He looked at her sideways, as if turning his head was too arduous. Still she felt him seeing into her, that ability he had always had. That thing that had attracted her to him in the first place. Back when they first met, when she'd been young, newly wed and regretting it, such a look from him had seared straight through the barriers of faces and skulls to the top of her spine. He had been in love with Freya back then, which he had confessed early in their brief fling. Back then Emiliana had felt she could compete.

'I concealed one or two things from you.'

He raised his eyebrows. Unable to bear that slanted look of his, watching instead his fingers drawing casually into a bunch on the wooden rail, she cleared her throat. 'About Saffron Jeuck.'

He didn't respond. She watched a sheet of the mist drift slowly off the nearer reaches of the hills and erase the lowlands in the distance. She blinked tears from her eyes. He would never visit again, she supposed, and it was unfair. While he tried to help a girl who was doomed, because he was obsessed with a woman who was dead, here she *was*. She had been prepared to elope with him for the twelve years she had been married.

'Saffron's dead,' she said.

She dared a glance at him. His lower jaw was jutting out, as if he were smarting from a punch. It took him for ever to say anything. Mist appeared in the ditches of the craggy fields between Enghem-on-the-Water and the hills, as if the main body of descending fog was piping it ahead underground.

'How?' he asked finally.

'Suicide.'

'Not glass?'

'Because she was turning into glass, yes.'

He closed his eyes and remained motionless, taking it in. In the long while before he next spoke, the mist felt its way closer, groping out of the ditches like an old blind creature coming out for a forage, nibbling boulders, fingering its way through grasses, squatting on an insipid brook.

'This is news,' said Carl.

'I didn't want things to work out like this. I thought, after all, Ida might be okay where Saffron was not. It's not that the treatment did no good at all. It kept the glass from spreading for months.'

His fingernails were digging into the wood of the rail. His knuckles were white. Otherwise, he was very still. 'It wrecked her body. We've seen the weals and burns on your video. The logic of the remedy was to leave flesh that played dead, not flesh without strength.'

She nodded sharply. The hills were beginning to vanish entirely in the thickening air.

'Is there anything else?'

'I want things to be different. I would never wish what's happening to Ida on anyone. And you should know, Carl, that you can be—'

'Is there anything else about Saffron Jeuck?'

She gulped. 'I heard the suicide made it very quick for her in the end. I don't know much more than that. When she left my care it felt like it was *working*, Carl. It was only afterwards that I learnt something was wrong.'

The mist seemed now to billow and expand almost suddenly, as if the earth had exhaled a deep breath on a cold day.

'Get out of my sight,' he said.

She trotted down off the deck and away across the broken pottery of shingle and pebble. She rushed away from him, taking fast panicked steps, until her shoes were wet and sinking through spongy ground. She kept going, never looking back, until she found she was treading uphill and the mist was all around her. Then at once she came to a dead halt. How dare he banish her from her own house? Except . . . in truth it was Hector's house, and this landscape belonged no more to her than it did to Carl. She turned back to face Enghem Stead, although it was unclear in the mist whether she was facing the right direction. With her next step her foot cracked through an iced-over puddle. She stopped again. She did not want to go back. She wiped her black hair back from her face and took slow breaths to compose herself. She would go somewhere else.

CHAPTER 32

The mists had blossomed as far as Enghem Stead. Vapour swelled so close to the deck that Carl could barely see beyond the handrail.

His mind was elsewhere regardless.

Only when Freya went travelling did he find out what love was. At university he had spent the grim nights when she had returned to her halls or house switching her off in his head using metaphysics, airport thrillers, Gnostic heresy or soft porn. Anything to distract. Then graduation's knockout blow. Freya left to travel in the Far East: Carl dragged himself into an academic career. Sometimes he went weeks without sleeping, not because he was incapable but because he couldn't bear to. Exhaustion caught him at inopportune moments. He had waking dreams of Freya washing cuts from her knees. He remembered a walk in the High Street when every pedestrian had bleeding kneecaps. A policewoman prodded him awake on a bench outside a supermarket.

He took to discussing Freya with himself at night, drinking whisky with his reflection. People lived and died for ideas. Wars were fought for their precedence. But he couldn't look his reflection in the eye as he said that, because he felt in his heart it was degenerate to love simply the idea of a person, the ghostly shape where hot flesh had been.

He sat forward in the chair and stared into the formidable monotony of the mist. He wondered how he was going to break the news about Saffron to Ida, and he had got nowhere with his wonderings when she came out on to the deck to join him.

The other night, when she'd shown them all her feet, Emiliana and Midas had dematerialized as readily as Enghem in this weather. So had the furniture, the walls, the winter and *time*. The shapes of her legs had resurrected feelings in him that felt ancient. He had remembered her mother's legs.

Last night he had persuaded her to show him the glass again. Her ankles had become almost purely transparent and the surfaces of her shins were insubstantial. The skin was turning from white to translucent, and beneath it were trails of blood in crystallizing veins, like fossilized worms. Seeing them threw him back to the quad in that summer from his youth, the smell of the dying grass and the clatter of Freya's bike crashing on paving slabs. It was as if he had seen the blood seeping from Freya's kneecaps with one eye, while the other saw the blood locked under the surface of Ida's shins. His brain had meshed the two together cruelly.

'Carl,' said Ida.

He sprang off his chair to offer it to her. She

eased herself into it as an old woman might. He could smell her. A scent much more natural than Emiliana's, which had been so evidently concocted in a lab. He couldn't remember Freya's smell, but he took consolation that she would have smelled like Ida.

'Carl—'

'Ida, I've had some . . . bad news from Emiliana.'

She looked concerned. He hung his head.

'What's happened, Carl?'

'You know I've always cared for you. That's been my absolute imperative. Your mother . . . when she was suffering . . . I wanted to do what no one did for her.'

Ida drew in an exhausted breath. 'No one could cure her, Carl.'

'But I wish I could have been there for her, don't you? Do you hold it against me that I wasn't?'

She didn't answer.

'Your father didn't inform me. Hell, Ida, *you* didn't inform me.'

'You hadn't been in touch for a long time. Dad said anyone who wasn't interested in Mum alive shouldn't be interested in her dead.'

Carl snorted derisively. The mist moved gently across the deck, making Ida look out of focus.

'He was going through enough, Carl, and truth be told he never liked you. As I'm sure you know.'

He sat back in his chair, rubbing his jaw. 'I was made to feel that she would prefer me to stay out of touch . . . But I brought it up,' he said, 'because

I wanted you to know I can't bear the idea of you suffering a drawn-out end like she did. And . . . and it's all a sham.'

Ida was as composed as a china doll. 'What is?' she asked slowly.

Carl held his hands to his head. His entire life had been shaped by her mother. Everything he had done. What he had become. Here was all that was left of Freya and he had achieved nothing except to deceive her. 'I wanted to . . .' he began, then started again because his voice had sounded puny. 'I wanted to help you, remember. I wanted to help your mother like this.'

It was very quiet on the deck. 'Jesus,' she said faintly. Even her slight movement, reaching for the nearest of her crutches, made a noticeable rustle. 'This isn't about my mum.'

'I *tried*, Ida.'

'It isn't about you either, Carl.'

He thought about the glass of her feet. He imagined he could feel her pain in sympathy, the cold burns down her legs.

'I need you to help me,' she said, voice quaking.

'Y-yes,' he stammered. 'Of course. I should . . . I should check your legs. Let me see your legs again.'

Her fingers closed around the wooden handle.

He ran his hands through his hair. He had only two thoughts. First, that he had to find another way to save her. Second, that he had to see the bloodied knees of Freya Maclaird.

'Carl. Just drive me to Ettinsford. That's all I want you to do.'

He scowled. 'Where's the good in that?' He clapped his hands. 'Come on, show me your legs. Take off your boots and your socks. I'll help you, Ida, I'll help you better now it's just the two of us.'

'Please drive me to Ettinsford.'

He bunched his fists. 'Get a grip on yourself, girl! We need to figure this out. You and me! There's no time for that wretched little boy.'

She slapped him.

He felt it all rush to his head. He lunged towards her skirt. She shrieked and lashed at him but her blows felt faint as raindrops. He pinned her in the chair with one arm.

'Let go of me!' he heard her scream, as if from a distance. Likewise a glob of spit that hit his chin felt intangible like a memory. Breathing hard, focusing on her skirt and the body beneath, he reached down with his free hand and lifted the fabric up to her hips. She wormed in his grip, but his strength and the immobile weight of her legs fastened her to the chair.

Her legs. The skin of her thighs was a battleground of swollen red weals and tough white skin, but he had eyes only for the faint shadows of blood preserved behind her shins.

He heard Freya yelling. Her head thrashed about. Again it seemed far off.

She cracked the crutch against the side of his head.

He let go of Ida's hands and she struck him with

both bunched fists, cuffing him hard on the jaw. He barely felt it, took a step back from her and sat down with a thud on the wooden planks. He held both hands up in surrender. The world shrank.

She grabbed her crutches, white-faced and sobbing hysterically, and swung down the steps of the deck, making painstaking progress away across the shingle. Carl watched her tumble into it and clamber back up. The mist closed around her.

He bowed his head, aware of his life repeating itself with a sad reprise. He had remembered so much about Freya since Ida had first arrived on St Hauda's Land. Now the things he had not remembered came back to him. Ugly and insecure moments. When he had seen her lips working a deep kiss on another man on a dance floor, and the feeling when she had opened her eyes and met his fraught expression with a scowl. The time, after he had walked her home one night and they were both fuzzy with alcohol, when he tried to put his arm around her waist, and she gently patted it away, and he tried again, and she slapped it aside and stormed into her house. The words she had said to him that night, that he had inked out of his memory. He wondered how much of his life he had secretly blotted away in this fashion. How much of his world he could really be sure of.

He closed his eyes and listened to his heartbeat, getting older inside him. He heard Enghem Stead creaking. He felt the throb of his pulses, the slight wheeze that accompanied his breath these days.

After a long spell had passed, and the mist had begun to thin, he heard footsteps. He looked up to see Midas Crook, out of breath.

'What do you want?' asked Carl with bile.

He spluttered in surprise when Midas grabbed him by the collar and yanked him so hard it nearly budged him off the deck. 'Where is she, Carl?'

He swatted Midas away with a backhand punch, flipping him on to his back. 'What are you talking about?'

Midas clambered back up. 'Ida! What did you do with her?'

'Fuck off,' he said.

Midas leapt forward and grabbed Carl's collar again. 'Look at me,' he hissed, 'and tell me what you did to her.'

Carl realized he had never looked this particular Midas Crook in the eye. He had always put that down to the boy's tiresome shyness, but now he couldn't be sure. Because there was a raw, unpredictable look of desperation in Midas's taut grey irises and pinprick pupils. He had never seen anything like it, in father or son.

'I-I was not myself,' he said carefully, 'so . . . I tried to . . . She went outside.'

Midas spat out his disgust and raced from the house and into the white mist.

Ida surely couldn't have got far, but he was terrified she somehow had. The bitter cold made a blue haze on puddles before his sprinting feet shattered them into fountains of ice. Particles of snow explored the mist. There would be more soon, the heaviest of the winter. Clouds of it would lay themselves down to die on the earth. He cast his head left and right, imagining Ida under a frozen sheet of ice, snow and fog whitening her out of existence.

The snow swarmed against the translucent curtain of the mist, and suddenly, as if it were made from this interplay of weather, he saw something cantering through the haze. It sprang like a gazelle, its white legs as thin and supple as saplings. It paused and he stumbled after it, nearly catching it. There were packed muscles under its coat, muscles that rippled on its haunches as it bounded away again. He fancied he saw an elegant head and a flash of steely blue where its head met its neck.

He sprinted after it, tearing through a sudden screen of undergrowth that appeared out of the mist. His footprints crunched over those left by its pinched hoofs.

His path was suddenly blocked by a toppled tree, blooms of fungi covering it like cork roses. The creature leapt, cleared the dead trunk in one bound, and vanished into the mist on the other side. Midas jogged to a halt in its wake and stared around him. Somehow he had been led into thick woodland. The fog was thinnest here, perhaps absorbed by the trees that stood close together with interlocked arms, cracked bark and hollow trunks.

Then he saw the animals.

A robin tweeting on a branch was paling from chestnut brown to fine white. Its legs became white wires and its eyes became hailstones. Its breast remained a red thumbprint for a second, then that also faded, through pink to crisp white.

It fluttered to another tree where it snatched up a white spider in its beak. Moments before, the spider had been an invisible brown against the bark. A white squirrel, which had been hopping through the loam, darted up the tree and sat on a bough, clasping its paws as if in prayer.

Further up ahead, someone lay in a coat powdered with snow. He rushed towards her.

'Ida?' he hissed, 'Ida, can you hear me?'

She opened her eyes. Her teeth rattled. 'Midas, I'm so sorry.'

'Don't say stupid things. God. Are you hurt?'

The winter was inside his coat and under his shirt, frosting his lungs, but even in the freezing anxiety of the moment the fact that he had found her made his heart hot. 'Put my anorak on. Don't lie down or it'll get wet and you'll get even colder.'

'Don't leave me.'

He helped her up so she could lean on him. She was as cold and heavy as ice, her dragging feet leaving a dented trail in the snow. It took them some time to make their painstaking way back to the car over unkind roots and spongy earth. They followed the footprints he had left in snow or mud, until Enghem Stead appeared like a mirage out of the mist, although all he cared about was his muddy little car, parked nearby. There was no sign of Carl. Her feet clinked on the car door as he helped her in, but by the time he had propped her on the back seat a tinge of colour had returned to her cheeks, and this made him glance up at the opaque sky, grateful it had held back its heavier snows. He got in beside her and closed the door.

'Sh-shit it's cold,' she said.

'I know. I'm sorry.'

She nodded drowsily. 'Your coat. Thanks.'

'It'll warm up in the car.'

'Hug me.'

'I . . . I'm sorry?'

She opened her eyes a crack. They couldn't focus. Her irises were ash between red eyelids. 'Put your arms around me.'

Carefully, he reached around her with both arms so his fingers locked across her back.

'You have to squeeze,' she whispered, 'or it's not a hug.'

He squeezed gently. They leant like that against the seat for a while, the warmth from each other's bodies sustaining them until the car's heater took over. 'We'd best get going,' said Midas, pulling away.

She whispered something he couldn't quite hear. He bowed his head to her lips to listen. 'You have to be bolder,' she whispered, '*please*.' Then she pushed her face into his. All his features seemed to spasm and twitch as she squeezed his lips with hers and touched his teeth with her tongue. Although her skin was freezing, her salty breath and saliva were piping hot. He couldn't move his own lips while she kissed him. He could only jerk them open and shut like a wooden dummy. But to his amazement, it felt good.

CHAPTER 33

Midas was doing everything he could do to appear natural and confident as he helped Ida into his house, even though her whole body was pressed up against his and he could feel with his chest the shape of her ribs and breasts. She held him as he helped her into the sitting room, setting her down in an armchair.

That evening, when she'd changed, it struck him how unhealthy she was. The shadows cast by her high cheekbones had climbed into darkness around her eyes. Her lips were chafed and her hair organized in an artless tie. She wore a knitted jersey and a long grey skirt that made her legs look like a chunk of flint.

Midas puffed up the sofa cushions, on which he planned to sleep tonight. 'The weatherman says tomorrow will be brighter. We can start finding a way to fix you again.'

'That's kind of you, Midas. But really . . .'

'We'll think of something. Some new lead will crop up.'

'I'm sure we will, but as far as I'm concerned tomorrow can wait as long as for ever.'

'Okay. You take my bed, I'll sleep down here.'

'Will you help me up the stairs?'

He felt the soft delicacy of her fingers as he took her hands and lifted her from the armchair. Her waist was thin and firm. Being so close to her still made him tense, but it was tempered by a nervy excitement. Her legs scraped on the wooden stairs as he hauled her up them one by one. Then he dashed back down, grabbed her things and rushed them up to her, finding her leaning on the bedroom wall.

'I'm too cold to get changed,' she said.

He helped her on to the bed and tucked the duvet over her.

She grabbed his collar and yanked him on to her. Her lips pressed his, springy and desperate. When he tried to speak she kissed harder. One of her hands sank into his hair and her nails scratched his scalp. Her other hand ran down his spine. He was immobile atop her not because he was petrified but because he was enthralled. After a while her kisses slowed and they parted lips.

He battled with his tongue to be the first to say something. He managed, '*Wuhhmmm.*'

'Kick off your shoes, Midas.'

He did as he was told. She started to kiss him again, grabbing his thigh and driving in her fingertips. His hands lay limp at his sides. *Oh God*, he thought, happily. One of her hands got under his vest, then scraped past his tight belt . . . He made a gargling noise. 'Relax,' she hushed, unbuttoning his shirt. 'What's the matter?'

He shook his head. 'Nothing. Honestly.'

She removed his shirt and he felt the first rumours of relaxation: muscles turning to jelly. Instead of lying like a toppled statue he flopped like a rag doll. His lungs filled up with Ida. She led his hand up her silky waist. He inched his fingers over her flesh, over the grooves between ribs. She snatched his hand and pulled it under her bra where it seized up again like a gauntlet. She kneaded his fingers. They were supple again. There was soft tissue under his thumb.

She slipped off her top and unfastened her bra. For a moment the motes of shadow her breasts made hypnotized him, but then he noticed tears in her eyes and rolled off her. She blinked the tears away, but he'd noticed the marks on her stomach.

The flesh around her navel was patterned with swirls of cod-white skin. They reached up from her waist and traced over her belly, drawing a whirlpool around her belly button. They accentuated the pitted texture of skin until it looked more like citrus rind. Each pore treasured a speck that sparkled in the moonlight. They were the blueprints for glass, a boast of transformation to come. He wondered, terrified, what alterations glass had worked beneath the cover of underwear, dresses and skirts.

He was still staring when her hand pressed against his groin. She looked at him for approval. He nodded. She removed her skirt. He gulped.

'What?'

'Nothing.'

The skin of her hips had turned entirely to the dead white of the marks on her belly. Her legs were colourless all over. The inflammation caused by the poultices had mostly died down but the skin was left a rubbery white. Towards her knees the skin seemed translucent. The pink of tendons showed under a membrane of glass. In the transparent lower reaches of her shins, bits of muscle remained like confetti wilting in watery gutters. And on the outside of her right knee, where she had bruised it at Enghem Stead, there was a patch of glass ahead of the rest of the transformation, set into her skin like a little window. It offered a view of crystallized bones like specimens in a jar.

She pulled him back on top of her. It was impossible to feel the flurry of experiences at once. The heat of lips; the feathery weight of her hair; the flash of veined white in an eyeball; chest rising and falling. She swallowed. The fine soft skin of her neck. The tightness of her stomach against his. The cushioning of her breasts. The coldness of her knees. Her inflexible joints. The dead weight of her legs.

At first he thought her pinched expression was one of pleasure, but when her gasps reached a tortured pitch he slowed down. She covered his face with her hands.

'It hurts,' she whispered, 'like there are knives in my pelvis.'

He withdrew and lay lightly against her.

'I think there's glass inside me, Midas.'

She gasped and clutched her stomach.

'Ida!'

'I'm okay, I'm okay.'

In a patch of milky translucence on her hip he could see something maroon throbbing . . . Was that an organ? Her colon, her bladder, her womb? Her torso, arms and face glistened heavily with cold sweat. Amethyst-coloured veins strained on the insides of her thighs. She looked ancient and stretched. In an involuntary movement he reached out and grabbed a handful of her hair.

It was the touch that made him realize he loved her. Warmth from her scalp. Grease from her locks. He entwined his hand in her hair. It shrank through his moving fingers like sand. They lay together for a long time. Somewhere outside, a dog barked. He could barely believe he had lived so long without wanting to touch. Photography had made him forget the necessity of this feeling.

She reached over and stroked his cheek. He flinched, then relaxed. 'Midas, I want something.' She took a deep breath and stared at the ceiling. 'I can't stand being uncertain any more.'

He waited. Realized that you didn't always have to speak.

She closed her eyes. 'I want to stay with you for however long there is left.'

The barking dog outside fell silent. Midas thought he could hear snowflakes touching down on the windowsill, and somewhere in the house a bubble gulping through a water pipe. They lay in this quiet until he heard her breathing slow down. He rolled his head on to its side and saw her eyes moving rapidly beneath closed eyelids. He stayed awake, thinking how this moment was like the trapped time in a photograph. The moment would stay for ever in stasis. After relishing this for a while, he dozed off to sleep.

CHAPTER 34

The snow was melting in the bogs. Minuscule snow fleas, made dozy by winter, unsealed their chambers of ice and emerged into a morning's sunlight, preceded by probing forelegs. A lone otter took a cold bath in a pool that had been frozen a week before. The blue of the sky soaked into the unhealthy yellows of the reeds and lilies, turning them muted green. A trio of fish that had been locked in river ice tested their fins and began to swim again.

Henry swept books and insect drawings off his desk and placed the pregnant cow gently in the warm nest of an old bobble hat. She nestled in the fabric to rest her swollen belly while he prepared his things. First he set up an electric heater with red filament aglow on the desk. Then he took a leather wallet from a drawer and opened it, revealing the set of doll-size forceps he'd especially fashioned out of tweezers and pins. The cow moaned and drove her face into the wool of the bobble hat, her tail swishing against her flanks.

He drew the hat gently closer and slid his thumb under her throat and between her front legs to prop her on to her feet. She managed to stand, but her wings kept twitching and needed to be kept clear of Henry's midwifery. He had a special harness for the occasion, which he fastened lightly around her shoulders. Attached to the harness was a simple card partition that kept her wings spread and safely away from her rear.

He closed his eyes and calmed his heartbeat. There had been accidents in the past, especially in the earlier days, but most of the births in recent years had been a success. And yet . . . He had been distracted from the herd of late by thoughts of Evaline and Ida, and he didn't want that to cause mistakes during such a delicate operation. He took a sip of gin and let its taste set him back at ease. He selected a pair of forceps and held it between thumb and forefinger, concentrating on the metal until his hand was steady. Then with utmost precision, he widened the tiny pincers and slid them into the cow's rear. You couldn't judge the forceps' grip on the calf within, you had to follow a kind of gut feeling about how much pressure to apply. Holding his breath, he drew the calf out and laid it in the light. Placenta drooled behind it. The calf was cocooned in a yellow birthing sac that stretched as it tested its limbs. Its mother, panting with relief, staggered around and began to lick the sac from its head, revealing a black curly head with a white spot on its nose. Across its back, hard to distinguish from the sac, were the lilac membranes of its wings. Henry sat back beaming, folded his hands in his lap and watched.

It always moved him, this licking away the afterbirth. It always hammered home the point that passion wasn't exclusively human. It always marked its physicality. He toasted the new mother with his gin. Tenderness and emotion went hand in hand with bits of gut and blood.

He wished he had experienced it for himself.

It was odd what a little interaction could do for you. He left some food out for the moth-winged cow and went to the bathroom. He scrubbed himself at the sink, then went downstairs to eat some stale soda bread, in the hope that it would settle his stomach. He was going to drive to Martyr's Pitfall. Two or three times in the past he had gone there, but he had only got as far as to spy on Evaline. Each time he assured himself that the woman he had known remained absent from the frail body he observed in secret. Not once on those visits had he announced himself, but he planned to do so today. He tried to iron a shirt but couldn't remember how. He was agitated and ironed heavy creases into the old fabric. Wearing it anyway, he poured himself a tumbler of gin and drank it hastily before setting off.

Driving towards Martyr's Pitfall he felt his nerves like war drums, a feeling increasing as Lomdendol Tor's blunt head grew nearer, capped with dull seams of snow. He crossed the zigzagging bridges on to Lomdendol Island and felt the tor's shadow like a bad smell. These lower slopes of the giant hill were clustered with weedy trees whose bark was starred with dead fungi. Between them you could spot the austere fronts of houses and retirement homes. He noticed that many more were boarded up since last he came, their FOR SALE signs fallen down and covered in mud and tyre tracks. The younger folk of St Hauda's Land had left with the whaling trade and the people who remained were sunk into gloom and inactivity. This brought him a smile, since it helped him imagine the archipelago inhabited by moth-winged cattle alone.

Evaline's helper, Christiana, answered the door and of course didn't know him. He'd forgotten he'd need to get past her to speak to Evaline. He stood for a moment ignoring her politely concerned enquiries ('How can I help you? Are you lost?'). Then he leapt into the house, dancing past her and bolting down the hallway, flinging open the sitting-room door and jigging on the spot as if fighting off gnats. Evaline stood and shushed the protesting Christiana with a finger to her lips.

'Uh,' licking his lips and tasting the gin. 'Uh . . .'

'H-Henry Fuwa,' she said.

He had been so preoccupied, he realized, with finding the courage to get here that he had not thought what to say when he arrived.

The room took on a distant quality. He was within an arm's reach of Evaline, yet he felt as if a glass barrier stood between them. He could no

322

more reach for her than he could reach for her tea tray or crouch to touch the carpet.

She had begun to cry, he realized now. Her default expression was so close to tears that it took only the subtlest of muscle movement for the ducts themselves to open. Nor did her posture of clasped hands and sloping shoulders change. Really only her cheeks differed. They shone like a bog stone shines where a new brook is born.

So much had happened since they had last seen each other, but only time gave it weight. Life had been routine since the moment he first set eyes on her. Comfortable, yes, but no particular day stood out from the others. The cumulative importance of all those years was nothing compared to their single day together with the dragonflies on the river-bank. Yet somehow those compressed years were responsible for this invisible barrier dividing Evaline's sitting room into two, apportioning that side to her and this side to him. It was the most tangible thing in the house. He reached up and could feel it in the air. Their faces were no more than two feet apart, but this was as close as his hand could get. She raised a hand of her own, so that their vertical palms were inches away. Their fingers were separated by a pane of air only as thick as a thumbnail, but he couldn't so much as smell her perfume through it, couldn't feel her breath.

They stayed posed like this until Henry's elbow ached, and when he lowered his hand Evaline copied him like a reflection. She returned to her place in the chair, fixed her eyes on the view of her snowy garden, and took her cold teacup in her hands. She held it to her lips and sipped. He exited quietly, shutting each door – to her room, her hallway, her house – with the infinitesimal care he had learnt through years of tending moth-winged cattle.

Outside, Lomdendol Tor's shadow muffled everything. There was no traffic, and a cat in the road padded into a snowy hedge, careful not to crumple any leaves. His car snorted at the silence as he left Martyr's Pitfall. He would return to moth-winged cattle and the burr and clickety-clack of swamp sounds, and he wouldn't come back here again.

CHAPTER 35

On the rooftops of Ettinsford, melting snow
let clean patches of slate emerge, plasmic
bodies of light agleam where furred white
had been for weeks. At St Hauda's Church, an icicle
that had formed hanging from the nose of the statue
of the saint dripped away into the brass folds of his
robes. The Ettinsford strait swelled as water courses
gurgled down the park slopes to join it. Cars drove
slowly on wet roads, headlights turning cobbles into
light bulbs. In Midas's yard, a blackbird sprang back
and forth under the gutter, then was hit by a bomb
of snow. It squawked and indignantly shook its
feathers. Droplets fell from gutters and pinged off
the dustbin lid, where trickles of water felt their
way indecisively across the tin. Lumps of slushy
snow fell free of the trees overhanging his fence,
sending shivers through shrubs.

Midas hummed to himself as milk to make hot
chocolate simmered in a saucepan on the hob. His
whole body felt cleaner this morning, as if something
toxic had been wrung out of him. It wasn't sex that
had done it. It was something outside of his body,
outside of Ida's. A collision of sorts.

That morning he'd taken five minutes just to climb out of bed because he was so careful not to disturb the sleeping Ida. His bed had always been a functional object to enter when sleepy and exit when rested, but Ida's head and bare shoulders on its pillows transformed it. Her hand curled up at her chin and her pale hair bunched at her neck were ornamental in ways the glass parts of her body, hidden under bed sheets, could never be.

He had taken the battery out of his clock to ensure its ticking wouldn't disturb her. He had prayed for silence from the melting snow outside. When a car honked and her eyelids fluttered and he realized she had to wake at some point, he determined to make it a peaceful awakening. Hence the stealthy breakfast he was preparing for her now.

The doorbell rang. Irked by the interruption, he poured out the hot milk. But it was probably just Gustav and Denver and they'd understand that this morning was one he wanted to keep private.

He found Christiana on the doorstep, fiddling with the cuffs of her coat sleeves. The road behind her had been salted, and mushy snow made it look like an ash waste.

'Hello,' he said.

'Mr Crook, I've come to bring you a few of your things. From your mother.'

'My mother doesn't have any of my things.'

Christiana looked irritated. She turned and headed back to her car while Midas watched. He stepped outside and shut the door behind him so the cold couldn't trespass upstairs and wake Ida. He stuffed his hands into his armpits.

Her car boot was loaded with cardboard boxes.

'They're not mine,' he called, knowing exactly whose they were.

'But it's time you had them. They're gathering dust.'

'Good. They can gather rot for all I care.'

'That's up to you now.'

'What's brought this about?'

'Your mother's just ... getting older, Mr Crook.'

'Please don't call me that.'

'That's your name, isn't it?' She began to unload the boxes on to the pavement.

'I'll destroy them.'

'Fine.'

He threw his hands in the air, but soon she had finished unloading the boxes and was getting back in her car. She drove away, her tyres churning up trenches in the mush of snow. A minute or two later he trudged out to the pavement and began to carry the boxes inside.

Before he died his father had halved everything he owned, packed this half neatly and taken the other half on to the boat. Midas expected these boxes to be full of the same books, journals, diaries and papers that had fuelled the boat's quick flames. Only they were too light. Each was labelled neatly with a packing date, in his father's handwriting. By the time he had carried them inside, the hot

327

chocolate he had prepared for Ida was already getting cold.

Ida woke and stretched. Getting out of bed was becoming harder. She considered calling to Midas for help but pictured it and felt pathetic. Instead she dragged herself across the carpet to the mirror.

She lifted her T-shirt the way Saffron Jeuck had in Emiliana's video. The trails of hardened skin on her belly looked worse this morning. They had creased her flesh as she slept, leaving red lines running vertically towards her breasts.

She turned one leg to see into the patch of glass on the outside of her knee. Through it she could see squirts of blood still shooting over the cross-section of her kneecap, its marrow bubbled purple and grey like a chicken bone.

She sneezed into her hands, then had to wipe them on her T-shirt because she couldn't get to the tissues in time. She felt disgusting. She took off the T-shirt and tossed it on to Midas's laundry pile. The motion sent stabbing pains up her sides and into her armpits.

The glass was speeding up. It had spread so fast in the last week that she believed were she to sit like this at the mirror for an hour observing herself, she'd see skin lose its lustre and translucence become clearer. The glittering marks that had made a whirlpool shape on her tummy would soon fill in, so that her whole belly would be glazed, its skin rubbery. Then it would start to turn transparent, and not long after that things like her kidneys and intestines would turn to glass. She didn't like to think what would happen to her when they did.

She dwelt for a moment on a memory from girlhood: smearing her tummy with a spiral of glue, then tipping a whole pot of opal glitter across it.

She stretched for her crutches and pulled herself around the bed to the window, twitching back the net curtain. It was Ettinsford's market day and shoppers trod through the melting snow, headed to and from the stalls. A pair of schoolboys in tatty blazers furtively shared a cigarette. Two elderly ladies watched them from the cover of a postbox, muttering darkly to each other. Ida suddenly felt ancient and decrepit. She let go of the net curtain and covered her face with her hands, grimacing silently into them.

In the end, the thing that made her capable of tying up her hair, putting on a fresh T-shirt and skirt and battling down the stairs, was the man below and the isolation of his lifestyle. With Carl gone and Henry Fuwa right all along about the impossibility of cures, she felt a bittersweet relief in the loneliness of this little terraced house. It had few visitors, no television, hardly any view. It was just her and Midas in here, tucked away from the world. Here she could turn quietly into glass, with only love to distract her.

She found Midas bunched up at the kitchen table, covering a photograph with the flat of his palm.

'Midas ... Good morning ... Please don't pretend everything's all right.'

He lifted his hand off the picture and held it up

for her to see. It was the lone photo of his father, pulled off the wall. The face had been stabbed open by a pencil.

'You said that was your only copy.'

'It is. Do you know why I did it?'

She waited.

'To see if I'd feel bad. And of course I didn't.'

'There are boxes stacked in the hallway.'

'They're his, of course. My mother's helper brought them here this morning.'

'They're your father's?'

'Yes.'

'Are you going to tell me what's in them?'

'I haven't looked.'

'But . . . Midas . . . I would have thought . . .'

He flung his hands up in the air. 'Thought I'd be so stupid as to look? *God*, Ida! Each one is a fucking Pandora's box!'

'That's the kind of thing your father would say.'

She hoped making that comparison would shake him up, but it only made him look gloomier. If she had her mobility she'd spring across and kiss him violently, but by the time she'd lurched around the table the moment didn't feel right. 'Look,' she said, taking his hand instead (the skin was cold, the fingers limp), 'I remember when my mum died some of our friends went through her things for us, so all we had to confront were the important bits. Why don't I get rid of the boxes for you?'

He murmured something and shuffled about in his seat, staring at the kitchen floor.

'Was that a yes or a no?'

'You can get rid of them if you promise that's all you'll do. Only . . . your curiosity will get the better of you. You'll open them. You won't resist telling me what's in them.'

'I'll resist.' But he was right, she suspected.

'No, Ida . . . they'll stay closed. Maybe I'll lock them up somewhere. I never use my sitting room anyway.'

'That's ridiculous.'

'You think so?'

'Are you snapping at me, Midas?'

'*Yes*. Because *you* brought all this about.'

Her fists clenched. 'You can either apologize, or I can just leave.'

'Sorry. I didn't mean that. I just—'

'Are you going to let yourself be beaten by this . . . by this damned feeling things should never change, however fucked up they become? If you're angry at me for making your life uncertain, you might as well grow a moustache and put on some fucking spectacles and *become* this figment of your imagination you think you despise.'

'If it was imagination alone I'd—'

'No! All you are is the body sitting in that chair! Your dad isn't with you, Midas, not even in spirit. You keep going back to him so you don't have to take responsibility for the things you despise in yourself. I've *got* to be blunt with you because there's no time!'

He swallowed. 'Come on, Ida. There'll be time for us.'

She rolled her eyes.

'Ida, wait, where are you going?' He trotted after her.

She was already among the boxes. She tore savagely at the tape that held the first one shut. With his knuckles in his mouth Midas watched her turn the open box upside down and shake its contents on to the carpet. 'You can't . . .'

She ripped open another box and upended it. Dust and clutter fell in a shower.

One by one she tore through each package. When she picked up the final box she hesitated. 'This is your last chance.'

He stepped closer and took it from her. He shook it experimentally, but it didn't rattle. Everything would be compactly arranged inside. He picked off the tape. Smelled the old air as he peeled back the seal. Then he screwed up his eyes and turned the box upside down. Amid a brief rush of falling objects, something bounced off his toe. He looked down and saw his father's spare glasses spilled from their case.

Seeing the mess of objects on the floor, he wondered now what he'd expected. A morning suit, which in the box had been neatly folded, lay mangled on the carpet. A yellow rose, dried to a crisp, was still pinned in its lapel. A digital watch had stopped at 2:32 p.m. A toy car lay on its side. Midas gingerly picked it up. The metal was cold and the wheels jammed. *Midas Crook* was handwritten in a boy's script (not his own) on its underside. He cupped it in his palm. It weighed next to nothing. These items were just his father's leftovers. He felt no fear of them (he paused for a moment to check he hadn't missed it). No books, no papers, no communiqué from the afterlife. Just . . . junk. He looked to Ida, who was smiling proudly. He realized he had expected some kind of pharaoh's curse but he had not been struck down. He smiled back. It was not so hard, this bravery.

He couldn't stay upright any more. With a sigh of relief he sat down and lay back, among his father's old things and their dust.

'What are you going to do with them?' she asked after a while.

'Throw them over a cliff,' he murmured.

She cackled.

'Sorry,' he said.

'What for?'

'I hadn't meant for this morning to be like this.' He got up. 'There's something else, too.'

He went to the cupboard under the stairs and removed a miniature safe. He spun its lock through several combinations, hesitated when it clicked at the right one, then yanked it open with grim determination. He pulled a book from within, as if it were a blockage from a wastepipe.

'What is it?'

It was bound in black leather, with a grey ribbon stitched into the spine as a bookmark.

'His filthy book. First draft. Handwritten.

Passed down to me.' He grinned. 'Never. Even. Opened.'

'Good,' she said, 'that's good.'

His father woke in the night, heart rattling in his chest, and stumbled into the bathroom to cough into the sink. In the colourless dark he saw only grey fluid sliding grudgingly down the plughole, but he could taste blood and bile and when he pulled the light cord he saw spots of red in the basin, speckled with glass crystals the size of pinheads.

Unable to sleep, he went to the attic to finish taping and stacking his boxes. Then he lay with his hands over his eyes, surrounded by scrunched-up balls of paper: botched attempts at written explanations. All of his words were taped away in that other set of boxes downstairs, packed with his books and papers ready for flame. For a moment a smile floundered on his lips. He enjoyed the idea that life had been halved. His bookish, academic life had been severed from this life boxed in the attic, this remnant collection of experience and feeling.

He ran his cold hands across the surface of his body, feeling the bony arms, the smooth bald scalp, his cock and balls (thinking of their short effort in the creation of his son).

He tried to worry about what Midas would think of him. He didn't care about worrying for Evaline (she'd find that other man, no doubt, that man who mailed her dead dragonflies) but he wanted to worry for the boy. Yet . . . every time he tried to he

334

felt the sharp star of glass nuzzling his diaphragm, the pressure of blood forced through his veins. Then he felt fearful and knew what would happen to his body. He had done his research. He did not want to leave a petrified statue for others to gawp over.

At last he wrote *Dear Midas*, and upon writing it felt the other words he wanted to say flowing down his arm and into his pen-hand, as if these first two were the bung keeping the others at bay.

He wasn't sure if the Midas he was addressing was his son, or himself, or some amalgam of generations. At times he wondered if it were Evaline he were writing to, or his own gentle father with whom he had ended on such bad terms. Or perhaps his austere mother, or someone as yet a stranger to him: the offspring of his son, who he would never know, or a daughter-in-law, who he would never know. The only thing for certain was that writing had never felt like this: it was confessional, personal, where it had been a procession of theories and criticisms before. Pages filled with black lines like convoys of ants, and even when his heart burned and weighed like molten rock he managed to keep the words flowing. They ended abruptly, but they were exact. He knew he need not redraft these pages. When he tried to put down his pen, the muscles of his hand had cramped in their writing position.

He had written almost exclusively about the glass blooming in his heart. About the empty noise of his heartbeat, like a wineglass struck by a fork. About the pain he experienced when labouring up a flight of stairs, or walking too briskly down the street to buy a newspaper. The same pain that stabbed him whenever his pulse was set racing. A stroke from his wife's hand could do it, could make his chest fill with spikes. A photograph of a library that his boy had left as a gift on his study desk had done it, had wrung his oesophagus and dug claws in his lungs.

He leant back in his chair and wondered what should now become of these new pages. It was plainly too late to hand them over: it risked the formation of an emotional moment, and such a thing might deter him from his course of action. No, a better idea had already come to him. He tapped his forefinger along the spines on one bookshelf until he found the first draft of *On Beauty*, which he'd had bound in leather that was dark as black treacle. It was useless returning to bed, for now both the pain in his chest and his excitement were keeping him a-buzz. He put on his tweed jacket and corduroys and went to the car with *On Beauty* in one hand and his newly scrawled letter in the other. Books. Reading. Magic of pen and paper. His boy had yet to discover it, but perhaps reading this letter would be the turning point. He'd written of everything that had terrified him and more. He had described the X-rays, the moment he first confronted that dark, transparent cartography of himself. He believed this letter would be the connection between father and son he had always dreamt would spark, since the day the boy was concocted.

He drove out under the stars, along dead-of-night roads, all the way to Glamsgallow. He parked outside the little college bookbinder, the letter and the leather-bound draft readied on his lap: waiting for daybreak, opening time, a chance to set things right.

Midas and Ida drove south towards Gurmton, picking up the high, cliff-top road. A fog was heaped on the sea, making it hard to tell how high they were. When they parked at a deserted view-point and Midas dragged the boxes to the very cusp of the land, he looked as if he were standing on the banks of a lake of clouds. Puffed white pillows stretched to the horizon. It was more heavenly than he would have liked.

The first thing he pulled from the boxes was his father's morning suit. He held it up to the wind, which grabbed it before he had even let go, whipping the trousers out of his grip then stealing the jacket. The clothes flailed away into the fog. His father's spectacles followed, catching in the air like a spinning top. A set of whalebone poker dice, rattling away into the clouds. An old neckerchief he had never seen his father wear, ducking down through the vapour like a waterlogged butterfly. Piece by piece he let his father's remains ghost away, and when they had all been tossed over the cliff into the clouds, he hurled the cardboard boxes after them.

Finally, there was the book, which Ida handed to him with some ceremony. For a moment he had second thoughts and wondered whether, if he could bear to decipher its academic scribble, he might somehow know why its author had abandoned life. But as he held it in his hands, ran a finger over the cover, was careful not to bend the spine as he opened it for the first time on to still crisp pages, he had a vivid memory of his father performing the exact same ritual motions. He ripped the pages from their binding and chucked them furiously into the air. They battled the wind like terrified creatures, flapping against each other.

Then an unexpected thing happened: he yelled involuntarily. 'No!' was what he yelled. He reached for the madly dancing pages, his father's weird script jiggling in the sky, but they were already blowing far out of reach, away across clouds. He tripped forward as he lurched after them, and Ida had to grab him to stop him from blundering over the edge. She yanked him back from the cliff and he lost his footing and fell sideways towards the grass, grabbing at her arm and accidentally pulling her with him. She shrieked as she fell, but his body cushioned her landing, and although she puffed and wheezed for a few minutes, she couldn't have been too distraught, for she then laid her cheek against his and remained on top of him, their faces pressed together looking seaward, at an endless terrain of clouds.

They lay like that for he didn't know how long, him marvelling at how light her body was, except for down around her knees, where he could feel the way the glass bound her to the ground.

Then he felt a tear against his face. Alarmed, he reached to wipe her cheek. Her skin was soft and dry. She smiled. It had only been a raindrop. Another plopped into the grass beside them. Pillars of the sea mist had risen into the air above them and were expanding into clouds of rain. Ida, carefully, sat herself up. He got to his feet, helped her to hers, and was leading her back to the car when she stopped him with a gentle tap on the hip from one of her crutches. She pointed with it to a spot in the grass where a crumpled page of paper was caught. The rain tip-toed around it.

He remembered how he had choked up as the pages of the book had flown into the clouds. He approached this remaining page nervously, then snatched it up.

The rain and moisture on the grass had blurred the ink, spreading every letter into a watery blotch of blue and black. It was indecipherable, apart from the first two words, set apart at the top left of the page.

Dear Midas.

It brought a lump to his throat. By now the other pages would be miles away, through the opaque mist, but it didn't matter what was written on them – his father's effort and secrecy were enough. If the words were hurtful, his father would have spoken them freely, never going to such covert trouble. Midas, very deliberately, screwed up the page. But he didn't throw it after the others. He pressed it into his shirt pocket, turned to Ida, and dredged up a smile that turned genuine when she pressed her lips to his.

Unlike the southern coast where Midas and Ida now lay, the eastern shores of the archipelago were clear, and the cliff tops overlooked a cove of spiky rocks and wrecked ships. Henry Fuwa sat with legs dangling over the cliff and the wind flapping his trouser legs. He took Midas Crook's glass heart from its carrier bag, which the wind dragged at once high into the air, scrunched up and revolved on the spot before puffing out like a blowfish to send soaring towards the rocking horizon.

He laid the heart on his lap. The colour of his trousers shimmered through it.

'You and I rarely met,' he said, 'but even so I have tried hard to understand you.'

Puffins hollered on a distant pyramid of rocks.

'I realize now it hasn't been *you* that's nagged me through the years, but what was *happening* to you.'

He tapped the glass heart with his fingernails.

'Of course, you handled it badly, took it out on others. Never faced it. So I'd hate you to think I kept this out of sympathy. Your hold on me was just . . . A delay while I tried to understand. Now that I do . . . I've realized what a coward you were in the end. For killing yourself rather than fighting. Because . . . *What if?*'

He picked up the cold glass heart and judged its weight on his palms. He could sense the cliff drop through his wellington boots. The wind swept back his hair, smattered his face with sleet and plied his lips from his gums.

He thought about the body from the bog. 'You stopped hoping, didn't you, a very long time ago, that there was a "what if"? So *what if*, even had you transformed entirely into glass, you could turn back again?'

He didn't believe in it himself. But his point was that there was little more than belief to be had.

He casually tossed the heart over the cliff. It plummeted. It smashed in time with enraged waves. An explosion of froth twinkled below as a thousand studs of glass and water expanded and shrank in a final vapid heartbeat, before pattering into the sea.

He sighed. His thoughts were full of orbiting Evalines. 'I don't think there's a *what if* either,' he said, 'but I still hope to find one, somewhere.'

CHAPTER 36

With Midas out, working at Catherine's, Ida didn't find his home so cosy. She realized she was simply awaiting his return and decided to get out of the house. She laboured uphill against snowflakes wending their way down, and came to the nearest place she could think of to sit undisturbed. The trees in the grave-yard of the church of Saint Hauda reached clawed arms towards their brethren in the woods further uphill.

The only soul in the church, she sat on a cushioned pew and breathed the smell of old candle wax. A stained-glass window portrayed the heavenly host impassively observing Saint Hauda's flight across the Ettinsford strait, carried over the water by a flock of sparrows. The colour had faded from the glass and it was lit now, as she supposed was inevitable, in monochrome. White flowers bloomed in a vase on the altar. She presumed the flowers had come from Catherine's.

A vicar crept from a vestry door into the church hall, swiped the hymn numbers from their board and vanished again. A bible lay on the shelf attached to the back of the pew in front of her. She slid it gently aside and laid, in its place, her head on the wood.

As a kid she had witnessed a landslide. A cliff giving in to the water. She had been picnicking with her mother and father on the opposite side of the bay where it happened, looking on as the brilliant sunlight found the warm gold in the cliffs. It had been a calm day and the sea was flat and azure. Then suddenly the rocks across the bay were sliding seaward, as if they had been chopped up by a cheese wire. Cubic boulders came free of the coast in slow motion, trailing a yellow glitter of sandstone met by a spray of froth in midair. In the space of thirty seconds the shape of the cliff had changed to a mangle of rubble and grass, and the sea stroked over the amber stone the land had given up on.

She had sometimes wondered what had happened invisibly to the insides of that cliff. What hairline cracks and hidden chasms had stealthily prepared it for its final surrender. In the last few days there had been aches in parts of her body that had never ached before. A pain in the inside of a rib. A pain up the length of her spine. A pain in her inside thigh that had felt the size of a cavern.

She looked up at the other stained-glass windows in the church. A variety of saints had all faded out of colour, just like Saint Hauda had. It would take someone with biblical knowledge on the level of her father's to know which figure was which; to

Ida they were all impassive. Beautiful ghosts. A virginal woman with an urn was nearest. Looking through her face and robes, Ida could make out the motion of a tree in the graveyard beyond, shaking its branches in the wind.

She shook herself, then; struggled up and left the church on her crutches, the echoes of their placements tapping off the roof above her.

Midas spent his morning shift driving bouquet deliveries around Ettinsford and its surrounding hamlets. The last delivery on his list took him up to the granite pillared ridgeway past Tinterl. The ridge was a spine of stubby hilltops leading all the way across the islands to Lomdendol Tor itself. He hadn't been up here since his father's funeral and had been surprised when the order came in. The address given stuck in his mind from childhood: the uninhabitable crags around Wodenghyll Force, a vehement waterfall the size of five houses whose spray announced its presence like the smoke from a bonfire. Driving uphill from Ettinsford, it seemed that every crack in every boulder bled a trickle of crystal water fuelled by the heavy snowfall. Unlike most things on the islands, the grey rock-faces and barren, crow-hunched slopes were as large as the ones he remembered from childhood. Minor falls blew from rock-faces into deep pools, splashing water across dented roads.

The waterfalls of Tinterl ridgeway had never endeared themselves to tourists. Even the gushing

fury of Wodenghyll Force couldn't draw the island's
visitors away from beaches and marine life. It was as
dramatic as any great work of nature, but it lacked
grandeur in its savagery. On the old island map of
his father's, Wodenghyll had the longest piece of
annotation.

a howl echoing off hillsides.
saw thrush once sweep through water then crushed
– bones bent and scrunched.
here nature is self-loathing – every jag of rock
an eyesore.
good.

Creepers and juicy black mosses had grown across
the viewpoint above Wodenghyll Force. Midas's tyres
burst them like slugs as he parked. The bouquet sat
beside him in the car, a narrow sheaf of sticks and
flaky petals. Spray from the Force greased the sky,
but he could still see a great distance across the
island's cloud-logged woodland. He couldn't see a
single house to which he could deliver the bouquet.

There was, however, a familiar car: the only other
vehicle parked at the viewpoint.

Carl Maulsen slouched in the driver's seat chewing
his fingernails. Midas's first thought was to call the
police, but there was something demolished about
Carl's posture. The start of a scruffy silver beard
hung from his chin. Midas awaited the intimidated
subordination he'd felt in the past around Carl, but
it didn't materialize. He walked over and tapped

lightly on the window, enjoying this new confidence, what Ida said was bravery. Carl hesitated before winding the window down.

'What's this?' asked Midas.

'An apology.'

The back seats were piled up with rugs and pillows, a rucksack and a suitcase. Body odour wafted from the window.

'Have you been sleeping in there?'

Carl opened the passenger door. 'I can't go back to the cottage. Hop in? Please?'

Midas shook his head. He'd leant closer to hear what Carl had said. Every other time they'd met, Carl's voice had been bold and treacle-rich. Now the spaces in his sentences were full of the falls' fury.

'I'm going away, Midas. Perhaps to America. Away from these islands, that's for sure.'

Midas was silent.

'I think places take hold of us and we become mere parts of the landscape, taking on its quirks and follies. There are places on the mainland – perhaps you are too young to understand this – I can't return to without feeling, without *becoming*, things I had thought tidied up and finished off. My university campus, a particular beach, a certain cinema. Just because of Freya Ingmarsson. She's why I moved to St Hauda's Land, don't you see? Even though she was already dead when I moved here. She was a sun and boats person and this place was nothing like her. It was a good place to get away from her. But I brought bits of her with me. A horseshoe, a Christmas card. I tried to start again, but I brought bits of her with me. When Ida came to stay . . . Midas, it only served to remind me just how *much* I loved Freya.' He groaned, covering his face with his bear's hands. His nicotine teeth were slanted and saw-like. Midas had remembered them as straight and white.

Midas stared at the monstrous shape of spray rising from Wodenghyll Deep where the falls drilled open the lake. The spray gobbled dainty snowflakes as they fell.

'You're a coward, Carl,' he said, feeling a level of resolution he had barely known even days before. He wondered if this feeling was the one Ida meant when she talked about longing to sit on a boat in steady waters. A feeling steady as a spirit level, supported by great depths of tamed pressure.

'You're too afraid to admit the world doesn't revolve around you. You think even the landscape is subordinate to you. You can get pretty far in life with an attitude like that, I can tell that even though I've never had the nerve myself. People respect you when they're frightened of you. But I don't think you can be in love and be like that.'

Carl's hands were shaking where they rested on the steering wheel. 'I loved Freya.'

'But nobody could say the two of you were in love, Carl. There's a difference, and I think in the end the difference was that she was as frightened of you as everyone else.'

Since there was nothing more to say, Midas turned and walked back to his car. He threw the bouquet on the ground and drove over it on his way home to Ida.

Carl remained in his car with the door open. The spray drifted in, making the inside feel like a damp room in an old house. Carl felt like a piece of its furniture rotting from within. He looked at the immediate horizon, the sudden drop into Wodenghyll Deep, and knew all it would take would be a turn of the ignition and a stamp on the accelerator.

He imagined the water slashing around him, pushing him down to the lake bed, face first, no air, grit in his mouth and bones of fish. It was that or to carry on, move somewhere new, wait for the unappeased feelings in his gut to regurgitate. He couldn't hope for any end, and if he provided one of his own devising, then what? Carl didn't believe in an afterlife, even though he had needed one when Freya died. He had been stronger than that.

But suddenly strength seemed to him the failing that Midas had come out and claimed it was. Being strong had misled him, while a weakling like Midas wormed his way towards love, and *found* it. He laughed loud and bitterly, then stopped laughing abruptly.

These emotions had ruined him, this craving for a woman long gone, coming so powerfully from some bottomless well inside him that his best hope seemed now the dispossession of his body. He considered that to drive over Wodenghyll Force would be to go beyond bodies, to the nowhere where Freya was. Where at least Charles Maclaird was not. Yet.

He turned the key in the ignition. The engine fizzed and died. He tried again, but it wouldn't spark. He climbed out, lifted the bonnet and thumped the machine parts beneath. The engine would not start. He zipped his jacket up tight and felt the spray from the waterfall infiltrating his clothes. He was cold. He tried to start the engine again in desperation. Cursing the car, he took his mobile phone from the glove compartment and turned it on. Its battery had died. He had been sleeping in his car and had not recharged it.

A sudden fury gripped him. He roared, spittle flying into the spray and faint snow then flying back on the wind to hit his jaw. The noise of his outburst swallowed in the never-ending battle cry of the falls.

He would fucking well *walk* down to Tinterl, collar the rector of the church there, or break open the door of some cottage or other and demand the provision of shelter from the cold. He was not above using force and threats if he had to.

He paced off, staggering slightly in a wind that had begun to howl up the side of the ridgeway, lashing him with even denser spray and freezing drops. He kept walking, thundering along the road, stamping through the trickles from the smaller falls, bounding over deeper rivulets. Then he misjudged one jump and got both feet drenched. His toes went instantly cold and he thought of Ida hobbling away from him at Enghem Stead. He felt sick of being within himself, sick of having done all the things he had done. It was good that the Crook boy had found her.

A brilliant white sky hurt his eyes.

The road rounded a corner. He felt the wind peeling back his eyelids. Darts of sleet stung him and he walked with his shoulders squared against the splattering ice. He plodded on, finding it hard going, skidding on trails of water frozen across the tarmac. He turned another bend and stopped. To his left the hillside sloped away, to his right it rose steeply, and from this height a great sheet of snow had slid down to cake the road. He took a deep breath and tried to climb through it, but his foot sank and he fell. He scrambled onward on all fours, each arm and leg sinking deeper than expected. When finally he rolled out of the snowdrift on the other side, his teeth chattered and his breath crystallized in the air. Wiping moisture from his face, he tried to guess how far he had to go. The road drooped on and on ahead of him, snaking around rocks and crags into the sleet-obscured distance. No sign of Tinterl Church or any other building.

A sickly panic set in. Had he come the wrong way? He couldn't see back past the snowdrift. He staggered onwards.

The sleet thickened, meshing into a feathery wall. For a moment he thought he saw a woman's figure made from the particles, her arctic hair fluttering in the gale, but she had her back turned and he couldn't tell whether it was Freya. She vanished as quickly as she appeared. His limbs were stiff and unresponsive. He realized he would not make it to Tinterl Church. He wondered whether Ida's legs felt as numb to her as his did now. He lay down in the snow in the middle of the road.

CHAPTER 37

She watched the vapours from peat flats rise, made visible by cold. The milk-white of the sky reflected in channels of water and a rat that lay dead at the side of the road, tail and hind legs crucified by tyre treads.

They drove in comfortable quiet past trees wrapped in fleecy belts of green moss, past soupy pools and tracks of frosted peat.

It seemed that every time she forgot the absence of flesh beneath socks, forgot about glass locked around her legs by bolts made from her own bones, someone intent on curing her shattered that serenity. Midas had insisted they visit Henry again, to clutch at straws while precious days drained away.

Cures and preservation had been Carl's talk. All that bullshit he showed her of Saffron Jeuck. Talking in vague terms about containing her condition.

The cottage approached, the ivy leaves on its walls rising in the breeze like shackles. She forced a weak smile for Midas, wanting only to sit with him and drive through endless landscapes.

Henry wasn't home.

Peering through a grubby window, they could see the cottage was a mess. Books were spilled open on the sitting-room floor amid heaps of paper.

Midas scratched his head. 'What now?'

A bird cried piercingly somewhere in the bog.

'Midas,' she said as they stood side by side in Henry's garden, 'to tell you the truth I'm happy Henry's not here. I don't want to look for a cure any more.'

'But . . .'

'Shhh,' she said gently. 'I want to show you something.'

She led him to the pen of the moth-winged cattle. She tried the handle. It was not locked. He followed her through the outer door and they smelled at once the pungent stink like battery hens. She opened the interior door to reveal the room of jingling birdcages.

She leant one crutch against the wall and used the hand it had freed to take one of his. She stepped into the centre of the pen and told him to stand very still.

The herd adjusted their flight to stream around them, a musty-smelling cascade of fur and wing. Ida gasped when a bull landed on her scalp and combed its horns through her hair. Another settled down beside it, and one on Midas's shoulder, and another and another until the whole herd bristled on their shoulders and scalps, snorting and shaking their little heads, flitting their wings and stamping their match-head hoofs.

Then they began to low musically across the gap between them. She pulled him closer by the hand until they stood within inches of each other, the cows humming and the bulls snorting in symphony. A calf with bluebell-coloured wings leant against its mother, tilted back its head and gave a moo like the note of a flute.

'I'm not going to be cured,' she whispered. 'Let's forget about it from this moment on.'

CHAPTER 38

On maps of the islands the sands north of Clammum-on-Drame were an outstretched hand trying in vain to ward off arctic winds. Geologists claimed the sands had long ago been craggy highland plains, which an earthquake in antiquity had humbled to sea level. As evidence, cuboids of granite rose out of grey beaches, flat-topped or sheared at diagonals.

Ida and Midas drove the raised concrete road that traversed the quicksands, leaving tyre tracks in the deep layer of sand blown over the route. Their destination was Clammum Knoll, a gently sloping hillock at the northernmost point of the sands.

They sat huddled close together, on a bench at the tip of the knoll, watching the sea or looking back across the shining beaches dissected by the road and flooded channels of saltwater. Sombre storks and curlews plodded this way and that, and a cormorant croaked on the husk of a wrecked boat that lay on the beach like a whale's skull.

Northwards was an opaque horizon. This was

the wind's first stop since sweeping over glaciers and pack ice. Today it simply whispered and didn't dent the water face.

'I always wanted to go to the North Pole,' said Ida, pointing into the distance.

'You will.'

'I wouldn't last two seconds.'

'You don't know . . .'

The salt from the ocean dried and cancelled out the salty tears in her eyes. She remembered her father salting a fillet of cod with his mind elsewhere, when the bad feeling between them was strongest. She surveyed the infinite sea before her and wondered how much salt you'd find if you boiled off all the water.

'Have you ever seen the seabed?' she asked, knowing he hadn't. She wanted to talk about it and relive it through doing so. 'Deep down it's like twilight. You can see salt trails in the water like ghosts.'

Midas shook his head, smiling. 'I've never seen anything like that. It always surprises me how much more you've managed to do than me.'

'Not for much longer.'

'Don't talk like that.'

'All I'm saying is . . . I love just sitting with you, like this.'

The world was as monochrome as the day they'd first met, the sea as dark as vinyl. The cormorant on the wrecked hull took off and flew low over the black water.

'Midas . . . I'd love to sit like this on a boat with you.'

'All right.'

'What?' She hadn't expected him to say that.

'All right,' he said, slower this time.

She pressed ahead before he had a chance to back out. 'The weather forecast is clear for tomorrow. We'll rent the boat and go out as far as we can. As long as the sea's clear, I should be able to row a bit.'

He gulped. 'Okay.'

'Midas! What's brought out the seafarer in you?'

'Actually, I'm still terrified, but . . . a lot of things. Tearing up my father's book was . . . liberating. I owe you for that.'

'Ah, so you want to repay me?'

'No. Um, well yes, but not with this.'

'Right?'

'I don't think I can repay you enough.'

She rolled her eyes. 'Don't be so serious.'

'But . . .' He hung his head.

She shoved him playfully. He sat back up, looking hurt, so she shoved him again. This time he shoved her back and she squealed as she toppled over and lay on her side on the grass.

'Jesus,' she groaned, 'I can't even sit up.'

'Sorry.'

'No, no, just help me up. My stomach's cold. Freezing. All around my hips.'

He helped her up.

Their spot was a heightened level of concrete

that the tide would have to rise six feet to cover, so the knoll was safe from water. The sunset, like a blacksmith, was beating the sky into glowing red blades.

They sat quietly and watched it glow. She laid her head on his shoulder. He laid his against her crown.

'I should take a photo.'

'No. Just remember it, and us in it.'

He swallowed.

She smiled. Here was rightness of place and time. They kissed. The wind trickled over them.

CHAPTER 39

Before his next shift at Catherine's, he left Ida a bunch of pale yellow narcissi on the table. She sat among them writing Christmas cards, which she'd asked Midas to choose, since she felt weary at the thought of shopping.

He had tried to pick cards she'd like. She knew, from old ones he'd kept, where his own tastes lay. Black-and-white photos of Christmases past. Stony-faced mothers holding the hands of smock-wearing children on cobbled streets. Gaslight lampposts aglow in reels of snow. Church doors decked with spindly holly wreaths. Despite these monochrome images he loved, the ones he'd selected for her were pretty and colourful. A set of four designs all showed photos of deer in snowy glens. A speckled faun stared wide-eyed from a holly thicket where red berries brought out the ruddy sheen of its fur. A doe stood among a fallen oak's horizontal branches, wearing a comical cap of blue-tinged snow. A stag and his mate rubbed elegant necks under boughs hung with green mistletoe.

She opened the first Christmas card and plugged an ink cartridge into her fountain pen. Without concentrating she wrote *Mum and Dad*, then tore up the card and opened another to write only *Dad*. She put her pen down, breathing heavily. A hot cramp squeezed her bowels and made blood rush to her head. She concentrated on breathing.

Before Midas had left she'd told him that she was feeling better. She didn't mention that her hips were filled with a new, hot kind of paralysis. Like an insatiable rash on the underside of her skin. A woolliness in her muscles there was interrupted regularly by these blazing pains. She could guess what it meant.

Her fingernails scraped the table's paintwork as the pain flared again. She gritted her teeth. The agony subsided and she wheezed. When she had told Midas about feeling better, the relief on his face got the biggest smile yet out of him and he kissed her freely without hesitation.

It was still true, even though her body might hurt more than ever because of him. Him and her.

She sighed. Imagining turning to glass made her feel as if a trapdoor had opened up inside her and all her courage had fallen through. She thought how young she was, to be suffering like this, and how that made it seem all the more undeserved. Yet she had done all those youthful things, and even when she'd plummeted (the air whistling over her ears, the bungee cable spiralling behind her) she'd felt nothing as compulsive as the will she felt now, to cling to Midas. It would be impossible to break the news that she knew she wasn't getting better.

She could feel the encroachment of the glass like an animal feeling the tremor before an earthquake. He would not understand if she told him.

She had felt a collision with him and known that she had wanted this her whole life: to crash for just one moment into another person at such a velocity as to fuse with him.

That moment had come not at the height of a night's passion, as she'd expected, but in the morning when their eyes opened at the same time and felt for focus in each other's. They were newborns, wide-eyed, sharing their first breath of the world. Then it was over as quickly as it had come. Midas had blushed and looked away from her. She had reached out to hold his face.

Now that she had felt that moment, all she wanted was to feel it again. When he had walked out of the door for work that morning she had felt the temperature of the room drop, the ache in her pelvis redouble, the skin across her hips go sore. She supposed in the meantime it would be pleasant enough to pretend there was a future.

She wrote *Merry Christmas Dad, from Ida,* blew on the ink, put the card in the envelope, then hesitated with her tongue an inch away from licking the gum. She took the card back out of the envelope, the lid back off her pen, and wrote

> *. . . also, Dad, there's a chance we may not see each other for a little while. I wanted to tell you how happy I've been lately. I met a man.*

I don't know whether you'll get to meet him any time soon so let me tell you all about him. He was very shy at first, but I saw to that. He has a small house in a small town on an island. You'd like it here. As you'd put it: you can hear yourself think at night. He's a photographer. Most of all, you should know I'm in love with him. I think you said once that love should be what matters. I wholeheartedly concur.

She blew on the ink, having run out of space on the card. She put it in the envelope, sealed it, and savoured the taste of the stamp on her tongue.

Overnight the head of a fat old rose in Catherine's had shed petals like burnt bits of ribbon into a glass vase. Midas stared sadly at the warped red planets in the water's cosmos and thought of Ida's legs. That morning they'd woken in time with each other and he hadn't recognized the feel of his own bed or the noise of the street outside. Hadn't recognized the feel of old blankets soft on his skin. Hadn't recognized Ida, had seen her as if for the first time. As if she were the first thing he had ever seen.

He put the healthy roses into a new vase and poured the contents of the first into the sink. Petals whirled around the stainless steel then crumpled in the plughole. He went to the window and arranged tubers of bleached wood among satin tulips. There was something conspiratorial about flowers. He often sensed, when he was alone in a room of them, their petals whispering on a frequency beneath human hearing. Outside, a weak fog contained the street and made it look like a sound stage pumped with dry ice. The town beyond was only imagination.

He sighed. He wanted this shift to end. Wanted to return to Ida. Even though that afternoon they would be going out in a boat (of which he was terrified).

He had felt paranoid all day. First thing that morning he'd erased all the photos he had of Ida. He'd watched her as she slept while he booted up his laptop. Her hair was in a frizz, her lips were chafed. He hoped she was sleeping well. He didn't want her to wake again groping at her ankles as if trying to disprove a nightmare.

His photos had all been of her feet. They weren't *Ida*. That was why he'd erased them.

Light didn't conduct truth as once he'd thought. There was nothing you could do to preserve truth. Light was only of use as a metaphor for the ungraspable moment. Until there was a kind of camera invented that could return you entirely to a moment from your past, pictures such as those were no use. At first he'd felt a thrill upon deleting them. Without them he had only her flesh, hair, glass. Reality had been liberating. Only now, surrounded by the familiar, pollinated air, dealing with the humdrum demands of customers, he was beginning to doubt his wisdom.

363

The door chimed and opened. A flap of wind quivered the tulips. Midas remembered Ida entering Catherine's not long ago, with only a slim walking stick to support her. This time it was Gustav, which meant his shift was over.

Gustav looked staggered. 'What's got into you?'

Midas was jittering about on the spot. 'I'm going out to sea. On a boat with Ida,' he said.

'This girl's really done wonders for you. I'd never in a million years think I'd see the day when you get on a boat. It was more likely you'd get in a bloody spaceship.'

Midas, pulling on his jacket as he passed him in the doorway, grinned with a mixture of happiness and terror, and bolted away back home down the street.

Gustav shook his head and took his seat at the desk, unpacking a sausage and barbecue sauce sandwich and the day's newspaper. He had been through it cover to cover and was halfway through rereading the sports pages when the door chimed and a woman in a chic black raincoat stepped timidly in. She had long black hair and wasn't wearing any make-up to cover the bags under her eyes.

'I'm looking for Ida Maclaird,' she said urgently. 'Do you know where I can find her?'

Emiliana Stallows had spent the past few days on the mainland. After she had left Enghem she had telephoned a seafront hotel in Glamsgallow to book a night's accommodation, but she changed her mind the moment she checked in. She had stood for a minute or two at the reception desk in the cosy lobby, ignoring the receptionist's questions, unable to think about anyone except Ida Maclaird. Then she had asked for the return of her credit card, shouldered her bag and headed out along the rain-soaked promenade to the ferry terminal.

She hadn't enjoyed the crossing. The ferry had rocked from side to side so severely that, looking out of the window, the dark sea seemed parallel to the glass. The saving grace was the small feeling of purpose the journey gave her. All the time she held, tight in her fist, the crumpled address of Saffron Jeuck's family.

Their home was hard to find, in a residential estate in a newly built town whose roads were narrow and whose houses were compressed in ordered rows of clean brick. There was an awkward moment when Mr Jeuck answered the door, the first of an entirely awkward afternoon.

Emiliana had known that Saffron took her own life because of the glass. That had always seemed a ghastly enough end to the story, and to pry into the details of the girl's final acts seemed cruel. Only now was Emiliana gripped by the hope that something could be learnt from the whole sorry tale. Something for Ida.

Leaving the Jeuck house, having heard the opposite of what she'd hoped for, she burst into tears. In her last hours, Saffron had yelled for her father, and he had run to her to sit with her body propped up against his. Together they had watched an unexpected final phase of the transformation into glass. In the days preceding, Saffron had complained of a feeling of weakness, as if her body had been engaged in a long battle which it was now, through sheer exhaustion, surrendering. As the flesh gave in, the glass entered at unprecedented speed. Long before, father and daughter had discussed what they would do in such circumstances, but Mr Jeuck's hands were too shaky to open the safety cap on the little white bottle of pills. Saffron had to open them herself, tip them on to her tongue, and swallow with a dry gurgle.

'You've got to tell me where Ida is,' Emiliana insisted, leaning over the counter in Catherine's. 'It's urgent that I speak to her. Or Midas. Can I speak to Midas?'

'Slow down,' said Gustav calmly. 'They've taken a boat out to sea. They could be anywhere, as long as it's on the ocean.'

She thumped the counter. 'It's just . . .' she said despairingly, 'she's very unwell. And I have some terrible news she has to know . . .'

'There's no way to tell her. And even if there was, are you sure she'd really want to hear it?'

The cliffs here had been torn open recently, leaving chalky caves where blocks of debris had fallen on to the beach. Two dilapidated jetties poked into the water, one of them broken in two, with a scuttled and rusting whaling yacht beside it. Sheets of its hull jagged from the water ahead of its snapped mast.

Ida reclined in a rowing boat and watched Midas pace up and down on the intact jetty, its planks juddering with each step. She watched in admiration. His neuroses were still there, only now he was going to defy them. He just needed his warm-up. He growled, bent himself around to face the boat and bent away again, scared like a ghost to cross water. She held out a hand. He took such a deep breath she swore she saw the air bend as it surged into him. Then he leapt and the boat bucked as he landed in a heap. He clung to the wood with his nails, like a drenched cat, not realizing this was what he had been struggling towards, not trusting water enough to let it keep the boat upright. Only when the vessel was floating peaceful as a sheet of paper did he experimentally remove his hands from its sides.

After that he sat quietly with knees huddled to his chest while Ida rowed. She'd worried she'd not be able to brace herself without legs, but the glass anchored her and gave her a centre to heave from. They headed out to sea. The shore became a chalk line on a stone wall.

The sandy seabed looked like it was smelting into the water. The clear vault turned into hazy depths as they rowed further out. Fine sea mist phased the horizon into a blank atmosphere smelling of salt.

She was content just to look at him while he, dumbly grateful, responded in kind. She suspected that brotherhoods of monks in shadowy abbeys felt the same electricity of kinship in the air.

To use his own father's analogy, that Carl had repeated to her on a day not so long ago when snow had cooped them inside his cottage: there were still garments to be shed. She smiled at the idea that she had at least got Midas down to his socks and his Y-fronts. There were more layers to a person than an analogy of vests and anoraks could sustain, and she suspected that while you were peeling the outer layers away, new ones were being stitched together on the inside.

A pattern of spume, frothed up by the oars, floated behind the boat like a wedding dress. She wondered if she would ever have married him, and that surprised her so much she felt the idea of it almost rock her out of the boat. She'd never thought of marriage like that before, never felt comfortable picturing herself in a dress with a hanging train and a suited groom offering a ring.

'What's wrong?' Midas asked.

'Nothing.'

It couldn't have been like that of course, since she'd never have been able to stand at an altar feeling blood in her calves pumping around her wriggling toes. But pretending things were just beginning made her head feel pleasantly light.

'What's wrong?' he whispered.

'Nothing.' She held the side of the boat. 'Just a little seasick. That's all.'

'You told me you'd never been seasick in all your life.'

She rubbed her eyes. 'I suppose there's a first time for everything.'

In truth, her thighs ached with a new kind of latent numbness. She couldn't feel anything in her legs, but she had a hunch there was something there, something building up. She shook her head and looked out to sea for a distraction. She saw one at once.

In the water huge, elegant bodies moved. A narwhal pod. Funny, she thought, how invisible such huge creatures could make themselves under only a little water. She remembered she had dived once between a mother humpback and her calf. In cyan equatorial oceans.

The whale bodies grew more defined as they swam higher in the water.

'Thank you,' she said, 'for coming out here with me.'

He was watching her anxiously.

Not far away, a spiralled spike parted the water and rose like a spear. Another pierced the surface and saluted beside it. The two tusks touched blindly.

'Don't be frightened,' she said.

'I'm not frightened. Well . . . a little.'

The tusks were followed by blunt heads with stargazing, infantile eyes. Whale bodies tore open the sea as if it were wrapping paper. They bulged to the surface crisped with barnacles, their blubber streaked with flashes of black and white like obsidian and quartz. They defied the weight of water for a few moments before grudgingly slipping back under the sea, disappearing in craters of ocean, leaving only a puff of breath hanging in the cold air.

Then tails raked the water. Bubbles fizzed on the surface.

Midas was engrossed. It was dawning on him that he had never considered what the sea was like when it wasn't set against the land. It was another planet.

The last and largest narwhal tail creaked into a salute and stretched its heart shape against the sky before slipping under. The pod was diving deeper, disappearing where light couldn't follow.

Midas turned back to Ida with an awestruck smile on his face.

She was leaning over the other side of the boat, making it rock closer to the water. He scrabbled forward and seized the oars she'd left hanging in their sockets.

'I'm okay,' she groaned, against the evidence.

'Just try to, er, breathe. Breathe calmly. This will pass over.'

She rested her forehead against the wood. She ran her hands down her thighs and squeezed her knees.

'We should get back to land,' he said.

He tried to row like she had. The boat spun. The

oars slapped uselessly and tossed beads of water through the air.

'Stop,' she pleaded.

She lifted up her skirt. A half-inch of faultless glass covered her thighs. Beneath it sheets of bruised muscle strained. He let go of the oars and they scraped back into their locks.

She grabbed him so tight that her squeezing fingernails stabbed his skin. Together they stared mutely at her knees. The joints had locked.

She opened her coat and lifted her jersey. Her belly's surface was losing its details of moles and follicles as they watched. Flesh was receding, leaving a flat screen behind. Purple ligaments within vanished like soil scattered by a brush. The light twinkled in her glass navel. It hinted at the silhouetted mass of her intestines moving beneath layers of hardening fat.

'We'll get to shore,' Midas croaked, reaching again for the oars.

She pawed her hands up his arms and held them tight. When he got the message she felt her way up to his neck and cheeks to force their faces together. They kissed with eyes locked on each other's. He felt her elbows and forearms tighten. Grip slacken. Warmth of her ribs against his palms go cool.

Her soft skin leadened. He ran his hands through her hair. Held her cheeks.

Her lips plied his. Her tongue counted his teeth. Her eyelashes dripped tears on to his face.

Her grip on his arms went flat. Her lips were a

fading clot. She butted her head against his. The lenses of her eyes gelled.

The black dots of her pupils became pinpricks; closed like locks; were gone. For a moment her head was a glaciated rose, then it was empty.

He started to shake and cried, 'Help!' for all the good it could do. He was still held in her frozen embrace. When at last he withdrew his hands from her hair, unable to look at her face, he heard snapping. Glass fibres that had been her hairs clung to his fingers and cut criss-cross lacerations into his skin. Her arms still clutched his shoulders. He would have to contort himself to leave her.

Hidden in a tightening ring of sea mist, he lost track of how much time was passing, although each moment felt long and painful, each intake of breath like lifting a great weight. The mist grew greyer and dimmer. He was not aware of it. He was only aware of the ongoing movements of his body compared to the utter stillness of hers. His stomach rumbled and he loathed it for doing so. His gaze remained locked on his lap, and only after what must have been hours could he summon the courage required to look at Ida again.

Her glass face, transfixed in a kiss, was a mask over nothing. He shuffled closer, feeling the boat lurch and the water slosh beneath. He could see through her empty eyes into solid glass. 'Where have you gone?' he asked, desperately reaching out and touching again the laminate surface of her cheek.

In this block of cold silica the thoughts and will of a person had been. A will that he'd felt tug his own out of inertia and make him more than he had ever been before. He could not understand where that had gone now. It was not in her body . . . unless the crossed wires of thought and feeling that made up a person were kept somewhere deeper, in the heart or guts as he had so often felt in himself. He grabbed the bottom of her jersey and raised it to expose her glass waist. The blue of the top she had been wearing showed through her back and out of her stomach. Her belly was as empty as her head.

He let go of her jersey and wiped his eyes. Tears as transparent as Ida hung between his knuckles.

Her hands were still raised to hold his shoulders in an embrace. Feeling ponderous, he knelt in front of her and wormed back into her grip, re-entering the circle of her arms to rest his heavy head against hers.

In this way he remained, sobbing gently in time with the waves, until he saw a yellow light flash through the mist.

Reluctantly, he untangled himself from Ida to peer out across the water. An orange boat veered towards him. Lifeboat orange.

He looked back at her sparkling features and suddenly foresaw a future of interrogations. The examination and cross-examination of her body. Newspaper reports, television pictures, photographs. The glass girl of St Hauda's Land.

Her coat hung about her now like a dustsheet.

The beam of light from the lifeboat flashed through her head and found impurities, dots of curdled discoloration in the glass. He leant forward to kiss her one last time, but pulled away at the cold hard touch of her lips. Her mouth had looked moist for a moment, but it had been a trick of the light. Her hair had no depth, only the scratched surface of a block of glass. She was not, he realized, Ida any more. Which made what he had to do, with the lifeboat bearing down on him, incrementally more bearable. Just bearable enough to place his weak hands on her shoulders and shove with all his small might. She rocked, teetered, then plunged overboard, hitting the water with a splash. The momentum made the boat rock precariously, and all at once its slippery wood bucked under his feet, and Midas was tumbling after her.

The sea rushed over him and ice-cold water transplaced the air. There was an eternity of liquid below, into which Ida was sinking. A bubble trapped in the cavity of her mouth (a hot and supple mouth he had kissed) escaped like the mimicry of a final breath. He let out an involuntary roar that sent saltwater rushing into his mouth. The current whirled him on to his back underwater and he watched the trail of his own last breath chase upwards after hers towards the molten light of the surface. He tried to turn back over and swim after her as she sank, her clear body and billowing clothes becoming dimmer, dimmer. But swimming was impossible, either going up or down. He managed only to flip and sink at gravity's speed, with a weird quiet coming over him. His vision doubled, quadrupled. The sea was a hundred bright circles.

He missed her so terribly.

Then he was reversing, be it up or down he had no idea. All he knew was that he was being wrenched further from her, and it made him scream (but there was no air) and it made him cry (but tears couldn't form underwater).

There was an explosion of light and a cacophony. His back hit a hard surface. His body gave a spasm and he thought he was being electrocuted. Bristled lips were at his, hot and tasting of sweat as they forced air into each alveolus like a pin. He tried to push them away but he hadn't the strength. When they had finished with him he was rolled over on his side where he lay weeping, watching his tears drop on to the rocking deck and blur with the damp there.

He remained in this pose for some time, with blankets piled over him and his hair slopped freezing across his face. He felt the gulf that had opened between Ida Maclaird and Midas Crook. Each clapping wave on the lifeboat's hull sounded like an apocalypse. Eventually he could distinguish voices from the overwhelming sounds of the sea and the gulls. He could feel a grip on his shoulder and hear a familiar voice.

He looked up.

Gustav was red with worry. 'Hold on, mate,' he said. 'You're going to be okay.'

Behind him various coastguards watched with professional concern. Gustav's hand was clamped on Midas's shoulder. After a while the numb touch made Midas reach up, hang his arms around Gustav's neck and hold limply on. Gustav's broad arms wrapped around him and bundled him up. Midas buried his face in the hot red skin of his friend's throat and cried out. The noise faded on the expanse of the ocean.

CHAPTER 40

On a blustering morning soon afterwards, Henry Fuwa answered the door to Midas's knocking.

Henry's cottage smelt stale. A damp chill in the air made Midas fold his arms tight (he could still feel Ida's petrified grip: he had five fingertip-shaped bruises on each shoulder).

Henry returned with a pot of green tea and two china cups without handles. They drank carefully, neither man looking at the other.

'Did you love her?' asked Henry, his voice low.

When Midas spoke he fancied it came from his insides, maybe from some alliance of organs that didn't have a name. 'I didn't think I ever would love anyone. But yes, I did.'

Henry nodded. There was honesty between them where suspicion had marked some of their previous meetings, born from the knowledge that what had happened could never really be discussed with anyone save each other, and that after today they'd never be able to bear meeting to discuss it again.

The wind cooed in the cottage walls. Midas closed his eyes. 'I wanted to say I always hoped things would work out for you. Regarding my mother and so on. Um, and say that I'm going.'

'Going now?'

'Going away from St Hauda's Land.'

'Ah. Where to?'

'I'm not sure yet. Although I've packed my bags.'

They fingered their teacups. Midas's hands still stung where Ida's hairs had cut him. The healing cuts were leaving faint scars like the pattern of bark.

The chair legs scraped on the floor when he got up. He held out his hand. They shook briskly and parted. Midas walked out over bog soil covered in fine snow.

CHAPTER 41

Months later, the turquoise sea carried a creaking boat and Midas Crook away from an unfamiliar archipelago, away from low, sandy islands whose olive trees and noisy towns basked all summer in a heat that had turned Midas's skin a warmer shade and his hair from black to deepest brown.

He was wearing red, for the first time in memory. The ferocious colour dazzled him when he looked down at his body. Red all over, a red wetsuit exaggerating the knobbiness of his knees.

Flying fish jumped from the water, fins flicking like moth wings before they submerged again with claps. A whole shoal leapt and landed in a ripple of applause.

The instructor clapped him on the back. 'Are you ready?'

Midas nodded and pulled on his tight plastic mask. He plugged the oxygen tube over his lips.

They dived. He still couldn't get over the rush, not just of the fluid world around him, but fluids in his brain bubbling to adjust to the pressure. The blue water was the home of sequined fish swishing between coral towers. He swam down farther, kicking his legs in the rhythm he had been taught, constantly forgetting he didn't need to hold his breath. Soon, at the bottom, scudding across a seabed jewelled with shells and tickling anemones, he plucked up the courage to swim a little farther from his instructor than he had the day before.

That was his plan: swim farther and farther afield each day, until he could safely dive alone.

Until he could dive in foggier oceans. In paler, stiller corners of the world.